# SH

# NOT

# HERE

To Maverick—
Happy Reading!

Mandi Jyll

# SHE'S NOT HERE

ISBN-13 978-1-7325557-0-9
ISBN-10 1-7325557-0-2

Cover Design: Damonza

www.mandilynn.com
www.stoneridgebooks.com

# SHE'S
# NOT
# HERE

## MANDI
## LYNN

Also by Mandi Lynn

*Essence*
*I am Mercy*

*For Mémère,*
*The one no longer here*

# Chapter 1

8 months ago

Tom was sitting in the chair, his arms stretched out in front of him. He was smiling; he always smiled, but it never reached his eyes. He had his shirt buttoned all the way, just how he liked it—the fleece ironed to a crisp, fresh look. His peppered hair grew over his ears. He needed to go to the barber.

"Okay, Tom, how are you feeling today?" The doctor sat on the other end of the table. His white jacket was a stark contrast to Tom's shirt, a bright amber-plaid.

"Great," Tom said. His answer was short, clipped as it often was.

"How did you get here today?" The doctor was playing with the pen on the table, his notepad at the ready.

"Uhh," Tom let out a laugh as he turned and looked around the room. There was a moment of panic until his eyes met with the woman standing behind him. "This little lady right here." He put his arm out to touch her hand.

"And what's her name?"

Tom looked at the doctor again, but this time his face dropped. The thick waves of hair, the dimple in her cheeks, the way she seemed to sway to the side—none of it was familiar. His eyes dimmed and his shoulders slumped.

A crushing pressure built up in the woman's chest as Tom struggled to remember who she was. It was not the first time he had forgotten her name or called her someone else, but the blow was painful all the same.

"That's Jessi," he said, but the woman could hear the unease in his voice.

The woman stood behind Tom. She wanted to sit beside him, but at that moment it felt easier to stand and pace than to sit and do nothing.

"I'm Willow, your daughter," she said. She put her hand on his shoulder. He looked up and smiled, but the corners of his lips didn't touch his eyes. With her tanned skin and her dark eyes, she was a mirror image of her father, but there were always these moments where he didn't recognize her.

"Oh, yes," he said, but the confusion was still there.

"How has he been?" the doctor asked, this time turning to Willow.

"Same as always. Waking up in the middle of the night, forgetting things. We need to repeat a lot, but he's still getting around fine. Sometimes he sings to himself, but I can't always understand what he's trying to say."

"When he talks, does he slur?"

"No, not that I've noticed."

The doctor shook his head and opened a file with Tom's name written on the edges. Willow looked around the man's office. Dr. Gadel. Esteemed researcher in neuroscience. Case study after case study, and here he was, looking for new patients willing to volunteer their bodies to science in a hope that it would not only help them, but others.

"Well, as I'm sure you know, all of Tom's symptoms are signs of advanced Alzheimer's Disease. You're here to learn more about the clinical trial?"

"That's correct. My husband has been researching Alzheimer's on the side of his medical practice. He stumbled across some of your case studies in his research. We've tried a lot of things, but nothing seems to slow down the progression of the disease."

"Your father was diagnosed," Dr. Gadel looked down at the papers in front of him, "six years ago?"

"Yes, and the past year has been especially hard. He's been forgetting who people are, where he is. He's not himself anymore."

Willow placed her hand on her father's shoulder as she spoke. He smiled up at her, having no idea she was talking about him. That's how the conversations seemed to go in their house. Willow and her husband could talk about Tom for hours, just feet away from him, and he would never know.

"So you're considering having your father be a part of the clinical trial?"

Willow took a breath and pulled a chair out next to her father to sit. He stared at her wide-eyed, and for a moment, she let herself think he was still there. She looked into his chocolate brown eyes and felt herself reaching out to him. Did he know the decision she was forced to make?

"My father has been sick for a long time," she said, still looking at him. He blinked back, lost in some other world. She looked at the wrinkles around his eyes, the way his shoulders fell forward. "There are some moments when he speaks and it's like I have my father back. Maybe a memory has sparked in him, or me, or maybe both of us, but in that moment, I'm not wondering if my father is going to be okay." Willow stopped to take a breath and turned towards the doctor. The corners of his mouth were inching

3

down, his body completely still. "But those moments are becoming far and few. It doesn't feel like he's there anymore."

As soon as she said the words, she felt as if she needed to take them back. Of course, her father was there. She held his hand, his cold and fragile hand, but the man she knew growing up? Where had he gone?

"You want your father back," Dr. Gadel said.

"I'm afraid there's not much else to hold onto."

"I can't make any guarantees the trial will work," he said. "In fact, I can't say it won't make him worse. Everyone is different, but I will do everything in my power to make sure your father is a good match for this trial before we move forward. This means blood tests, MRIs, anything that can tell us as much as possible as to how your father's brain works. But even then there are some things we can't predict."

"I understand," Willow said. She looked at her father, but he was staring at his hands.

"The trial is for a new drug I've been working on. It's part of an experiment that has been touched upon by scientists from around the world, but it originated in New Zealand. It started as a way to develop  a sort of anti-venom for Alzheimer's, but before you can develop an anti-venom, you must first have a venom. Naturally, a disease has no venom. What the scientists in New Zealand were working on was a venom-like solution that replicated the effects of Alzheimer's."

"Is that possible?" Willow ran through her years of nursing school knowledge on how venoms and poisons and diseases worked, but each seemed to be a separate entity. However, Willow knew that all it took to counteract a venom was to find the matching anti-venom. Could it be that simple?

"They created a serum. It was injected into sheep, mice,

4

anything that would allow scientists to directly observe the effects of Alzheimer's on the brain — granted, not a human brain."

Every muscle in Willow's body tensed, and she reached out for her father's hand before Tom had a chance to know what was going on. She could picture her father in an examination room, a faceless figure standing close by ready to make an injection. What would it do to him? She stood up from her chair, and Tom looked back at her, his mouth gaping open. He was not an animal to be tested on.

"Willow, please sit. I'm not suggesting we do this type of experiment on your father."

Her heart beat against her chest, and her blood pulsed at her temples. If her father hadn't been there with her, she would have left the room before he had a chance to say anything else.

"I'm talking about a new serum that was created as a direct result of the anti-venom that was produced. They observed the animals that had been injected with the venom, studied their brains, the effects and why it affected it, and then created an anti-venom after years of study."

A thin layer of sweat was still coating Willow's skin. She looked at her father, the dazed look in his eyes, and sat back down.

"Did the anti-venom work?" she asked.

"It did," Dr. Gadel said.

"But it only stops the progression of the disease."

"In some cases, the brain was able to recover and return to a normal state, as if they had never been injected with a venom in the first place."

Her breath caught and tears sparked her eyes. When she walked into the appointment today, she told herself one thing: do not hope for results. She covered her face with her hands and put her elbows on the table. What he was saying, it wasn't supposed to be possible. After years and years of working in a hospital, she knew that there were just some things you could not fix. But could she be wrong?

"What would my father be doing?" she asked.

"He'd be injected with an anti-venom, Derilum. I've been working with a team of doctors to produce this drug, and it's been approved for clinical trials. When I met your husband at a conference in Boston, I was presenting the drug to a panel, and he approached me afterwards asking for my card. He had read some of my research articles on the project."

Willow nodded her head. Randy had given her Dr. Gadel's card as soon as he got home from the conference, but she had been afraid to call. It sat at the bottom of her purse for a week before she called to make an appointment.

"Do you really think it would help?"

She felt a spark of life that she hadn't felt in months. She never dared to let herself hope. Each doctor appointment ended in disappointment, but a flutter in her chest told her to stay.

"I think it could save your father's life."

# Chapter 2

Sam was coughing when she woke up. The alarm clock in her room read 3:21am, and when she looked past it, she thought she could see thick, black smoke filling the air.

She pushed her cover away and ran across the room, pulling her door open as more smoke piled in. Her thin cotton pajamas felt thick in the heat of the room. Sam wanted to run through the hallway, to the stairs that would lead her to the entrance of her house. Instead, she found herself standing at the doorway, turning her back to the thick smoke that was curling around her body. Her parents. Avery. Where they already out of the house? She put a foot forward, back in the direction of the stairs, but the smoke filtered through her lungs until coughing was the only thing left she could do. The fire alarm in the house blared, the only sound she could hear until her ears began to ring.

Sam knelt to the floor, pulling her t-shirt up to cover her nose and mouth, but it did little to filter the smoke. She wanted to scream out, to see if her family was still in the building, but any move to make a sound only left Sam struggling to breathe.

Sam covered her ears to block the sound of the alarm, but she could swear she could hear something far in the distance, a thud—like someone was walking up the stairs. She crawled across the floor, her eyes watering from the smoke. She closed her eyes, begging the stinging sensation to go away. Everything felt like it was on fire, but she didn't see the fire yet. There were no flames, just the heat and the suffocating smoke. She put her hands out, feeling her way in the darkness. She took shallow breaths, looking for clean air but never daring to look up. When she inhaled the thick trails of smoke, it became difficult to even cough.

"She's here!" a rough, muffled voice said. Or at least that's what Sam thought she heard. Her hands were shaking when he found her. Thick arms wrapped around her and under her legs until she was off the ground. Sam reached out and tried to speak to the man, to tell him her parents and sister were somewhere. She tried pointing in the direction of their rooms.

"It's okay," the man said, his voice muffled through a large respirator mask. His jacket had a light that flickered, the only brightness in the smoke. The man carried Sam down the stairs, the sound of his breathing through the respirator the only comforting sound inside the burning building. As he carried her down the stairs, the air grew dense and the smoke grew thicker. The fire was just around the corner, and as the flames grew higher, they seemed to possess their own sound of screeching as they ate away at the home. Memories of her life begged for escape as they were forever lost in the billows of smoke.

The flames blazed a magnificent orange until it was the only thing Sam could see. She was inches from the door in the arms of her savior. She wanted to run out of the house, but with each breath she took, the farther away the doorway seemed. By now, she had no oxygen; she was just a ragdoll in the fireman's arms.

There were other voices in the house, all just as muffled as the man who carried Sam. The team of firefighters rushed to find anyone trapped inside the house and to put out the flames that flowed from the kitchen and took over the home. The flames reflected off the masks of the firefighters, and the men seemed to blend into the chaos. It was a dance between fire and man. Each lick of the flame brought a renewed sense of urgency as they rushed to quell the fire.

"I've got her!" the man carrying Sam shouted as he stepped through the doorway and away from the fire.

The air cooled the instant the firefighter stepped through the doorway, but when he looked at Sam, she was limp in his arms. There was a thin coating of ash on her skin and pajamas, and the EMTs rushed around her, pulling her onto a stretcher and holding a respirator over her mouth. Bodies crowded around the young girl as they checked her vitals, and she was laid out on the stretcher. The team talked in rushed voices, operating as one to bring life back to Sam.

Avery was still coughing when she broke through the barrier of smoke. The moment she felt the fresh air on her face, she wanted to collapse to the ground, but her lungs wanted to cave in on themselves, making it impossible for her to catch her breath. Her eyes watered as a firefighter led her to the ambulance, and she was placed on a stretcher.

"Just lie down," a voice said.

Avery looked at the women whose hand was on her arm. Her grip was gentle as she kept Avery on the gurney, and an oxygen mask was slipped over her face. The streams of air felt too cold, and she pulled the mask from her face.

"Sweetie, you need that," the EMT said. She placed the mask on with gentle hands but tightened the elastic so it wouldn't come off as easy.

"Where's my parents?" Avery said. She tried to sit up, but the women pinned her in place.

"Don't worry, we'll find them," was all the women said as she hovered over Avery's body.

More EMTs rushed to her side, taking vitals, poking and prodding at her until she couldn't keep track of how many people were standing around her anymore. Through the mass of bodies, she saw Sam laying in the stretcher across from her with no sign of life.

"Sam?" Avery screamed, but her voice didn't have the power. Instead, her words were a rasping against her throat.

"It's all right, she's going to be fine." A woman stepped in front of Avery's vision so she couldn't see her sister. Avery sat, holding the respirator to her mouth, her breathing fogging the plastic cover over her nose and mouth.

Avery looked around in the dead night, her house a candle in the dark. Snow fell around the scene, a peaceful blanket coating the chaos. The lights from the firetrucks and ambulance flashed across the neighborhood as people slipped out of their houses to see what all the commotion was. Faces watched from the border of the scene as their neighbors' house was engulfed in flames, a blazing light in the otherwise dark night.

"There we go." Amidst the chaos, those were the words Avery heard. Just a whisper. They came from the EMT standing over Sam. There was a deep, damaged wheezing sound, and when Avery looked over, Sam's body was moving again, her chest heaving with each breath of air. The team of EMTs were blocking her vision, making it impossible to see Sam from the waist up, but she was there. Fire hoses were pulled into place, and water was poured over their home. Sam's cough was a comfort.

And then Sam was being rolled away. Avery was on one stretcher and Sam on another, and each were being pulled in opposite directions until Sam disappeared behind the doors of an ambulance. Sam was sealed away, leaving Avery in a sea of strangers.

"Wait," Avery said. Her voice was softer than a whisper. Through the fire of the night, the click of the doors of the ambulance echoed through the air. "Wait!" This time Avery could hear her voice. The first snow of the season glittered the ground. She should be cold in the freezing night, but the fire held her too close.

"It's gonna be okay, we're getting you to the hospital," an EMT said. He stood beside her, his body moving in rhythm with the rest of his team. His voice was calm. Tears pooled in Avery's eyes, but she wasn't sure if it was because of the smoke or because Sam was out of sight and her parents was nowhere to be seen.

"Sam's in that ambulance, let me go in that ambulance!" The man Avery had just spoken to was no longer listening. He was talking to the other EMTs in code or words that she didn't understand.

"Where's my parents?" Her eyes kept going to the man that had spoken to her. He worked on putting ointment on a burn that was on her leg — she hadn't even felt it. It seemed her whole body was on fire.

"The firemen are working on rescuing whoever they find in the house," he said, rubbing the cool ointment into her skin. Avery stared at her scorched leg; it shined when he put on the ointment.

"It was just us in the house. Me, my parents, and my

sister, Sam." Avery watched the other EMTs float in and out of her vision. She was in the ambulance now, still on the stretcher. The doors were open, leaving room for anyone else the fireman might find. They needed to find someone else. They needed to find her parents.

Avery watched outside the door as the firemen worked far off into the flames. They poured gallons upon gallons of water into her home, washing the house away, until all that was left to see was rubble. The flames didn't want to die. Avery imagined the fire hose freezing in the cold air, but the flames never being extinguished.

Then there was another stretcher. Without even realizing it, Avery's dad was pulled in, and the moment she saw him, she wished she hadn't.

— — — — —

From the outside, Massachusetts's Dover Memorial Hospital seemed quiet. The night was dark, but the building was bright. Patients inside were calm; most had long been asleep, yet miles away, a house was on fire. There were still flames trying to fight their way to grow and destroy. The fire had started in the kitchen, though no one knew that just yet. It would be hours, days even, before the fire marshal found the cause. Until then, there was just smoke and flames and ash.

Avery was separated from her dad once they arrived at the hospital. The drive was short, but to Avery it seemed to last hours. She closed her eyes as two EMTs worked in the small space, making sure her father could breath. The sound of lungs fighting to breathe echoed in her mind. When they carted her out of the ambulance, there were tears staining her face.

"Dad?" she tried to say, as cold air coated her skin until goosebumps formed where the burns had taken residence. A nurse heard her and took her hand as her father was taken away by another team of nurses.

"He's going to be okay, sweetheart." Avery didn't see the nurse that spoke to her. Everything was moving around her, and she wasn't sure where she was. She was rolled into the hospital, across other moaning patients in the emergency room. Her dad was no longer with her; Sam was nowhere in sight.

The nurse never let go of her hand, but she didn't speak up again. The lights in the hallways were too white, but when Avery closed her eyes, all she could see were flames. Cold, crisp teardrops left cool trails of relief against her burnt skin. She couldn't breathe through the tears, and coughing followed soon afterwards. With each cough, her body lifted, her muscles taunt.

"It's okay, just breathe." It was the nurse again. This time, Avery could see her, her dark hair coiled in braids. The woman held up the respirator again — Avery hadn't realized she had dropped it.

— — — — —

Sam was on the other side of the hospital, conscious, but just barely. Streaks of blond hair were strewn across the pillow, sprinkled with ash. The stench of smoke coated the room. There was one nurse who seemed to hover over her the most. She didn't speak to her patient as she worked in quick, thorough movements. Her hair was pulled back into a braid, thick curls poking out around her face.

"Come on," she mumbled to herself, working quicker than her hands would allow. She hooked Sam up to an IV; the girl hung on by a thread. There was a slow drip as the liquid made its way into Sam's bloodstream. There were other nurses rushing around the room trying to keep Sam alive. She was no longer coughing, but her breathing was shallow. There was a constant supply of rich oxygen to her lungs, machines and tubes running across her body, burying her under the life-saving devices.

"We have an identification on her," another nurse said, rushing into the room. She held the chart full of Sam's information pulled up on the computer, from her vitals to her weight. Sam Ellison, age 16. It was simple information, but with that, she was more than just a patient. She was someone with a family, with a story.

"Willow, is she stable yet?"

Willow tucked loose strands of hair behind her ear. "Almost," she said, staring at the machine that read Sam's vitals. "Come on."

Sam was pale in her bed, paler even with the dark soot staining her face. There were lines of clean skin around her eyes from where tears overflowed from coughing.

"Do we know where her parents are yet?" Willow asked.

"Not yet, but the EMTs on the scene said they pulled two adults out the fire — most likely her parents," the other nurse said. She put Sam's chart back in place at the edge of her bed and moved to leave the room.

"Wait," Willow said. She held Sam's wrist, a habit that'd formed over the years from always having to check for a pulse. "What condition are they in?"

The nurse shook her head as she stepped out the door. "Not good."

# Chapter 3

7 months ago

"It's okay," Randy said. The waiting room was long left behind, and now Willow stood in the doctor's office. Tom was sitting on the cushioned bed, paper crunching beneath him.

"I'm just not sure," Willow said. She was on the phone with her husband, Randy, trying not to pace in the small room. When she had checked her father in for his appointment, a nurse came in to check his vitals. Now, she was left to fill out one final piece of paperwork to say Dr. Gadel would not be held responsible for any side-effects during the use of Derilum.

"How's your dad?"

Tom was sitting, his back hunched forward. The corners of his mouth were pinched down, not because he was upset, but because he wasn't happy. It was one of those days Willow could look at her father and not recognize him.

"He's fine."

"What's your gut telling you?" Randy said.

Willow's hands shook as she held the phone. She tightened her grip.

"My gut is telling me we don't have a lot of options."

"Do you remember what your father told you when he first got diagnosed?" he said.

When Willow looked over at her father, his lips were moving in a soft rhythm like he was singing, but no sound came out. His eyes were fixed on the floor.

"He said, 'don't let my disease become your disease,'" she said, repeating her father's words. The moment felt like it had happened a lifetime ago.

"He'd want this for himself and for you, despite the risks."

Willow hung onto Randy's words. She blinked, and a tear ran down her cheek. She brushed it away before her father could see, though she knew the chances of him noticing were slim.

"I know," Willow said, her words on the verge of a cry.

"I love you," Randy said. His voice was soft, and when Willow closed her eyes, she could imagine they were both home and she was in his arms, away from this hospital.

"I love you, too," she whispered.

"Good luck, sweetheart. You're doing your father well."

She tried to nod with his words and looked to her father. Tom lifted his head slightly and looked at her, but his eyes were lost.

"I'll talk to you when I get home," Willow said, a moment before the call ended.

The silence that remained after she hung up the phone felt heavy. A clipboard sat on the counter, a paper held in place with a blank line for a signature at the bottom. She took the pen the nurse had given her, and with the all care she could muster, she signed her name. She expected the moment to feel final, but the weight in her chest did not lift.

A knock at the door sounded a moment before Dr. Gadel

walked into the room.

"Good morning, Willow. Good morning, Tom," he said, turning to each of them and foaming his hands with sanitizer by the door. His eyes passed over the clipboard with Willow's signature. He took it and sat in the chair across from Tom. A nurse slipped in through the door, pushing a small tray with implements towards Dr. Gadel.

"Thank you, Lisa," he said before the nurse left the room. "Did you have any questions?"

He turned to Willow after he looked over the paper. She had signed everywhere she needed to. All that was left was to inject Tom with the serum and observe what happened.

"How long will it take to see results?"

"Well, assuming it works, it would be as soon as twenty-four hours that your father's brain cells stop dying. From there, we can hope they begin to grow back and multiply like healthy cells. We'll have to coach your father and bring him back up to speed. He can't re-gain memories that he's already lost, but we can certainly help him retain new memories."

"Okay," she said. She was afraid to look at her father and know that what he'd lost was forever gone.

"Do you still want to do this?" Dr. Gadel stood from his chair and rolled the tray closer to him. Implements were arranged across the tray in a perfect order. There was gauze, a syringe, dressing tape, alcohol wipes, and most importantly, a clear purple liquid in a vile.

"I'm sure." Willow stepped toward her father and took his arm. He looked back at her, and Willow could imagine her father the way he used to be. If he were there, he would have smiled in that moment.

Dr. Gadel slipped on rubber gloves and brought the tray

over to Tom.

"Dad," Willow said. "Dr. Gadel is going to give you a quick little shot."

"Yeah, yeah," Tom said. He put his hand out to dismiss her away. When he did, her eye caught sight of the purple bruise on the top of his hand from the IV he had a few days ago when he came in for a test. Purple also skirted the inside of his elbow where a nurse had drawn blood from his arm. The bruised skin cried out for help.

Test after test, all in caution of Derilum. And somehow, each test came out negative. No adverse effects predicted. But there was always a chance.

"Alright, Tom, I hope you don't mind shots." Dr. Gadel used alcohol wipes to sanitize a portion of his arm. Tom didn't say anything as Dr. Gadel worked. He watched Dr. Gadel moving, his sight never straying. Could he remember being prodded by a needle just a few days ago?

Gadel filled the syringe with the purple liquid. It almost glowed in the stark white of the room. His hands worked fast and fluid as he stuck the needle in Tom's arm. Tom didn't flinch or look away. It was Willow who took a step back.

"I love you," she whispered to him. His eyes didn't lift to meet hers. "You're doing so well."

She saw the fluid drain into her father's skin, and from there, there was no going back.

# Chapter 4

Dr. Fischer stood over his patient. His hair was disheveled, and his scrubs were stained with God-knows-what. Around him, nurses seemed to operate in a blur. They were all on a mission, a mission that was familiar to everyone that worked in the ER—save a life. Each of the staff members woke up in hopes of saving lives, to not let another heartbeat die out. The rush of energy filled the room with a desire to move on, to keep working no matter how bleak a patient's outlook seemed.

The man on the table, the stranger in front of him, was fighting for breath that couldn't get through to his lungs. A nurse had him hooked up to an IV and a ventilator machine that did nothing to help against the smoke that had filled his lungs.

There was a hum of machines in the room, all drowned out by the medical staff working to save the man's life. His eyes were closed as bodies moved around him. There was a burn across his chest—some of the hair on his scalp looked like it had been singed off. But he didn't seem to be in pain. The skin was red, almost glossy in appearance. Patches on his chest were wired to the heart monitor, the beeping too inconsistent.

A nurse handed Dr. Fischer a long plastic tube, and with careful hands, he slipped it down the man's throat. The goal? To allow him to clear his airway and breathe. The man didn't respond. Behind the doctor, the heart monitor played a pattern of beats that grew farther and farther apart.

"Damn it," Dr. Fischer mumbled.

There was the prolonged hum from the heart monitor. The sound filled the room; it was the sound that took everyone's breath away. The man's life-line floated the air, mocking everyone in the room. Every nurse and doctor knew what the sound meant. It reverberated off the walls as everyone froze and turned to watch the monitor. Some nurses began to step back; only one nurse continued to treat the burns on the man's body.

A few seconds passed. Dr. Fischer counted the moments.

"Time of death: 4:16 a.m."

He stepped back and looked at his patient. He didn't need the heart monitor to tell him his patient was gone. He could feel it. Each time a patient died, there was a pressure in air, an energy that left the room. It's something Dr. Fischer could never describe, but it weighted on his shoulders, a whisper of a person waiting to be released. Something swept through the room, bringing with it a dark cloak. He wondered if the nurses could sense the change, or if it was just him. When Dr. Fischer looked back at his patient, the man's body was limp, his skin already discolored from the smoke.

The death was followed by a moment of silence. The nurses' faces were bleak as they stepped away from the man laid across the bed. The tube was still down his throat, the IV still in his arm. To anyone else he might just look asleep or under anesthesia, but the feeling of loss was all too familiar for the team.

"Damn it," Dr. Fischer said again. The words echoed across the room. They didn't know who this man was.

– – – – –

The hospital bed wasn't comfortable. Her dry, sandpaper skin brushed against the sheets. When Sam finally woke, it was the stiff sheets that she noticed. Minutes passed before she saw the IV in her arm or the tube in her nose giving her oxygen. When the room came into focus, she thought she could still smell the smoke in the air.

"Good morning, sunshine," a voice said.

Sam turned to see a nurse at her left hand. "Can you tell me your name?" she asked. She smiled gently. In her hands she held a hospital band, not yet around Sam's wrist, but about to be.

"Samantha Ellison," Sam said. Her voice hurt when she spoke. She needed water.

The nurse nodded her head and wrapped the band around Sam's wrist. Sam's skin felt raw. She remembered the fire, and she supposed her skin could be burnt, but wouldn't the nurse have treated her burns?

"Do you want to try to drink something?" The nurse held out a cup of water over Sam and pointed the straw towards Sam's mouth. She took a sip, not realizing how thirsty she was until the water slipped down her throat.

"Thank you," Sam said.

The nurse smiled and put the cup down on the table next to her bed. The bed was surrounded by a curtain, forming its own private room.

"Is my mom going to be here soon?"

The nurse froze for a moment. By now, all the victims of the fire had been identified. Two girls were found upstairs, two adults downstairs where the fire had started. The fire alarm hadn't gone off.

"Samantha," the nurse said.

21

"Sam," she corrected her, but she felt ashamed of speaking. She wasn't ready to hear what the nurse was about to say. Sam remembered the fire, of course she did. Part of her didn't think she'd make it out of the fire. Instead, she ended up in the arms of the firefighter. If she was safe, the rest of her family had to be.

The nurse smiled gently. "What's your mom's name?"

The nurse already knew. She knew both the names of the adults that were found in the fire, but she couldn't stand to look into Sam's eyes until she knew for sure that those were her parents.

"My mom's name is Cheryl, and my dad is Daniel."

The nurse stood across the room. It took her a moment to speak. "Let me talk to the doctor." The nurse walked out of the room before Sam could say anything else.

Sam reached across to the table beside her and took a sip from the cup of water. When the doctor finally walked into the room, Sam was only thinking about how chapped her lips felt.

"Hello, Sam, I'm Dr. Fischer," he said. He was a young doctor, his dark hair cropped close. His scrubs were clean now, a fresh pair that replaced the ones that had been covered in his previous patient's blood. His eyes were ringed with dark circles. "How are you feeling?"

"Sore, dry." She coughed, her throat feeling raw, and brought her hand up to cover her mouth, only to remember she had a tube across her upper lip, leading oxygen into her nose. Her skin felt like it had been pulled taunt. Every move she made, her skin protested.

"You'll be coughing for a while. We want to keep an eye on you, to make sure the smoke doesn't give you any long-term effects. That's what the nasal cannula is for, to make up for any oxygen that may be having a hard time reaching your lungs because of the smoke." He pointed to the tube under Sam's noise.

Dr. Fischer didn't sit. In fact, there were no chairs in the room. There were just curtains, machines, and wires. "I was the doctor that worked on your father when he came in."

"But he'll be okay, right? Does he have one of these like me?" Sam pointed to the nasal cannula. The doctor's face shifted, and she knew she was wrong, very wrong.

The news set in. For some reason she had assumed she was the only one who had needed medical help. She had assumed, or maybe hoped, she was the only one who had been too close to the fire.

"Your dad was found just outside the kitchen. It's not confirmed yet, but authorities are saying that might be where the fire started. We can only assume he tried to stop it from spreading. He had severe burns. He died within a few minutes of arriving at the hospital."

The oxygen continued to travel through Sam's nose and her lungs, but she couldn't breathe. "Where's my mom?" She wanted to cry—it took too long for the tears to form, and when they came they felt all the more painful.

Dr. Fischer frowned. "When the firemen pulled her out of the fire, she had already passed. They think maybe she found the fire first, tried to stop it, but it got more out of control." He was babbling. He shouldn't be telling her this. These are things the police or social services handle. It wasn't his job to tell a girl she's an orphan.

Sam didn't look at him, she couldn't. She looked at the cup, still in her hands, no longer full of water. She felt tired.

"Can I have more water?"

Dr. Fischer didn't question her. He stepped forward, took

the cup from her hands, and pulled the curtains aside so he could leave her little room.

Sam watched him leave, was thankful once he left, and let out a soft, painful cry, and after a moment it was over. She was numb, and she didn't want to cry anymore.

— — — —

There was no warning for the news. She didn't ask for the news. All morning she had been asking for something, any bit of information to know her family was okay. She had finally fallen asleep when a police officer came into the room.

"Avery," the man said.

She sat in her bed, her body sinking into the sheets. She felt sick, like she was going to throw up.

"Avery?"

She heard him.

"My name is Officer Caldwell."

She heard the stranger as he introduced himself.

"Your parents passed away. I'm so sorry."

Her consciousness faded in and out of focus. Passed away? Were those the words he said?

"They're gone." Avery's voice was rough when she spoke, but she wasn't sure if it was because of the smoke she had inhaled or the fact that she was trying to contain the sobs that demanded to be released.

"By the time your mother was discovered, it was too late. The team of doctors and nurses tried to revive your father, but there was nothing they could do."

Avery could remember the last time she had seen her father. His body was laid parallel to hers in the stretcher. She only caught glimpses of him—his red, shining body. It was an image she tried to push from her mind. But she heard him. She heard his echoing cough, how it sounded as if his entire body was being heaved out of the earth. There were moments she wondered if there was blood in those coughs, if his body was beginning to give up on expelling the smoke. Apparently it had.

"There's a social worker here who's going to be speaking with you." But before Officer Caldwell could finish speaking, Avery interrupted.

"Where's Sam?" The words came out as a demand. When Officer Caldwell looked into her eyes, he saw so many things: fear, anguish, desperation. Her mouth hung open, her eyes wide, tears making a steady flow down her face.

"You'll have to talk to the social worker. She has more information."

The officer stood in the curtained room. In a moment so private as learning the death of her parents there were no walls, just thin cloth.

"Avery Ellison?" An older woman poked her head into the room. She wore a pencil skirt with a loose, bright pink blouse, and she held a leather-bound notebook close to her chest. Her hair was dyed blonde; the way a woman might do when her hair is completely gray. Smile lines and laugh lines etched her face. "My name is Paula Tiller. I'm your social worker."

Officer Caldwell looked Mrs. Tiller over quickly, and seeing she had the situation covered, made his way out the door.

"Good luck, Avery," he said. Avery searched for sarcasm in his voice, but his words were sincere, and that made it all the worse. She didn't know the officer, but as she watched him part the curtains to make his way out of the room, she felt tears brimming. Is this how it was going to be now? Being passed from stranger to stranger? Avery was nineteen—practically an adult—but for now she felt like a child.

"Avery, I've been looking over your file since I've arrived, and I have good news for you," Mrs. Tiller said.

Avery wondered if she was serious. Good news? Avery could feel herself shaking. Her legs felt on fire under the thin sheets of the bed, and she remembered that there was a burn on her shin.

"Can you call in a nurse?" Avery said. Her voice was weak, filled with tears. She wanted to sleep and hope that when she woke up she was home again.

"Oh," Mrs. Tiller said. She began to turn to step out of curtained room.

"There's a call button." Avery pointed to the button on the chord next to her bed.

"Right." Mrs. Tiller turned again, this time walking over to press the call button. She smiled at Avery, but her smile cracked whatever glue had been holding her together.

"I'm sorry," Avery said. "I don't—I just—I just want to sleep right now." She struggled to speak. The cries were coming in hiccups, and she wondered if the whole hospital could hear her.

A few second passed while Mrs. Tiller stood, having no idea what to do with her young client, until a nurse stepped in.

"Avery?" the nurse said.

"My leg hurts." Tears were fresh on Avery's face as she spoke.

"It's okay, we'll just put more cream and a new bandage on. It was almost time to do that anyway."

The nurse got to work, pulling the sheets up and revealing Avery's leg, her shin wrapped in white gauze. The nurse used soft fingers to unwrap Avery's leg. The burn screamed against the nurse's touch as she worked, but the physical pain felt lighter than the emotional.

Mrs. Tiller stood in the room, not saying a word. She opened the folder in her hand, read over something quickly, and stepped forward.

"Avery, would you like to speak with me later?" Mrs. Tiller wasn't pushy when she spoke. She was gentle, and for once, she didn't smile.

Avery brushed tears away and looked to Mrs. Tiller. Her words were clear as she spoke. "What's the good news?" She wanted to smile, but a frown formed instead.

"Before your parents passed, they made arrangements. Your grandparents will have full custody, but because you're over eighteen your future is entirely up to you." Mrs. Tiller smiled once she finished speaking. Avery thought of her future, one without her parents, and it seemed too bleak to imagine.

Mrs. Tiller watched Avery. After she finished speaking, Avery looked away and watched the nurse work on her leg instead. As the nurse re-wrapped the gauze, a silent tear slip down her cheek. She didn't hear Mrs. Tilling leave, but she supposed she had, because when she looked up again it was just her and the nurse.

# Chapter 5

4 months ago

Tom's bed was made perfectly. The corners tucked into the edges, crisp, like they had been ironed. The pillow had been smoothed; the way Willow always left it. Every morning, Willow would fluff the pillow, place it in the perfect center of the bed, and then smooth the pillow case. She never made her own bed. Each morning she woke up, she would abandon her bed, sheets strewn about, husband still fast asleep. Usually by the time she made her way out of bed, Tom was already somewhere in the house.

Willow had always thought about what she could do to keep her father in bed. The option of locking the door to his bedroom always entered her mind, but then anxiety would overrule. What if he fell? What if he needed to leave the room, but she couldn't get there in time? So, she kept the door unlocked.

A sensor pad was on the floor, right above where Tom usually stepped to get up. If he put weight on it, an alarm would sound so Willow could know her father was awake. When it failed to go off multiple times, she littered the room with baby monitors and became accustomed to being a light sleeper. Here she was, a woman in her forties, never had a baby, but had tested out all the latest and greatest baby monitors.

Willow pulled the corner of the sheets away. It was another day past, another ending. She was ready to say goodbye to that day and hope that when she woke up in the morning, things for her father would be better. Hopeful.

Arms wrapped around her waist. "Bed time?" Randy whispered in Willow's ear. He looked over her shoulder into the guest bedroom that had become her father's permanent residence. The room was pristine. The drawers to the dresser was closed, but Randy knew if he opened it all, Tom's clothes would be perfectly folded.

"Just about," Willow said. She entwined her fingers through Randy's and stepped away from the bed.

"Want any help getting him settled?"

"Is my dad still on the couch?"

"Watching another episode of Dirty Jobs. Want me to get him?"

Randy loosened his grip and Willow turned to look at him. Her eyes were a bright green. When he looked at them he could get lost, but her eyes seemed to wander off somewhere far. He held her in his arms, but he could feel her floating away.

"It's fine, I'll get him," she said, slipping out of his grip.

When she was gone, the air felt colder. Randy walked out of the room, careful not to step on the sensor mat on the floor. There was a quiet muffle of the TV in the living room and then it turned off.

"Dad," Randy could hear Willow say. Randy thought he heard Tom say something in response but he couldn't make out the words. "Dad, it's time for bed." This time her voice was louder.

Randy stood up and ran down the hall to the living room.

The TV was off and Tom was standing in front of the couch, but he held the remote while Willow tried to keep it in her grip. He knew if Willow tried, she could easily pull the remote out of Tom's grasp, but she always refused to raise a finger to him.

"Tom, you can watch TV in bed," Randy said. He walked towards Willow, and she released the remote. Her face was etched with shock and she stepped backwards. Tom pulled the remote to his chest and sat down on the couch.

"Move," Tom said. His voice was rough, and Randy knew he was having another one of his episodes. Tom looked at his daughter with pointed eyes until she cowered away.

Willow pulled her arms into her chest and slipped out of the room. Randy thought he could spot fresh tears coating her eyes.

"Tom, it's time for bed," Randy said. He learned forward and took the remote out of Tom's hand while he listened to Willow's soft footsteps as she walked upstairs.

"No," Tom said. The remote was out of his hands and the TV was off but his eyes were still glued to the screen.

"You can finish watching TV in your room." Randy took his arm with a firm grip, just enough for Tom to realize that the time for jokes was done. Once Tom stood, Randy loosened his grip and took Tom to his bedroom without another word.

As Randy pulled the sheets back he listened for Willow up the stairs.

"What are you doing?" The voice was Tom's, and it pulled Randy back into the moment. He helped Tom undress, fold the clothes, and put it on top of his dresser next to his bed.

Randy had a habit of not answering Tom. When he was first diagnosed he always made it a point to answer every question he asked, but as time passed and the questions become more plentiful it became a habit to just ignore them.

"What are you doing?" Tom asked again, and so the repeating began.

Randy worked as quickly as Tom would allow him to get his pajamas on. The fleece was loose against Tom's limbs, like he was shrinking into himself.

"What are you doing?"

"It's time for bed," Randy said, finally answering. "Just lie down, okay?"

"Where's Willow?" he asked. He lay back in bed and let Randy pull the covers over him. As he stepped back from the bed, he watched the mat to make sure he didn't touch it.

"In bed," Randy said.

The answer seemed to satisfy Tom, and he relaxed into the mattress, closing his eyes without a peep about wanting his television show turned back on.

Randy shut the glass door to the room, still watching Tom as he backed away. Willow had insisted on the glass door when her father first moved in. "We'll be able to check on him whenever we need to without being afraid of waking him up by opening the door." The point was true, but the glass door made him feel like Tom was a fish in a tank, or maybe it was the other way around.

"Willow?" Randy said as he made his way up the stairs. She didn't respond.

When he turned into their bedroom, he found her on the edge of the bed, sitting up, but slowly sinking into the mattress. She looked up when he stepped into the room and the anguish was coated in her skin. She was a bright piece of panic. The tears were still readily streaming.

"It's okay," Randy said as he reached across the room and took her in his arms.

Her body was shaking and she curled into him, tucking her knees up as she sunk into his chest. His pulled her hair away from her face and he turned her head into his chest to hide herself.

"Your dad is just having another one of his episodes, he's fine now." He ran his fingers over the skin on her arms. He could feel her quaking, and he held her tighter as if he could pull her back together.

"There's nothing I can do," Willow whispered. Her voice was disgruntled and thick.

"It's just part of the disease."

She pulled herself up and broke away from his arms. "Then what was the point of all this? What was the point of the tests, all the doctors, all this time, effort, money, hope that maybe he'll get better or at least stop declining. It's been three months since we started the treatments. Was all that for nothing?"

Willow was still sitting on the bed, but her body was strung high and alert. Her spine was as straight as an arrow, her arms holding herself away from Randy when they had once held him close. She was ready to flight.

"It's just been a bad day," Randy said. "These things take time." He reached out for her hand, and he thought for a moment she was going to pull away. Her body was stiff, but when he wrapped his fingers around hers, she began to thaw. With gentle movement, Randy pulled her closer. With each inch closer, she sank into Randy until he was holding her to him. She surrendered into his body, and as she relaxed the tension left her. She melted into him, each limb uncurling. She let go of control and the tears billowed over.

"I can't do anything," she said again. She mumbled the words to herself over and over until her words got so soft, Randy couldn't make them out anymore.

# Chapter 6

Sam tugged the tube beneath her noise. She stared at the threads of the blanket over her body, the only thing she seemed to be able to focus on at the moment. The hospital was cool, and the blanket was thin. Her body was rigid; her heart felt the same.

"Sam?" Dr. Fischer appeared in her curtained room, an older woman in a pant-suit beside him. Sam pulled the blanket up over her body, wondering how she looked in comparison. "Sam, this is your social worker, Paula Tiller. She wanted to speak with you."

"Good morning, Sam," the woman said. "You can call me Mrs. Tiller." She offered her hand out and Sam shook it; the woman's grip was loose.

Dr. Fischer slipped out of the room as quickly as he had appeared, leaving Sam with Mrs. Tiller.

"How are you feeling?" Mrs. Tiller stood at the foot of her bed, holding a folder of papers. She thought she could see Avery's name written at the edge of one of the folders.

"Tired," Sam said.

Mrs. Tiller let the corners of her lips lift and then her smile disappeared as if she caught herself. "Did you want to talk about what happened?"

Sam felt her eyes water and wiped the tears away before they could form.

"Um." A tear slipped. "My parents are both dead?" She didn't mean for it to come out as a question.

Mrs. Tiller paused at the foot of the bed and frowned. "I wish I didn't have to be standing here in front of you." She paused and tried to smile before thinking better of it again. "I wish it were your mom or dad here for you, but I'm here to make things easier for you. I'm here to make sure you're okay, and that we find someone to take care of you."

"What about Avery? Is she okay?"

"She is," Mrs. Tiller said. Sam felt herself wanting to smile as well, but it seemed like too much energy. "She's in this hospital right now. She's okay, a burn on her leg, but she's okay."

Sam's head began to hurt. She itched at the tube under her nose, longed for more oxygen. Her breathing felt too rapid and her airways still too tight. Her body was fighting against her as she tried to breathe. All the while, she tried not to think of her parents, but again and again their faces came to mind.

"Can I be alone?" Sam said. Her words seemed weaker.

"Are you sure you don't want to talk to anyone right now? It doesn't have to be me. I could find a doctor or nurse, just someone who will listen," Mrs. Tiller said. Her hands furled and unfurled in front of her.

A lone tear trailed down Sam's face. She shook her head, and it was all Mrs. Tiller needed to leave the room. Sam's breathing hitched once she left the room. The coughing started soon after and she let herself surrender into it. She closed her eyes and hoped for sleep. For now, Sam didn't want to handle reality.

– – – – –

There was gauze below Avery's knee. It was wrapped lightly around her leg, but it felt suffocating. Underneath the gauze, her skin was blistering.

"Ms. Ellison?" Mrs. Tiller walked into the room. "How are you feeling today?"

Mrs. Tiller was afraid of her steps as she took them, and Avery wondered how she ever became a social worker. She didn't move to take a seat in the room even though there was a chair next to where she stood and Avery wondered if she was planning on leaving again soon.

"Someone's here for you." Mrs. Tiller smiled when she spoke and the gesture seemed to hurt Avery all the more.

Avery pulled herself up in her bed. Mrs. Tiller turned to the door, and Avery followed with her eyes but the wrong person walked through the threshold. Avery imagined it would be Sam, and that the two of them could face their new life side-by-side, but instead her grandmother walked in.

"Avery?"

"Hey," Avery said. She looked her grandmother over and wanted to cry. When she blinked, she thought she saw her mom. The way she shifted back and forth on her feet, the way only one corner of her mouth seemed to tip up into a smile. She looked nothing like her mother, but the way she held herself made it feel as if she was staring at a ghost.

"Oh, sweetie," Shelly said. She had streaks of mascara under her eyes. "I came as soon as I heard. I wish I could have been here sooner." Avery looked at the clock. It was 7:08pm. Had this day not passed yet? Avery turned to her grandmother, wishing for the nightmare to end.

Shelly sat beside Avery on the bed, wrapping her arms

around her. Avery stiffened. Her body felt raw, her skin still too dry and burnt, but then she began to cry, to really cry since the moment she had arrived at the hospital. It was like a gate had been opened in her and now there was nothing she could do to contain her emotions.

"They're gone," Avery said. Her voice was muffled in her grandmother's hair. Shelly didn't cry. She was too tired to cry. She cried enough on the car ride to the hospital. Now, she held her granddaughter, whom she hadn't seen in so long, as she fell apart. Shelly's only hope was that she could pick up the pieces.

"I know," was all Shelly could say.

Mrs. Tiller found herself backing out of the room, shutting the door. Avery watched her walk away through watered eyes, relieved at her absence.

"It's going to be okay," Shelly said. Avery leaned into her chest, pushing the blanket away. Shelly saw the strips of gauze across Avery's leg and winced.

Moments passed in silence before either found the courage to speak. They sat curled on Avery's hospital bed, the sound of nurses and doctors on the other side of the door a constant reminder that things were forever changed.

"What caused the fire?" Avery said. Her eyes were red and worn, her cheeks stained. Shelly took a deep breath. It was the question that was being repeated throughout the clinical staff and police. It was the same question Shelly asked when she first heard about the fire. And she knew the answer.

"It started in the kitchen. The fire alarms in the house malfunctioned and didn't go off—they're still trying to figure out why." Shelly turned to look at Avery, but she didn't seem to react. "From what the police can tell, the oven was never turned off. The burners caught something on fire, and since there was no fire alarm, by the time the fire was noticed, there was nothing your parents could do to put it out—but," she hesitated, wondering if she wanted to speak the words. "But they wanted to try to stop it. Or at least that's what they think."

"I didn't turn off the oven," Avery said. Her mouth hung open and she could feel herself shaking. The tips of her fingers quivered. "I forgot to turn the oven off." Avery moved the thin sheets from her feet and stepped out of bed. Her skin stretched against the movement, raw and dry. She could still imagine the fire against her limbs, but she pushed past it and walked toward door.

"Avery, stop." Shelly got up and pulled Avery back.

"The fire was my fault," she said. She turned to look at Shelly, and the tears were there again. Avery didn't bother wiping them from her cheek. "It's my fault," she said, her voice squeaking.

"It's not," Shelly whispered. She pulled her granddaughter to her, standing in the middle of the room.

Avery tried to pull away from her, and Shelly let her slip out of her arms. Avery slid to the floor, her shin burning and her body shaking. "I was on a date. I got home late. I made a grilled cheese because I was hungry, and I must have forgotten to turn off the oven because—" she stopped herself.

"It's okay," Shelly said, but she didn't know what to do for comfort. She watched, helpless, as Avery sunk into the floor.

Shelly knelt down beside her, tried to hold her, but Avery just continued to push her away.

"It's my fault," Avery said, her tears ran hot onto the cold tile.

37

# Chapter 7

3 months ago

Willow was pacing outside the bedroom. The anxiety came rushing out through her body in sparks. She imagined them reverberating throughout the room as if they were something physical she could catch and use to bring her back down to Earth. She bounced with each step, eager to do something, anything but think, but that's all she seemed to be able to do recently.

"Please, Willow, this isn't good for you," Randy said. He was in the hallway with Willow, watching her pace. "You love your job, I know you do, but you can't work and take care of your father."

"No, I'm fine. I cut my hours at work. I'll be okay," she said. Her feet led her in circles.

Randy looked at his wife, his eyes always following her. "When did you cut your hours?"

"A few weeks ago."

"Honey, you've been looking more and more exhausted for weeks. If you don't want to look into nursing homes, maybe we can hire an in-home aid."

"No," she said. Though tired, her body seemed to awaken. "I don't want someone else to take care of him. I don't want him to feel like he needs constant care."

Randy looked at his wife. Her skin was pale, her face flush. Dark circles were painted under her eyes, and Randy tried to remember the last time Willow had gone to bed at the same time as him. She had a tendency to stay up late enough that he was fast asleep by the time she slipped into bed. Yet, she always managed to be the first one out of bed to go check on Tom even if he wasn't awake yet. Thin grey hairs speckled her temples—he was trying to remember if he'd ever noticed them before.

"He does need constant care." He tried to say the words gently, but he could see them slice through her. When she heard his words, her world seemed to stop—her pacing held still. Her green eyes glowed bright as the tear escaped. For a moment, Randy was afraid she would walk away, but instead she stepped forward and let herself crumble into his arms. She let her body melt into Randy's, his arms strong around her shoulders. She struggled for breath. He whispered into her hair.

"It's going to be okay."

When Willow closed her eyes, she could almost picture her father as he once was—a tall man, someone respected, someone that always held himself high. He had taught her to ride a bike, how to drive, he'd been the first one there to hug her when she passed her nursing exam—he had walked her down the aisle. There were some days she looked at her father and wondered if he was there. Who was this person in front of her that looked like her father? Surely it couldn't be him. But there were moments, rare and precious moments when Tom spoke up and it was like Alzheimer's had never laid its hand upon him.

"I love you, Willow," Randy said, his arms still tight

around her. He let his lips be drawn into the crown of her head and kissed her. "I love you because of how fiercely you love. I know you would drop the world to take care of your father, but you need to take care of yourself first. Whatever you want to do — quit your job, find someone to take care of your dad while we're at work — we'll be okay. But we can't keep doing this. You can't be in this constant state of worry because you aren't sure where your dad is or if he's okay."

"I know," she said. Her words were soft and her knees shook, tempting her beyond everything else to give up.

"What if I'm like my father one day?" Willow laid her head against Randy's chest and listened to his heartbeat in hope that the rhythm would calm her own.

"You won't be," Randy said. He brought her hand forward from where it rested on his chest and kissed the tips of her fingers.

"It can be genetic sometimes," she said.

Randy wanted to say something else, but a beeping came from Tom's room. Willow rushed away from his arms, and the moment they had was gone in an instant. The alarm was a common one — Tom has gotten out of bed. Sometimes it felt as if they were caring for a toddler

.

# Chapter 8

Sam woke up before it happened. Her body was electric when she slipped into consciousness. Her eyes were open, and she knew they were open, but she couldn't find the center of the room. She held still but everything began to turn. Her limbs felt jittery, and that's when it happened.

Sam's body was only shaking for a moment before a nurse ran in.

"Code blue!" the nurse yelled out. She stood over Sam's body as she convulsed. Sam stayed in the bed, her limbs never thrashing around to break anything. The nurse held Sam's IV out of the way and worked to turn Sam on her side. Another nurse ran into the room with an IV bag. She worked quickly to exchange Sam's previous IV bag for another. As soon as the tubes were hooked into place she squeezed the bag gently. Sam's body stilled and her limbs relaxed into the bed.

"Get Dr. Fischer," the nurse said.

Penny left just as quickly as she had come. The nurse kept Sam on her side and used the sheet of the bed to wipe the saliva that was at the corner of Sam's mouth.

"What happened?" Dr. Fischer walked into the room,

Penny trailing lose behind. He foamed his hands as soon as he stepped through the door and put gloves on.

"She was having a seizure when I walked by. From what I observed, it lasted about twenty seconds."

Dr. Fischer nodded his head and knelt down in front of Sam. He checked the machines around her bed for an abnormality in her vitals, but as far as someone who had just had a seizure, she was good. He checked her pulse anyways. Normal. Her eyes fluttered open, and when Dr. Fischer looked at them they were slightly bloodshot.

Sam rolled until she was on her stomach.

"Sam, you need to stay on your side for a little bit," Dr. Fischer said. He helped her roll back onto her side and she let out a groan. "How do you feel? Does anything hurt?"

"My head," she whispered. She rolled into her back and Dr. Fischer helped guide her into a position that didn't affect her IV.

"It's going to hurt for a little while, but you're okay."

Sam's eyes roamed around the room. She saw a nurse standing close to her, but couldn't make out what she was doing.

"Sam?" Her eyes sparked open when she heard the voice, and she turned to the door to see two familiar figures.

The figures walked closer until they came into focus.

"Grampy?" she said.

"What happened?" he said, but he wasn't talking to Sam anymore.

"Just take some deep breaths, Sam," Dr. Fischer said. She took a long, shuttering gasp. He turned to the couple that walked into the room. "I'm Dr. Fischer, I've been treating Sam and Avery during their stay." He held his hand out to shake.

"Paul," Sam's grandfather said. "And this is my wife

Shelly." He took the doctor's hand. "What happened?"

"From what I can tell, Sam had a seizure. I'm not sure why, so we're going to run a few tests and get as much information as we can."

"You don't know?" Paul said, his voice raising. Shelly stood next to him, holding his hand and she pulled on him as a silent way to ask him to calm down.

"No, sir, but we're working as quickly as we can."

"Well, you need to work quicker."

"Honey," Shelly said. She pulled him away from the doctor enough to make him notice someone else had walked into the room.

"Grandpa?"

Paul turned around to see Avery standing at the door. He wanted to scoop her up as soon as he saw her, but at the same time she looked too fragile. She took small steps as she came into the room, a small grimace pulling at the corner of her lips. Shelly stood close behind her at the doorway, looking past him to Sam who was becoming a science experiment to the nurses.

"Avery." As Paul spoke, relief washed through his body. She ran towards him as best he could, still limping. "You're okay," he said as she entered her arms.

"I'm okay," she said, but the words weren't sure. He hugged her delicately and she buried herself into his shirt. He was something familiar she needed.

"Sam?" Avery said, looking at Sam, her face lips turned down and eyes glossy and red. Avery turned to her grandfather, but he didn't speak. The wrinkles across his face were defined more than ever, and she tried to remember if his hair was this gray the last time she had seen him. Paul let go of her, and Shelly placed her hand on Avery's shoulder. "She's okay, right?" Avery looked to grandmother who wrapped her in her arms, kissing the top of her head before speaking.

"Sweetie, she had a seizure. They aren't sure what caused it, but they need to run tests," Shelly said. A flicker of hope poked through her exterior, but her eyes wandered to the corner of the room where Sam was laying.

Avery turned to her Shelly. Her face fell slack, the tears wanted to return, and they slipped like rain drops as she reached out for her grandmother's arms.

# Chapter 9

In the end, it wasn't Alzheimer's that killed Tom. It was a blood clot. Willow remembered walking down the street with her father, just as they always did after lunch, when he stumbled forward before falling to the ground.

"Dad?" she said. Tom's face was white. Willow's arms were around him, his body limp.

"Whhii..." He put his arm out, and Willow held him up.

She was helpless as her father vomited on the side of the road. There were birds chirping as she held him. She held onto him while she tried to reach for her phone in her pocket, but she couldn't reach and she was too terrified to let go of him.

"Miss?" A car had pulled up by now, a stranger sticking his head out the window. Willow didn't let him speak.

"Call 911," she said. The man nodded his head and within seconds she could hear him talking to the operator. "I think he's having a stroke." She didn't bother to turn to the kind stranger to see if he was listening, her eyes were all for her father. His face sagged, and she watched her father disappear in her arms.

"Hhheee," Tom said, though the words were unclear. He

began coughing that turned into wheezing. Willow laid him across the ground, placing him on his side in case he started to vomit again.

"It's going to be okay," she said. Her years of schooling to be a nurse ran through her head, but panic ruled out. What could she do? How was it she could save the life of a stranger but not her own father?

An ambulance pulled up, and by then Tom had stopped seizing. They worked around his body and placed it on a stretcher. She wanted to ask questions or stand by her father in case he opened his eyes to look for her, but to her the moment was frozen.

Her hands outweighed her will as she took out her phone and dialed Randy's number. He picked up on the fourth ring.

"Hey, sweetie." His voice was kind — it was always kind.

"My dad," she said, and finally it seemed the tears wanted to pour. The panic was evident. "I think he had a stroke; he's in the ambulance now."

She heard rustling in the background. The sound of a door opening. "You were on your walk? I'm coming. I'll be there soon." He hung up.

Willow stood, watching the EMTs lean over her father. He was hooked up to a defibrillator. He was covered in so many tubes she had to search to find his face in the chaos. Bodies rushed around her. Cars of strangers were parked on the side of the road, ready to help. But what was she supposed to do?

"Willow." Randy come up behind her, his hand finding hers before she collapsed into his arms. He was covered in sweat. Had he run all the way from their house? How long ago had he hung up the phone?

He brought her closer to the ambulance and spoke in rushed words to the EMTs. She hung on him, like a small child lost in a crowd and he never loosened his grip. He wasn't Randy anymore, he was Dr. Ash. Willow couldn't hear the EMTs as they spoke. Her father was in the stretcher, surrounded by machines that were supposed to save his life, but he was already gone.

— — — — —

She watched as his casket was lowered into the ground. The man she had once known, the father that had been with her every second of her life — he wasn't there anymore. He hadn't been there for years. He wasn't in the casket at her feet, and he hadn't been there when he died. It didn't seem fair for him to be gone. Was she supposed to continue, pretend like he had never existed? No. The memories of her father seemed burnt into her core.

Everyone that had come to the funeral were long gone. They had all said their goodbye and offered condolences before they left, and now it was just Willow and her husband. He stood farther back from the grave than her. She watched workers fumble awkwardly with the casket. Sometimes they looked over at Willow, waiting for her to walk away. When she could no longer picture her father in the grave, she turned away, Randy following close behind.

"You okay?" Randy put his hand out to his wife. Her face was dry, but the tears had been replaced by a raw numbness.

"I'm okay," she said, more to convince herself than her husband.

He opened the passenger door and she slipped in. The funeral tag was still hanging on the rearview mirror, and she pulled it off and put it in the glove box.

She couldn't stop picturing her father falling to the ground. He had been walking, then what? She had caught him, but what good does that do if it's a stroke? She could catch him a million times and there would always be the same result.

47

Randy sat in the driver's seat and looked over at her.

"Hey," he gripped her hand. "Don't do that."

She was being quiet. She knew that. In this car with Randy, she was not present. Willow was away somewhere she could not be reached, her mind floating somewhere far away. It was Randy's hand that seemed to pull her out of the fog, and with it came every emotion she tried so hard to repress.

"Do you think it's my fault?" She said the words so quietly she hoped Randy had not heard them.

"What?" He seemed angry when he responded, but he kept driving and for that she was thankful.

"I didn't do anything when my father fell. I just...I stood there. I wasn't even the one who called 911. A stranger did. I don't even know his name."

"Willow, there was nothing you could do." His words seemed final, frustrated, but most of all tired. When they pulled into the driveway neither of them got out of the car.

The silence didn't want to go on. Willow sucked in a breath. "When you got there, you jumped into action. Why couldn't I do that?"

Randy turned to her, wrapped his fingers around her chin and kissed her forehead. "Because the hardest patients to treat are the ones we love."

She wanted to let his words comfort her, but instead she looked up at Randy and felt herself falling. Not in the literal sense — no, that would be too easy — but in a much harder way. She could feel herself slipping into the darkness that sometimes consumed her when she wasn't careful enough to distract herself away from the reality of life.

"Jeremy," Randy said.

A tear slipped when Willow looked up. She was

consumed with the type of grief that took you far away, away from your own body, but with Randy's voice she would hear herself being pulled in again.

"What?" she said.

"Jeremy. That was the name of the man that called 911. He was driving to the store when he saw you and Tom on the side of the road. I talked to him — I wanted to thank him."

Willow looked at her husband, wide-eyed. The day her father died, she felt so trapped, much like she did now. If she thought back, she wouldn't be able to say what the stranger looked like, never mind his name. The details were so skewed from that day. She remembered the look on her father's face as she saw the light fade from his eyes, she could remember the stain that was on his shirt from when he spilled his drink at lunch, but the one person who stopped to help?

"He died twice, didn't he?" she said.

Randy looked over to her, his ears never straying from hers.

"When someone has Alzheimer's, they die first when they lose their memories, their thoughts, and their personality. And then they die again. We can no longer pretend that, that shell of a person is them anymore, we're forced to finally let them go." She choked on her words as she spoke. "I didn't want to let my father go."

"I didn't want to let him go either," Randy said. Their voices hung in the air. He looked at her; his hand was still gripped to hers. The car was hot and sweat was beginning to coat her forehead, her dress clinging to her body.

"Tell me about work," she said. He frowned when she spoke, but she wouldn't let her eyes leave him.

"Do you remember a few months ago, how I applied for a

fund to conduct research on Alzheimer's?"

The word made Willow cower, like it was a knife being skimmed across her skin.

"I remember," she said.

"My department was chosen for the funding. Our program can move forward. We'll be able to do more research, find out how we can put a stop to this disease — or at least how to curb it."

He was full of possibilities when he spoke. A cure. That was the dream. But Willow had been there before, had seen clinical trial after clinical trial fail. When her father was diagnosed, she wanted the best for him, but the best wasn't good enough. What difference could Randy make? What if there was no cure to be found? Did he know, with each day it felt like she was losing herself more and more? That soon enough, she was going to wake up and forget who her husband was?

"Good," she said, but the smile wasn't there.

She kept a paper in her pocket now, to write things down. She wouldn't lose her memories the same way her father had.

"Willow." He released her hand and let it fall to her lap. It felt like a betrayal to have him release her, but a moment later his hand was on her cheek, turning her face to look at him. Her fingers traced the warn piece of paper in her pocket. "I promise you, I will do everything I can to find a cure. I won't let this happen to you, or me, or anybody else ever again."

And she let herself pretend his words were true.

# Chapter 10

There were three people in the room sitting huddled together when Sam's neurologist walked in. The oldest two — the grandparents he supposed — looked as if life had hit them like a truck. They leaned into each other, neither able to support themselves. The youngest was a girl who looked about nineteen with eyes that darted around the room. She was the first person to spot him, and when she did, her demeanor changed. She lifted her head and sat up straight, but her hands stayed in her lap; a slight tremor shook her.

"Good evening," he said as he approached the group. They all lifted their heads. "My name is Dr. Randy Ash. I'll be taking care of Samantha during her time here. Though we meet under unfortunate conditions, I hope we can accommodate you all the best we can."

"Thank you," Shelly said. Her hands gripped around her husband's like a vice. Paul nodded his head toward the doctor, but the rest of his body stayed rooted in place.

The room stayed silent, hold for the hushed murmurs of the waiting room.

"Can we see Sam?" Avery said. Everyone tuned to look at

her and then towards Dr. Ash, waiting for an answer. Paul was already on the edge of his seat, ready to leave and find his granddaughter.

"Unfortunately, Sam is a bit under the weather at the moment. I'm not sure the best thing for her would be seeing visitors." Paul opened his mouth to speak until Shelly put her hand on his knee. His body relaxed and leaned into her again and closed his eyes, resting his head on Shelly's shoulder.

"What's wrong with her?" It was Avery who spoke the words everyone else was too terrified to say. Paul opened his eyes to look at the doctor, but he didn't lift his head.

"As of right now, she's sleeping. The seizure she had earlier took a lot out of her, and her body needs some time to recoup. We hope to perform a few tests soon to determine what caused the seizure, but we have to wait until she's stable."

"Do you think the fire had anything to do with it?" Shelly asked. Her arm was wrapped around Paul while her other hand reached out for Avery.

"It's possible that the lack of oxygen could have brought on a seizure, though it's not likely. It may have been a pre-existing condition that hasn't come to a head until now. The fact that she was already in a hospital is just luck. It's allowed us to give her immediate treatment to stabilize her."

Avery was sinking. Her body was heavy; her feet were planted firmly to the floor, but the urge to run was strong.

They weren't sure if they'd be able to stabilize her?

— — — — —

Willow couldn't ignore the beats of her heart. It made her panic to hear it so loud, like she was holding her head up to her own chest. She had been working with a patient, checking his vitals, when she lost her breath.

Sweat was coating her skin as her throat closed in on itself. Panic jumped through her veins, and her body urged her to do something, so she smiled to her patient, walked out of the room, and ran down the hall.

The corners of her vision began to recede, and she walked the halls, holding her head high. Coworkers walked by and smiled; she smiled back but the muscles didn't feel right. Black edged her vision, and she began to run when she thought she couldn't see anyone anymore.

Willow ran through the door of a patient's room that had been empty earlier, but she almost screamed when she saw someone in the bed.

Tubes lined the young girl's body. Her eyes were shut, but her chest moved in a steady rhythm. Willow backed away, but panic took over and she leaned on the edge of the girl's bed for support. The stranger never stirred.

This wasn't her patient. A white board on the wall read Samantha Ellison, and Randy's name was written at the top as the practitioner.

By law, they couldn't care for the same patients. Willow put her hand to her throat as if that would help clear her airways.

The girl in the bed stirred and shifted to the side. Her breath hitched, then she fell back into a slumber. The monitors and wires connected to her beeped in response.

Willow watched the rise and fall of the girl's chest and tried to mimic the movement.

The panic refused to leave her body. It moved like a current through her skin until it urged her to pace the room. She didn't think about her movements. She couldn't stop herself if she wanted to. Instead, she paced. She panicked. And she prayed for the moment end.

Was this what her father had felt like when he had an episode?

As soon as the thought entered her mind she couldn't forget it. Her heartbeat rose and her breathing thinned. She tried to remember why she started panicking but she couldn't. Alzheimer's. The disease haunted her. Could it be running its course through her nerve cells?

"Willow?"

Someone was at the doorway. Willow blinked until her eyes came into focus and saw that it was a nurse—Jenna. She walked into the room with a smile though questions littered her eyes. She put a folder onto the table next to the patient's bed.

"Are you okay?" Jenna asked. In the months since her father had died, she hadn't been going out with Jenna as much, but they always made sure to make time at least once a week to sit down and talk. In truth, Jenna was the only person who could keep Willow grounded, especially after her father had passed away, but now she couldn't speak.

Jenna walked closer to Willow, and she backed away and turned to leave.

"Sorry," Willow said. Her body couldn't hold still and she could barely make her words form between breaths.

"Willow?"

Willow heard Jenna calling for her as she paced down the hall to Randy's office. She only hoped Jenna didn't follow her and Randy wasn't inside.

She walked down the hall, only able to focus on what was directly in front of her. She felt her body swaying and knew if she stopped that she may not be able to start again.

Randy's door was locked when Willow found her way through the long hallways. She murmured a soft prayer as she slipped the spare key into the lock and shut herself into the small room. It was empty.

Papers littered Randy's desk, and dozens of notebooks were left open, each filled with illegible writing.

Her body was still frantic as Willow searched through folders of research. Her vision was blurred, but as the seconds passed, her head began to clear enough to read and she tried to focus as much as her attention on the papers in front of her.

He had been approved for his research, thank god he had been approved, but could he work fast enough to save her? She skimmed article after article written about Alzheimer's hoping to find something to ease her mind. The words swam around her, and her throat threatened to cut off supply of oxygen as she leafed through the pages. She knew the symptoms of Alzheimer's like the back of her hand, but to be a victim felt different — dangerous.

Willow wasn't sure how long she spent looking through the files. She expected her heart rate to calm, but it only edged closer and closer to hysteria the longer she read articles with hopeless fingers.

Willow opened a thick folder only to find her handwriting staring back it her. Page after page of Tom's symptoms, his medications, his good days. It was a medical journal Willow obsessively worked to create. Looking at it now was disturbing. She read the pages of notes over and over until she thought she saw herself in the pages and flung it away. She tried to breathe.

She pulled out another folder. All the other articles she had read so far had Randy's handwriting in the margins, but this one was clean. The article was about a trial that was being conducted in New Zealand — The Venom Trials. As she skimmed the pages, her heart dropped. Was this the trial Dr. Gadel had been talking about? A note was made about the drug Derilum. It was noted as failed.

Willow pushed the papers away, but she couldn't stop looking at them. The half thought-through drug they had used on her father.

The tears ran in violent streams when she finally picked up the papers again, this time pacing as she read.

The article made notes of the formula used to create the venom. She laid out the page out on Randy's desk, and her heart stopped. Could it be that simple?

Willow looked the chemicals over and over. Their grams, their composition — it was all there. If she wanted, it was as simple as going to the lab and putting it all together. She could perfect the serum, fix what everyone else had missed or were too afraid to try.

She took out her paper. Notes were written all over the margins. Things she needed to buy, phone numbers she needed to remember. But now, more menial things were etched into the page: lunch break is at 12:20, the trash gets picked up on Thursdays; things she used to know that felt like they were slipping. She wrote the chemical formula of the serum into a corner of the page that remained white.

Already the paper was worn, perfect squares folding into creases, a small rip in the center of the sheet from wear. She started writing on the paper the day her father died, and it was almost every day she added another phone number or name to the list. Randy's birthday. Yesterday, she added the date her father died with a Sharpie marker. With so many other numbers and letters already written down, it seemed important this one stood out. She would not let herself become that date.

The paper was soft and worn where it folded. A few more days, and it was bound to rip.

It was her father she thought about as she folded the page and slipped it back into the pocket of her scrubs.

# Chapter 11

Willow's shift finished long after the night rounds began. She knew the lab was going to be locked before she tried to open the door. Her badge didn't grant her access, but she knew Randy's would. He was on his lunch break when she slipped back into his office.

His white coat was on the back of his chair, his ID hanging off the breast pocket. Randy had a bad habit of walking around without his ID. It was something she reprehended him for almost every day, but today it worked to her advantage. She removed his ID and walked back out to the hall in the direction of the lab.

All she needed was to swipe into the lab, jam the latch so it can't lock and put Randy's badge back before he came back. She held his ID tight in her hands and departed down the hall. When she finally got to the lab, she was relieved to hear the click of the lock moving out of place. She took an old brochure off one of the nearby countertops and slipped it between the door-jam so it wouldn't be able to close all the way. She took a step back, Randy's ID still in the palm of her hand, and ran.

She had to put Randy's ID back in his office and get back to the lab before anyone else walked into the lab. She wasn't sure how high-traffic the lab was, but if someone else walked in and let the brochure fall, she had no way of getting in.

Randy's office was still empty when she got there and she clipped his ID back into place. He would never notice.

It felt like too much time had passed when she reached the lab again, but she was able to breathe again when she saw there the brochure was still sticking out the door. She took the edge of the brochure in one hand and the doorknob in the other, and she walked into the lab without issue. The room was empty.

She shut the door behind herself and unfolded the paper she had been keeping in her pocket all day. Her hands were shaking when she put on a lab coat and gloves and began to work.

The amount of time that passed was unknown to Willow. Underneath the latex gloves, sweat coated her hands as she mixed liquid and powder milliliter by milliliter. By the end of it, a light yellow, almost orange liquid came to rest at the bottom of the cylinder tube. No more than 5 milliliters, it almost glowed against the hue of the room.

The repercussions of it wasn't what struck her. It was the simplicity of it. In her hand was something that could ruin so many lives, but could also bring a cure. The study in New Zealand was making so much forward movement, but they were on mice. It would be years before they ever moved forward with human trials. Was that what was stopping them? Could a cure be as simple as testing it on a human?

Her father's face came into her mind. She remembered when Dr. Gadel first told her about the trial and she thought he was suggesting doing the venom trials on her father. At the time, she was appalled, but was that all it would take? One human life.

When Willow looked up again the clock on the far side of the room read 1:13am. She placed the tube in a holster and backed away, terrified of the thing she had created without even knowing if it had any real power.

Her fingers went numb. Leaning against the wall, she slipped the gloves off as fast as she could, throwing them to the floor. A counter was at her back as she watched the serum from across the room. She wanted to imagine it boiling over, bubbling until it burned away at the counter.

Looking at it was suffocating. She imagined injecting the solution into her skin, feeling how her father felt. Was he in pain? Did he know what was happening to him? The man he used to be seemed too far away. When she pushed against the thoughts, she could only remember the father of her childhood. The memories of adulthood were riddled, stained by Alzheimer's.

Heart beating, palms sweating, eyes crying, Willow stepped across the room, gripped the tube, and stepped into the halls.

The hospital hadn't changed. Long hallways going in every direction, signs directing to corridors that patients would never be able to find. But Willow found her way, lab coat still on, the cool air making no effect on her fogged mind. She took a syringe from a nurse's cart as she walked by. She walked until it was Samantha Ellison's room she entered.

She wasn't sure why it was Samantha's room she walked into. It could have been anyone, but as her feet carried her forward she found herself walking through the doorway of a girl who had already lost so much.

To have control. To find a cure. That was the goal.

To never let this disease course through her body. To never forget who she loved. To never forgot why she loved.

She stood over Samantha's body, the girl fast asleep. Flowers were beside her bed, a card buried in the petals. Sam's hair was skirted across her pillow, a knit blanket laid across her legs.

Willow didn't breathe—she couldn't breathe. Her hands were steady as she filled the syringe with the solution. She took Sam's right arm with a gentle touch and wiped it clean with alcohol. Still, she didn't breathe as she injected the serum into Sam's arm.

It was simple and without celebration. There was no thrashing as the solution made its way through Samantha's body. The girl continued to be undisturbed, and perhaps that was the most frightening thing of all.

Soon enough, the serum would make its way through her blood stream and into the nerve cells of her brain, stimulating the effects of Alzheimer's. Willow would stand by, watching, observing, testing until she discovered how to reverse the effects and create an anti-venom that would cure the disease.

Willow gasped for breath once the needle was pulled away from Samantha's skin, a red speck the only sign the needle ever entered her body.

# Chapter 12

S he was searching the room in a frenzy. If she wasn't digging through drawers, she was pacing. That was how Randy found her when he walked into their bedroom. Her hands reaching, her face searching.

"Willow?"

She stood up. Her arm was deep into the laundry basket, pulling out dirty clothes and throwing them across the floor. Where was the paper?

"What are you looking for?" Randy said. He came up behind Willow and started picking up the clothes she had tossed.

"Umm," she said, shoving her hand into pockets of scrubs, waiting for her fingers to skim the worn paper. "Some papers."

"What kind of papers?" he asked, turning to leave the room and search.

"Shit," she whispered. She had started laundry when she got home and instead of grabbing all the laundry that was upstairs she started off with the load she had brought down a day earlier.

Willow could hear the machine filling with water as she came into the basement. The door rattled against her grip as she tried to pull it open, but it was locked. "Dammit," she said. She hit the button on the machine to turn it off. It continued to fill for a few seconds longer before it finally shut off and unlocked with a click.

Her scrubs from that day were at the top — the bottom of the pant leg sticking up. When she pulled them up, they were half soaked but not fully, and thankfully enough, when she put her hands in the pocket she pulled out the folded piece of paper and there wasn't a drop of water on it. Her messy script stared back at her. Everything she was terrified of forgetting was held close in her hand.

"Willow?" Randy's voice echoed into the basement.

"Coming. I just wanted to grab one thing while I was thinking of it." She met Randy at the top of the stairs, keeping the paper tucked in the palm of her hand. His brows were snitched, but he eyes never wandered from her face. She let a smile coat her lips, hoping to soothe any of his worry.

Willow slipped past Randy to grab her wallet off the counter and the tucked the paper behind a credit card.

Randy looked back at her just as the paper disappeared out of sight.

"How was work?"

The memory didn't come until Randy wrapped his arms around her. She jumped when it happened. The face of the patient came into her mind, too vivid to be a dream. A motion of slipping a needle into the girl's skin haunted her. Willow's heart began its rapid beat as the realization of what she had done manifested.

"Good," Willow said. Her breath caught at the end of her sentence, and she pushed herself away from Randy.

"Are you okay?" He let his arms drop, but his hands still reached out for her.

"Just tired." She turned her back to him. The urge to pace

became immediate. "I think I'm going to head to bed early."

She kissed him on the cheek, the motion quick and fleeting. She let out a shuttering breath as she turned her back to him. Her face dropped once she was out of sight, and she prayed he didn't follow her.

"I'll be up in a minute," he said.

She blocked out his words, but not by choice. Her vision shifted from the stairs, the hallway, her bedroom, to the hospital, a syringe, the arm of a girl fast asleep. What had she done?

She collapsed into her bed. It was happening again — that familiar feeling of dread and panic all crashing together. Her throat closed and her head spun until her vision faded at the edges. She couldn't place herself in the room; all she yearned for was Randy's touch, but she was too ashamed of what she had done to let him find out.

How did she forget what she had done? How could she forget poisoning a girl, injecting God-knows-what into her body, for what? A cure? The cure only comes once the disease has begun to play, and the girl would have to be victim to scientists, nothing but a lab rat. Not to mention the fact that to conduct these experiments, it wouldn't be behind closed doors. There were vague memories of hope that she could find the cure on her own, but was it really possible?

A choking sob threatened to suffocate her, but she pushed the emotions away when she heard Randy walking up the stairs.

"Randy?" She was surprised at how composed her voice was.

"Yeah?" He walked into the room and lay next to her on the bed. He folded her into his arms, her back against his chest. She was thankful he couldn't see her face.

What could she say? He'd done so much, given so much,

and this is what she'd done. Samantha was his patient. Would Randy suffer the consequences of her actions? A knot formed in her stomach; she let a breath out.

"I love you," she said, and for a moment, she let herself be lifted away from the chaos. Maybe the serum had no effect on the girl. At least that's what she told herself when Randy kissed the skin behind her ear.

Her body didn't shake when she thought of the girl. Willow let herself breathe easy, inhaling Randy's scent, memorizing the feeling of her skin against his.

She found herself in a trance, trying to remember the ingredients of the solution, their chemical compounds, their side-effects. Could this give the girl Alzheimer's? Her stomach dropped at the thought, but there was the familiar electricity of an idea. When things begin to piece together like a puzzle, everything finally fitting in harmony, her panic was replaced with intrigue. She took a breath and spoke.

"Did you read the article about the Venom Trials?"

Randy looked over to her. "Like the one Dr. Gadel had been talking about?" She nodded. "I found the article, but I haven't had a chance to read through it yet."

"I read it." She paused, trying to judge the moment. Should she tell him? "It's a medical trial that's been going on in Europe." Randy sat up, propping himself with his elbow and waited for her to say more. "It's called the venom trials because they inject a serum into mice — it gives them symptoms like Alzheimer's. The brain cells begin to deteriorate; their short-term memory begins to go."

"Huh," he said. He frowned while he thought it over. "Do they think they can use it like venom? Like, when a snake bites you, you use the antivenom to stop the venom from continuing to affect the area. Is that what they're doing?"

Willow watched him. His brows furrowed, and he stared off into space, a crease forming above his eyebrows before he spoke again. "Venom is made up of protein, and so is the abnormal protein that is found in the brain of Alzheimer's patients. They're looking for the anti-protein then? Something to kill the protein that's damaging the brain. Interesting."

"Do you think it's something that has any value? Maybe they're onto something that can reverse Alzheimer's?" Willow asked. Her muscles were taunt, refusing to relax into the bed.

"No. Even antivenom doesn't reverse damage, it just neutralizes it. I imagine it would have to be administered continuously, because Alzheimer's is not a toxin that enters the body once—it's constantly present."

"But there has to be a way to reverse it," she said, her voice rising in octave, and this time she could hear the hysteria starting. She took a moment to compose herself, breathing and letting her heart calm before she spoke again. She hoped Randy either didn't notice the lift in her voice or was willing to let it slide. "There has to be something out there that's still to be discovered."

Randy let out a sigh and relaxed into the bed again, pulling her to him as he did so. "There's always something left to be discovered. No matter how much research is done, how many hours are spent in a lab, there will always be mystery of a disease: how it works, how it affects someone, how you cure it. There's never a definite answer. You know that, Willow. You of all people know that."

"But there might be a way." The frustration hung in her voice as she spoke. She didn't realize her hand was in a fist until Randy reached around to unfurl her fingers.

"There might be," he said. "But that doesn't mean we'll

find it, or those scientists in Europe will find it." His voice was soft, pleading for Willow to let the subject drop.

"You promised," she said. She stared out across the room. A picture of her family was mounted on the wall. Her father looked back at her. "You promised you would do everything you could to find a cure, so something like this would never happen again." Her body began to react before her mind could. Each muscle in her body clenched. Her emotions became something so strong it was physical. Her heartrate began to race again. The urge to run ran through her nerves, but she felt more rooted in place than ever.

Randy rubbed his thumb across Willow's hand. He was calm, she was chaos. They were two opposites colliding over and over. "My father died —" She was going to say more, but her voice dropped before she could finish.

"I know I promised," he whispered. Willow could hear the pain in Randy's voice. "I'm trying, Willow. Believe me, I'm trying."

Willow shifted to face Randy. He refused to look at her, not because he didn't love her, but because he loved her too much. He needed to be strong for her, but now he couldn't be strong for himself.

She let the room run quiet. For a long time, it was just the sound of the clock ticking in the corner that filled the room.

"Randy?" she said. She turned her face up to him but his eyes were closed.

"What are you thinking about?" he said, opening his eyes, and that's when she knew things were okay, for whenever she was upset, he asked that simple question.

"What if the Venom Trials used the serum on people? Maybe that's why Dr. Gadel failed? They've only tested it on animals? The full anti-venom wasn't tested on humans yet. That's a whole other brain composition. Don't you think that would open up new doors?"

Randy looked at her, and for a moment Willow felt a lift of excitement. Maybe he saw it too. He'd understand why something so inhumane had to be done. One life in exchange for thousands, maybe millions? Wouldn't it be worth it?

But then Willow felt alone. When Randy looked at her, there wasn't anger or confusion; there was just utter and complete anguish. Her sorrow for her father began his and with it, he folded in on himself.

He spent a long time thinking it over. His eyes wandered from the ceiling back to Willow, and each time he saw her, he realized how deep she had gone into her desperation.

"We could never do that," he said. "If we do that, we lose all humanity. You can't bargain one life for another, and if humanity is lost, what's the point?"

# Chapter 13

Sam's eyes were open as they walked into the room. Paul was the first one through the door, and he rushed to her side. Sam's head turned slowly. Her skin was pale, but a small smile crept up her lips.

"Sammy," he said as he wrapped his hand around her fingers. He was carful as he touched her, terrified to hurt her but afraid she might slip away if he let go.

Shelly followed close behind, finding her way next to Paul at Sam's side.

It was Avery who paused the longest at the door. She stared at her little sister, but when she looked at her, it felt like she was seeing someone else. Her sister was there, but something was missing, like Sam was just an empty shell. Her eyes were glazed through her smile. Paul was speaking to her in hushed words, and Sam was looking around the room, not hearing a word he said. When she did look at her grandfather, she seemed only to look through him.

"How do you feel?" he said. He brought a chair over to sit beside her. Shelly stood behind him, her arm on his shoulder. A silent tear had rolled down her cheek, but a smile was shining through.

Sam blinked, looked around the room, and looked back at Paul. Her body was molded to the bed.

"Sammy?" Avery took the final steps toward the bed and came to stand beside Shelly.

"Hey," Sam said, testing out her voice.

"Look who finally decided to wake up," Avery said, hoping the joke would bring her sister to the surface again.

"Is that why I feel like this?" Sam moved to lift her head but decided against it.

"What hurts, honey?" Shelly said.

"Just my head." She frowned when she left herself surrender into the mattress. "I feel like I'm in a haze."

"Paul, go get a nurse," Shelly said. He let go of Sam's hand and left the room.

"Where's Mom?" Sam said.

The moment hung in the air. Avery's stomach dropped, and Shelly froze in place.

"Sam?" Avery was the first one to speak. She looked over to Shelly who had turned her back to Sam, wiping a tear from her face. "Mom passed away in the fire."

Avery watched Sam, waiting for a look of registration in her face, but it never came. Beside her, Shelly was trying to compose herself before turning back to face Sam. Avery watched as Sam let the news sink in. Her eyes flickered from side to side, but she didn't look in any particular direction. Her body was still, relaxed almost, but her eyes grew red and her face grew limp. She was learning the death of her mother all over again.

"Where's Dad?" A small flame of hope flickered in her eyes as she looked at Avery, but it died just as soon as it appeared.

"Sam," Avery said. She wanted to say more, to explain,

but the breath was caught in her lungs.

Without any other words Sam understood, and she grew quiet. All three of them were like this when Paul walked back in the room, a nurse by his side. The nurse smiled when she approached Sam, but Sam's mouth hung open.

"Grandma?" she said. Shelly stood by her bed as the nurse worked over her. Sam's eyes flickered to each face in the room. She was still searching for her parents. She had heard Avery's words, but she couldn't get herself to believe them.

Shelly took Paul by the hand and motioned for the nurse to come over. Tears were running down her cheeks as she explained what happened.

"She can't remember?" Shelly asked, waiting for the nurse to give a reasonable explanation. Her voice was hushed, but she could barely manage to keep her voice down with the shock of the news. Paul was fidgeting as Shelly spoke, his eyes never leaving Sam.

The nurse spoke without ever giving an answer for what was happening. "I'll have to speak to the doctor." She kept saying it over and over, and soon Shelly and Paul stopped listening.

"Will she get better?" Shelly asked.

The nurse crossed the room and replaced Sam's IV bag before she answered. "The memories are there; they're just jarred a bit from the trauma. Give her some time to process what's happened, and she should be okay. We're going to do an MRI just in case to ensure there was no other trauma from the seizure. Let me get Dr. Ash." As the nurse spoke, her words became clearer, more confidant, but how much of it did the nurse believe? Or was she just saying all this to calm them down until they had real answers?

Paul gripped Shelly's hand as the nurse walked out the room.

"I'm getting an MRI?" Sam's voice was quiet as she spoke, but it broke the barrier in the room.

"Yes, sweetie. We just want to make sure everything is okay," Shelly said, but the words were spoken with a forced confidence.

Sam looked at Avery before she turned her face down to her hands. If Sam looked closely enough, she could see the veins beneath the frail skin. The IV stuck out of her hand. Every time she looked at it, she was afraid to move. Would it hurt her if she lifted her arm too fast? She tried not to image the needle in her skin.

"Sam?" Avery was kneeling beside Sam's bed. "Do you want me to go with you?"

When Sam looked up, she noticed a team of nurses around her. The doctor was in the back of the room, lines around his eyes, hair slicked back. He stood with his hands behind his back, perfectly patient. On Sam's right side, another nurse was at her IV bag, checking its contents. How had she missed everyone coming into the room?

"Dr. Ash says one person can stay while the MRI is being performed. Do you want me to stay? Or do you want Grandma or Grandpa?" Avery said.

"Can you?" Sam said.

Avery gave a small nod and as soon as she did, Sam's bed was wheeled out of the room and down the hallway. Her heart thudded against her chest, and for a moment, she lost sight of Avery. Just as soon as she disappeared, a voice came from far behind.

"I'm right here, Sam."

The motion of the rolling bed made her want to be sick. She pushed her arm out over the edge of the bed, reaching for

Avery. A hand caught hers, and she let herself relax.

Sam was pushed into a room that was mostly empty, save for a large machine that sat in the center. It was circular, with a relatively small opening in the middle, just large enough for a body. Connected to it was a bed that was nothing but hard plastic and a thin sheet.

One of the nurses slipped her arms behind Sam's back as she helped her sit up and switch to the hard length of plastic. Avery stood in the corner as she watched the nurses lead Sam into the machine. They spoke in soft, pronounced words.

"You'll have to lay very still while you're in the MRI machine. Avery will be right here beside you the whole time." Avery came forward from the corner of the room and placed her hand on her leg. "It's going to be loud," the nurse said, "so we're going to give you these headphones to help with the sound. Would you like to listen to music?"

Sam gazed up at the nurses as they placed the headphones over her ears. For a moment, everything was silent, and then there was music. She let herself drift as the nurses pulled something over her head. When she looked up there was a small mirror angled so she could see everyone in the room while laying down without having to move her head.

Avery was wearing a pair of headphones as well. A switch was flipped, and the room was filled with a loud pulsing sound. The sound beat through Sam's skin and Avery's hand tightened around her leg as she was pushed into the tight machine. She held still as the pulsing and rhythmic sounds continued around her. When she looked through the mirror above her, she could see Avery's torso, but not much else. The corners of Sam's eyes caught only a glimpse of the inside of the machine: close, plastic corridors. Music played through the headphones, but it seemed to do little against the sounds of the machine.

However many minutes passed, she wasn't sure. It had been too long by the time the nurses pulled Sam out the machine again. A layer of sweat was coating her skin when she was released.

"And that's it," a nurse said, helping Sam sit up.

Avery smiled at her as Sam sat up. She swayed to the side and a nurse kept her arm behind her back for balance.

Sam was hollow. The noise of the MRI machine was there as echo inside her mind. She could still hear it as she was wheeled out of the room. Paul and Shelly were out in the hall waiting for her when she left the room.

"How did it go?" Paul said.

"She did great," the nurse said. "We have her imaging, and I'm going to send them to Dr. Ash to look over. For now, we're going to send Sam back to her room where she can rest while you wait for Dr. Ash to come back with the results."

Sam was rolled back to her room and it only took her a few moments to fall asleep once she was placed back in her bed. The sounds of the MRI machine were beginning to fade as she drifted off into sleep.

"Did she seem okay?" Paul asked, turning to where Avery sat.

He was standing at the edge of Sam's bed as he spoke. Shelly was on the far end of the room, slumped over in a chair. Her head rest in her hands, propped on the arm of the chair.

"She seemed scared," Avery said. She leaned against the edge of Sam's bed, wishing the hospital had more than the hard, plastic chairs. "When they turned the machine on I could feel her body tense up. She stayed like that during the entire procedure, which is probably why she's so exhausted now."

Paul nodded, but his eyes wandered over Sam's body. He was looking for something, but he didn't know what.

"What is it?" Avery asked.

"I don't get it. How she's here. How she survived the fire, yet we don't know why she's in a hospital bed." He paused, letting his hand run over his face, the stubble on his chin. "How can a fire cause a seizure?" There was a hitch in his voice and he cleared his throat.

Avery watched Sam's eyes. They were closed, but if she watched close enough she could see a soft flutter. Was she dreaming?

"I don't know either," she said.

She wanted to offer Paul words of encouragement, but she was deflated of hope. Even with the silence of Sam's room, she felt like she could still hear the MIR machine beating around like it was going to tumble in on Sam.

"She couldn't remember her own mother's death! Isn't that something that sticks with you, no matter what?" When Avery looked over, Paul had walked away from the edge of Sam's bed and was pacing the room. His eyes looked red and his hands were restless at his sides.

"I would give anything, anything to forget that phone call saying that Cheryl was gone. I wasn't there when she died, but I remember the moment so clearly I'm afraid the memory of her death will replace the memory of her life."

His voice was rising as he spoke, but the more the words came, the more defeated he sounded.

"Children are never supposed to die before their parents," Paul said.

Avery stood up and crossed the room to where Paul stood. He was looking out the window into the parking lot of the hospital, watching families, people come and go. Avery followed his gaze before wrapping her arms around him. He hugged her back, but he couldn't get himself to look at her or anything within the room. Life had betrayed him and left him with this mess.

"Parents aren't supposed to die when the child still needs them either," Avery said. She followed her grandfather's gaze out the window to the birds that were flying high over the buildings. She wished for the freedom to fly away.

"I'm so sorry, Avery," he said.

She shook her head against his chest as he spoke. For now, the pain of her parents being gone was pushed away. She could open that box another day when Sam was awake and they could deal with it together.

"Do you think Sam will be okay?" she said.

"I sure hope so."

The sound of a door opening caused them both to turn. Sam's doctor walked in with a clipboard in hand and closed the door behind him.

"Is she okay?" the words echoed across the room again. This time it was Paul who said it.

Paul walked over to Shelly, tapping her on the shoulder to wake her up. When her eyes opened, she seemed bright for a moment, until she looked around the room and remembered where she was — why she was here. Within a few seconds, the light disappeared from her eyes and while she was present physically, her bright glow had left the room.

"I've been looking over the MRI scans and there doesn't seem to be any abnormalities," Dr. Ash said. Once the words were said, a collective breath was released throughout the room. "Everything appears to be normal, and we think that the memory lapse is either a result of shock or temporary damage caused by the seizure. Either way, with enough time and rest, she should be back to normal."

"And what if she's not?" Paul said.

Dr. Ash let the question hang in the air for a moment before he could come up with an answer. He looked over to Sam whose bottom lip hug open as she slept.

"Then it might be a brain injury that hasn't had the chance to surface yet. If she doesn't get better on her own, we'll do more tests."

"What about right now?" Paul stepped towards Dr. Ash. He wasn't a fighter, only for his family. Dark circles were ingrained under his eyes. Shelly stood up to hold onto his arm in a silent effort to keep him calm. "I don't want to wait until she gets worse to find out what's wrong with her. I want tests done now. I want to know now whether she's going to be okay or not."

Avery stayed by the window. When Paul spoke, she could feel his voice breaking. He was on the verge of tears, but he never cried in front of strangers, never mind the doctor that was supposed to save his granddaughter's life. So instead of crying, he yelled. Dr. Ash was just unfortunate enough to be on the receiving end.

"Paul." This time Shelly spoke, though her voice seemed to get lost among Paul's.

"No, Shelly, we've already lost Cheryl. I'm not losing Sam too."

"I lost Cheryl, too," Shelly said. "And Daniel." She held herself taller, but just barely. Avery watched her family as their anger formed the tears that they were too afraid to cry. "She was my daughter, too."

Dr. Ash held Sam's file in his hand, but he didn't look at it. He had already spent hours combing through it, looking for at least one thing to tell him what was wrong. He had it memorized by now. Sam was in perfect health according to the MRI.

"Sam needs all the help she can get," Paul said.

"Sam needs to heal," Dr. Ash intervened. "She can't heal if we're taking her from room to room, placing her in these machines, taking her blood, making her do all these tests — they aren't good for her." Dr. Ash finished speaking, letting his own frustration hang in the room.

"I'll take the tests." The voice was so soft among the uproar; it was just barely a sound.

Sam was awake and when everyone turned to her it was obvious that they had all forgotten she was there in the first place.

"Whatever test it is, I'll take it."

Paul and Shelly looked at each other. Was it shock or confusion that decorated their faces?

"Sam, we don't have any tests for you to take right now," Dr. Ash said.

"And why is that?" Paul was back on his feet, and Shelly retreated into her chair.

"Sam has been through a lot," Dr. Ash said, turning to Paul. He took a deep breath before he faced Sam again. "The best thing for you to do is rest. If you have time to heal, you might not need any further tests."

"I want further tests," Paul said without skipping a beat.

"And we'll cross that bridge when we approach it."

For a moment, all air filtered out of the room before Dr. Ash turned to Sam and looked over the machines that monitored her.

"How are you feeling?" he asked.

"Okay," she said. When she spoke, it was obvious she had been awake for the whole conversation. She shifted in her bed, self-conscious of the eyes on her.

"Why don't we let her rest? Time alone will do her well. Why don't you all say goodnight and call it a day?" Dr. Ash said, turning to Paul and Shelly.

Before Paul could say anything, Avery stepped forward to lean over the side of Sam's bed.

"I'll see you soon, okay?"

Sam gave a small nod, but her eyes were already starting to close.

"I don't feel right," she said. Avery frowned when she touched Sam's hand that was tangled among the wires. "It's like, there's this current flowing through my body, and it won't stop. It keeps me awake." Her words were contradictory as Avery watched Sam's head lull to the side. Her eyes were wide, but she fought to keep her head up.

Avery looked over to Dr. Ash who was writing something down. He looked up quickly and gave Avery a sharp look and nodded before he turned back to his papers and wrote what Sam had said. When Avery looked over to Shelly and Paul they were having their own quiet conversation.

"You'll be okay," she said, and she placed a small kiss on Sam's forehead. Her forehead still had a light sheen of sweat and Sam's look up to Avery as she backed away. Terror was alight in her eyes. She didn't want to be left alone.

# Chapter 14

Sam was awake when Willow stepped into her room. It was at the beginning of her shift, and she slipped in before anyone could notice. Sam was sitting up in bed, staring at the IV in her hand.

"Sam?" she said.

Sam turned her head to look at Willow, but her body froze. The nurse had an odd familiarity. Her body was electric, like she needed to run, but she wasn't sure why and she urged the feeling to pass.

"I don't feel right," Sam said. Her eyes were wide, and she looked at the needle in her skin like it was a foreign object.

"What do you feel like?" Willow said. She looked at the machines beside Sam's bed. Her blood pressure was fine, heartbeat high, but most likely due to her own fear rather than health.

"You know how there are those shock pens that people use for pranks? If you push on the pen it shocks you and you can feel the electricity going up your arm? Well, I feel like that, but instead of my arm, it's my whole body."

Sam kicked her feet out from under the blankets of the bed and looked over her body expecting to see something hidden in her skin that was causing the sensation.

"Do you feel sick?" Willow asked.

"I feel like I'm in a bubble," she said. "I can see what's in front of me, but it's out of reach."

"It might just be stress," Willow said. She stepped closer to Sam. She needed her to be calm, but most of all she needed Sam's trust. The possibility of the serum working made her stomach churn and head spin. She was ignited by the possibility of finding a cure.

"Don't say that," Sam said. There was a blood pressure monitor on the tip of Sam's finger, and she pulled it off. The machine beside her bed went blank. "Everyone keeps saying that, but I can't remember anything. My parents are dead, and I have no idea what happened."

Willow rushed over and slipped the monitor back on her finger. She expected Sam to pull away, but she never did. Sam let Willow work and settle everything back into place. Willow adjusted Sam's body until she was laying down and her head was resting against the pillow. "There was a fire," she said.

"I should know that," Sam said. Her voice was a whine. She was a child who had been left out on a secret.

"Your body is just trying to protect you. It can't handle the stress of knowing. It will come in time." As she spoke she wondered if it was the serum already at work. She watched Sam, looking for the vacant look in her eyes that her father always seemed to have before her died. Sam looked back at Willow, a glint in her eye that said she was still there. That was good, wasn't it? For a moment, Willow was disappointed that maybe the serum didn't work.

The monitor kicked back on, and Willow looked it over to make sure her vitals looked normal. She slipped out a small notebook from the pocket of her scrubs. Her folded paper fell out onto the floor and she bent down to pick up before Sam noticed. The notebook was for Sam. It was small enough that she could conceal it while still being able to write down everything she would need to document about the effects of the serum. She wrote in small letters, 'Doesn't remember fire or parents' death" and dated the page at the top.

"You're doing better than you think," Willow said. She closed the notebook, a burning guilt forming in the back of her mind. There was no going back now.

— — — — —

Sam pealed the tape off her skin and pulled the IV out in a slow, measured movement. A small pool of blood was left in its wake, and she hid it under gauze. She unclipped the small device from her pointer finger and the machines in her room went blank again. When her feet finally touched the floor of the hospital, it was a sweet relief to feel the cool tile again her skin, even if it was through a pair of thin hospital socks. She still felt like there was a part of herself that was beyond reach, but the floor beneath her feet at least made her feel present.

Sam pushed her door open and let the light of the hallway empty into the room. Her hospital gown hung open behind her, the only real piece of clothing was her thin underwear. Goosebumps lined her arms and legs, but she pushed herself through the door.

She hadn't bothered to see what time of night it was, but the sky was black when she left her room. In the hallway, nurses floated through the hall just as always, but there seemed to be a muffled hush as they worked. There was no urgency, no visitors, just the quiet of the night.

"Miss?" A nurse came up from behind Sam. She let her

hand linger on Sam's arm with a light, but firm grip. The nurse was ready to take hold in case Sam decided to take off. "Do you need help with anything? Do you need to go to the bathroom?"

Sam looked over the nurse. Her scrubs were bright green, her hair pulled back into a bun, but her face didn't seem familiar.

"No," Sam said. Once she realized she didn't know the nurse, her gaze redirected to someplace down the hall. She wasn't sure what she was searching for, but she knew she wanted to be gone.

The nurse gripped Sam's wrist and turned over the hospital ID band. She hadn't noticed the thin plastic around her wrist until then. She stared back at it, her name and birth date printed out on her wrist for all to see.

"Come on, Samantha, it's time for you to go back to your room."

She thought about running, but even though she was on her feet, she didn't trust her muscles to take her anywhere far. She swayed as the nurse kept one hand on her wrist and the other behind Sam's back to guide her back to her room.

"Here we are," the nurse said, turning the light on in the room as she stepped through.

She settled Sam on the bed and laid the blanket across her body. The warmth of the room drew her into a prison again. Whatever life and freedom she had felt when her feet touched the floor disappeared.

"How does your hand feel?"

The nurse held Sam's hand in her own, lightly massaging where she had taken the IV out.

"Sore," Sam said.

The nurse held her hand up to the light for a closer look.

"How about we switch hands?"

Before Sam could answer, the nurse was on the other side of the bed with her left hand, rubbing alcohol where the IV would be inserted. Sam watched as the needle was slipped into her skin, looking away only as she winced from the pain.

"There," the nurse said. She stood up, checking the IV line before putting the pulse oximeter on the tip of her finger to monitor her blood pressure. "I'm going to bring your nurse in to check on you. Have a good night, Sam. Try to get some sleep."

Sam watched her as she stepped out of the room. She felt more trapped than ever.

# Chapter 15

Avery was there when the phone rang at her grandparents' house. Paul was out visiting Sam at the hospital, so it was Shelly who stood up to answer the phone.

"Hello?" she said, there was a short pause. "Yes, speaking."

Avery didn't want to listen, but in the stillness of the moment she could hear the faint words of "fire" and "oven."

Shelly stood at the kitchen sink looking out the window of as someone on the other line spoke. Her face was stone. Avery knew Shelly had been crying in moments of privacy; she could see it some days when her eyes were tired and worn, but Shelly tried to make it a point not to push that onto Avery as well.

"Yes, thank you. Goodbye," she said, hanging up the phone.

Avery waited for her grandmother to turn to her and tell her what was said but she kept her back turned.

"Grandma?" Shelly covered her face with her hands before she spun around to look at Avery. She tried her best to conceal the emotions, but they spilled over through her frown.

"Was that the fire department?" Avery asked.

Shelly sat next to her on the couch and held the phone in her hands. She looked at the blank screen as if she was waiting for it to ring again.

"It was," she said. "They were calling because they're closing the investigation on the cause of the fire."

"What was it?"

"They couldn't come up with a definite answer." Shelly was going to continue talking, but she stopped as soon as she felt Avery stiffen beside her.

"What do you mean? That's their job. To investigate and find the cause," Avery said. Her voice was rising, and she knew she had to quiet down. "They can find the culprit of a murder with one shred of DNA, but when it comes to finding the source of a fire, they don't know? What if it was faulty wiring? Shouldn't we…" but Avery stopped herself. She only hoped it was faulty wiring.

"Sweetie," Shelly said. She rested her arm against Avery's back. "There are some things we'll never be sure of. The fire marshal said it could have been wiring, but it also could have been something as simple as forgetting to turn the stove off."

She knew the words were coming, but the tears still surfaced. She had hoped the fire was caused by a faulty switch, or lint in the dryer, something simple—a freak accident. But Avery had heard the word oven spoken over the phone, and she knew that the officer considering the oven as the cause wasn't just a coincidence, it was a possibility, and a strong one at that.

"There has to be more." Avery stood up from the couch. She was starting to panic. The blame had to be placed somewhere else, anywhere else.

"That's all the information they have," Shelly said.

"They need to find out why." Avery looked from the door

to the window and soon that's the way she began to pace.

"Avery, honey, sometimes they can't find the answers. They only have so much time in the day and they can't spend it all looking into the cause of a fire."

She was angry. Angry at her grandmother for not pushing the officer for more information when she was on the phone, at the fire department for letting the case close, but most of all she was mad because she couldn't remember if she had turned the stove off that night.

— — — — —

"Shh!" Avery was giggling, and her whisper was hard to conceal. "Everyone is asleep upstairs."

Eric was laughing when he followed her to the door. He watched the way she skipped through the night and up the steps to her house.

"Come on," Avery whispered. She led the way through the door.

Eric followed her through the house, keeping the lights off as they wandered. Avery navigated without missing a beat, and Eric held onto her hand hoping he wouldn't run into a wall.

Once they were in the kitchen, Avery turned on the light and turned the dimmer down until they had just enough light to see, but no more. She opened a drawer next to the oven and pulled out an old pastel apron that her mother had used so much its color was beginning to fade away.

"What would you like?" she said, putting on her best grin while Eric leaned against the counter.

"What does the chef recommend?" he said. He was tempted to touch Avery, but he was afraid if he did he would break the spell of the moment. Avery produced her own light in the room, even with an apron that was covered in stains.

"Grilled cheese a-la-mode," she said. She tried to smile in that sexy-flirty way that Sam was always talking about when they watched romantic comedies, but it felt a little forced. Forced or not, Eric seemed to smile just a little wider.

"Sounds delicious," he said.

Avery tried to be quiet as she tip-toed around the kitchen for cheese, bread, butter, and of course a pan. She noticed out of the corner of her eye that the clock on the microwave said 1:53am, and although she could feel the long hours of the day beginning to creep up on her, she pushed the threat of sleep away.

"Make sure you kiss him! I want details in the morning!" That's what Sam had just about shouted to her as she left the house to meet Eric at his car. She was terrified he might have overheard, but if he had, he showed no signs when she had gotten into his car.

"Want any help?" Eric said, watching her from the other side of the kitchen.

She turned on the stove and could picture Sam nagging her in the morning. A dim-lit grilled cheese dinner was the perfect opportunity for a first-date kiss.

She bit her lip while her back was turned before holding the tub of butter out to Eric.

"Why don't I teach you?" she offered. She hoped her nerves weren't evident in her smile.

He smirked. "Are you sure you want burnt grilled cheese?"

"I'll guide you."

In her head, she imagined the moment would be more romantic. She stood by his side as she let her hand linger over his, guiding the butter over the bread and placing it on the pan.

"So will your parents be mad if they found us down

here?" Eric asked.

"My dad might be. My mom is just like my sister. She wants to know all the details. If she knew you were down here right now..." She trailed off, a blush creeping up on her.

"What?" he said. He turned to her and she could feel her face heating more.

"Flip it," Avery said, gripping his hand with the spatula to flip the grilled-cheese. She was going to pull her hand away, but she could still feel Eric's eyes on her.

"What are you going to tell your sister?" Eric looked at her, his eyebrows raised and smile at his fullest. Avery pulled her hand away and cocked her head to the side, raising her eyebrow. He laughed. "I have two older sisters. I've seen them gossip after every date they've been on."

"Oh, that must have been fun," she said.

"A little awkward, yes."

They both smiled, and Eric pulled the grilled-cheese off the pan and set it on a plate.

"You eat. I'll make a second one," she said.

Avery picked up the loaf of bread sitting on the counter, but Eric took her by the hand. He wrapped a single arm around her waist and pulled her closer, just by an inch, but it surprised her enough that she dropped the bread.

"Sorry," he said, but he was laughing a breathless, nervous laugh.

They were looking at each other, neither sure of what to do. Avery let one hand linger on Eric's arm. They were both gripping the counter, as if it was the only thing holding them in place. When Eric lifted his hand from the counter and cupped her cheek, Avery felt something release. She leaned forward, terrified and awake, and kissed him.

He didn't seem at all surprised when she kissed him. It was like he was waiting for her, and when she was finally there, he embraced her. They pulled away only when they heard footsteps above their heads.

"Remember how I asked if your parents would be mad if they found us down here?" Eric said.

"Let's not find out what would actually happen," she said. Avery took the grilled cheese from off the plate and carried it out to the hall and to the front door. Eric followed close behind and stepped out the front door. She thought she heard someone upstairs and froze. Eric was already through the threshold and standing outside, watching her and waiting. She thought she heard a door close. Did someone get up to go to the bathroom?

Avery slipped out into the night.

"I'll talk to you later," Avery said quickly. She took Eric's hands and gave him the grilled-cheese before he could protest. She flashed him a smile before she leaned in a final time for a brisk kiss, and this time Eric did seem surprised. "Goodnight!"

She thought he was laughing when she closed the door, but she wasn't sure. By the time she was up the stairs, the bathroom door creaked open.

"Avery?" the voice was hushed.

Her mom's eyes were squinting as she turned off the bathroom light and entered the darkness. She wrapped her arms around herself as she walked, her hair sticking out in all directions.

"Sorry," Avery said. She was afraid to say why she was apologizing. Did she hear them downstairs? Is that why she woke up? Or could she actually get away with sneaking a boy into the house at 1am?

"Were you downstairs?" she asked.

"Yeah, I just got hungry. Midnight snack. Made some

grilled cheese."

Her mom looked her over but she didn't seem too concerned, just confused.

"I thought I heard someone in the kitchen."

"Just me," she said, trying to hide her smile as she started to walk to her room. "Goodnight."

She let a small smile form as her mom walked back to bed and she realized she got away with it. Avery slipped into her bedroom and once she hit the pillows she finally let sleep take her. Normally, it would take a few minutes, sometimes an hour, for Avery to fall asleep, but that night she slept fast and without any dreams.

The oven continued to burn in the kitchen, a loaf of bread too close heating in the dark night. A few minutes passed before the plastic around the bread melted and caught on fire. The kitchen burned, inch by inch, until the inches turned to feet and the feet turned to yards.

# Chapter 16

"Your date of birth?"

Sam looked at the nurse, but the nurse wasn't looking back at her. Her eyes were on a laptop filled with Sam's health records. Sam knew her birthday was in December, but now the date was lost to her.

"December," she said.

"Date and year?"

The nurse was waiting. It was a safety measure for patient identification, but for some reason Sam couldn't identify herself.

"December," she paused, bite her lip. "First?"

The nurse's eyebrows came together. The clipboard in her hand dropped a few inches, and she looked out into the hallway.

Was she wrong? Did Sam forget her birthday?

"I'll be right back, okay?"

When the nurse left, she seemed worried. Sam had never said what year she was born in, and she was happy the nurse didn't push because she couldn't remember, but had she messed up?

More than anything, Sam wanted to go home. Everything about being in the hospital felt wrong. She wanted to go home to her mom, dad, and Avery, but the more she thought of them, the more her stomach seemed to drop and ache.

In the back of her mind, she remembered Avery at her hospital bed, telling her that their parents were dead, but that couldn't be true, could it? She couldn't grasp at the memory fully, and the more she thought about it, the more terrified she grew. It was like she was waking up from a dream, but she still wasn't sure if it had been a dream or not.

Sam's eyes were darting around the room, begging to find some object that would upturn a memory when the doctor walked in.

"Good morning, Sam," Dr. Ash said.

He closed the door behind him when he walked in. The click of the door was soft, but Sam jumped at the sound. Her mind rolled over memories, trying to find fact from fiction, death from life. What was real?

"How did you sleep last night?"

He was sitting on a rolling stool, casual, leaning forward with his elbows on his knees. The picture of ease.

Sam felt like she was blinking too much. Could Dr. Ash see that?

The moment held in the air before Sam finally spoke.

"Fine," she said.

"Well, a little birdie told me you had some adventures."

She could feel her face crumple in confusion. Dr. Ash pulled his chair forward and checked Sam's right hand. Her skin was dark purple were there had once been an IV. In the center was a small, almost unnoticeable scab.

"There doesn't seem to be too much damage here, and you've got your new IV on your other hand I see." He nodded to Sam's left hand, freshly tapped. She stared at the tubing until, just vaguely, she could remember a nurse coming in during the night to put it in, but why had she come in so late?

"So tell me, Sam, when's your birthday? We like to have little parties around here for the inpatients," Dr. Ash said.

She was thrown. Was she going to be in the hospital for her birthday? It occurred to her she didn't know what month it was.

"What's today's date?" she asked.

"Sam," he said. His voice was soft, but firm. "I need you to tell me that, okay?"

She felt herself starting to blink too much again. She was waiting for Dr. Ash to get frustrated with her, but instead he seemed to shy away from her and give her space. She tried to come up with an answer, but it was like something was blocking her from accessing it. The longer she tried to unearth the information, the more she felt like she was fighting herself.

"Do you know what month it is?"

She looked around for clues, expecting a calendar to be hung in the room somewhere, but it seemed bare except for the machinery and tubes.

"June?" It didn't feel like a complete guess, but she knew the answer was supposed to come easier than that. As much as she wanted to believe she was okay, that the confusion of time was just because she was in a hospital, any hope seemed lost when Dr. Ash shifted in his chair. He didn't have to say it. She knew her answer was wrong.

"How about we skip dates? Do you like to draw?"

"I'm not very good at it," she said, but Dr. Ash was already getting up from his seat and grabbing his clipboard that he had put on the counter. He took the first page out and flipped it over so it was blank. He drew a large circle on the page and handled the clipboard to Sam, along with a pen. He took his phone out of his pocket and looked at it quickly before putting it away.

"It's about 9:15 in the morning. Pretend that the circle is the face of a clock. I want you to draw the big hand and the little hand and make it say 9:15."

She didn't understand the premise of the exercise, but she obeyed without much difficulty. Dr. Ash watched as she drew the hands on the clock without needing much thought.

"Good, now can you name three words that begin with the letter S?"

"Snack, Salt, Sugar," she said.

He laughed a little bit. "Got food on the brain?"

She smiled and relaxed when she realized that these questions she could answer.

"Someone will be in soon with food. Why don't we take a break so you can relax and eat? I'll be back later today, but press the call button if you need anything."

The button was next to her bed, but she dreaded ever having to touch it. The more the nurses and Dr. Ash seemed to see her, the more confused she got. She was living in a haze, and she wasn't sure how to escape it.

"Are my parents going to visit today?"

Dr. Ash was about to slip out of the room, but he turned around when he heard Sam speak. Her voice was clear and her eyes were tired, but her question rattled through the walls. He took a moment to jog his memory, looking over her file. *Parents: deceased.*

He wondered if he was having a lapse in his memory. Hadn't he been there when she was told? And there it was, in his own writing in her file.

*Notified of parent's death before arrival at hospital. Woke up from induced coma, wasn't aware of parents' death. Family had to explain.*

It was normal for some memory loss after traumatic events or stress, but her symptoms didn't fit that type of memory loss. If she had been told once that her family had passed away after waking up, why did she forget again? She exhibited signs of short-term memory loss, rather than the long-term that is commonly seen.

"Sam?" When he looked at her he couldn't help but see the eyes of someone innocent, having no idea of the harm that the world can ensue. "Do you remember why you're here?"

She blinked when she spoke. Maybe because it was a question she'd never been asked before, or maybe because she had simply never thought of the answer herself.

She looked around the room for signs. There was a blood pressure monitor clipped to her finger, an IV on her hand, but what else? She hadn't broken any bones, nothing hurt, but she didn't feel right. She couldn't fully remember her life before the hospital, but she knew something was wrong. Sometimes it felt like there was something stopping her from accessing part of memories to find answers, but most of all she could never get rid of the feeling of knowing the answer to a question, but not being able to grasp it.

"I know something's wrong," she said.

Dr. Ash pulled his chair back over and sat beside her.

"Can you tell me about it?"

"I can't...remember things. I know I'm in a hospital, and I know who my family is. I know Avery came, but I don't know why my parents won't come. And sometimes, if someone asks me something, I know I have the answer but I just can't...find it. I know I should remember, but for whatever reason I don't.

Sometimes my body feels weird, like there's this electricity following through me. Whenever that happens I can't sit still, and I'm afraid to be alone because I don't know what's happening, but I know that it's not normal."

"Do you think that's why you've been wandering around at night?" he asked.

"I don't remember doing that. I just remember a nurse came in to change my IV."

"She changed it because you had pulled the other IV out of your hand because you wanted to get up. The nurse found you in the hallway in the middle of the night."

Sam didn't want to believe him. For a moment, she tried to entertain herself with the fact that maybe he was just trying to play a sick joke on her. She hoped that was the case, but the longer she waited for him to say something else, the more she realized this was her reality.

"Where's Avery?" she said.

"She visited you yesterday with your grandparents."

"And she's not hurt?"

"No."

A wave of relief washed over her, but there was still an ache in her chest. "And my parents?" she asked.

Dr. Ash looked back at her, his hands shook as he stood in front of her. He didn't want to tell her. "They died in the fire."

She wanted to cry, but her body was betraying her. The tears never came, and she felt herself shutting down.

Dr. Ash watched her as she closed in on herself. Her face was wiped clean. He knew she heard and understood him, but shock was taking over. He could hope for a tear, but instead she seemed only to close herself away from the world that was surrounding her. Her face was stone as she looked around the room.

All her charts read normal. The clipboard in his hand held nothing but results that you'd expect to see from a typical sixteen-year-old, yet the way she acted and reacted wasn't what would be expected.

Sam shuttered as she closed her eyes. Her lips were pressed into a firm line and tension radiated off her and across the room. She was completely still until she released herself to let out a gasp for air. Dr. Ash watched, thinking she was finally going to cry and let herself be released, but it never happened. Her eyes were dry, but her body stayed tense.

"Dr. Ash?" A nurse peeked into the room. "You're needed in room 304."

He looked from the nurse to Sam and back again. The nurse seemed to pick up on the moment and stepped farther into the room to help. Dr. Ash stood up from his chair and met her at the doorway.

"She needs space," he said. "I'm going to check on her in an hour or so."

The nurse nodded and left the room. Before Dr. Ash followed, he turned back to Sam and saw that while her body was beginning to relax, her gaze was fixed out the window. Her mind was somewhere else.

— — — — —

Willow was afraid to step into the room. She had nightmares of what she had done. Over and over, she saw herself injecting the serum into Sam's body, and over and over she tried to stop herself but never could. The shine of the syringe was a fixture in Willow's mind. Sometimes, she thought it was a curse that she had been dealt, other times she thought it as a miracle of what may come. A cure.

When Willow looked at Sam, her eyes were red. Her head was rested to the back of the bed, but even that seemed to take too much of Sam's energy.

"Sam?" Willow said.

Sam blinked and a tear rippled down. She was exhausted even though she never left her bed. She had tried numerous times to lift herself just enough to look out the window, but even such a menial task proved to be too much.

Willow watched her as Sam let one cheek lift into a smile and it settled again into a slight frown.

"How do you feel?" She took her small notebook out of her scrubs and opened it to the last page she had written something. In fine cursive were all of Sam's medical information that may be pertinent in finding a cure. It felt immoral to hold onto the notebook, but she knew that if she was going to help Sam get better, and help anyone else with Alzheimer's, she had to take full advantage of the situation. Willow had stopped asking herself why she had injected Sam; now she only focused on fixing it so she could fix others as well. The cure came at a price, and she had already paid.

"Fine," Sam said. She looked over Willow from top to bottom. She was looking for something, though Sam wasn't sure what that something was.

"I'm here to do a few tests on you to see how you're functioning. Can you answer a few questions for me?"

Sam watched her. She never sat down like her doctor would and she wasn't sure why. There was a biting feeling in the back of her mind as Willow came closer and for a moment Sam panicked. She wanted to roll out of the bed, not caring if she landed on the floor, but only caring if she could get away. The machine beside her bed began to spike and she knew Willow could hear her heartbeat. The transparency terrified her.

"Can you name the four seasons?"

The question took her aback.

"Summer, winter, spring and fall." She watched Willow. She was holding a notebook but every now and then she could see her flip through the pages.

"Can you name four words that start with the letter A?"

"Apples, applesauce, ant, anteater," she said. "My doctor has already been asking me these questions."

Her jaw clenched. She was agitated.

Sam kept looking past Willow to the door, making sure it never bolted shut. The only thing that calmed her was the occasional nurse or doctor that walked by in the distance.

"I know, we just want to make sure there hasn't been any changes since he last saw you."

Sam wanted to fight back, but try as she might she couldn't remember when she had last seen her doctor. She knew he had been there recently, though just how long ago was lost to her.

"Can you tell me your doctor's name?" Willow asked.

Sam opened her mouth to speak but then shut it just as quickly.

His name? She supposed it must have been written down on his uniform, and that she had read it, and that maybe he had even introduced himself multiple times, but there was no memory.

"I don't know," she said. She tried to make the answer seem blasé, that it was totally normal that she didn't know or remember her doctor's name, but the words felt bitter coming off her tongue. She should remember, but she couldn't.

"What about today's date?"

It was the same question her doctor had asked and she still didn't have an answer, but this time she didn't want to try to give an answer.

"I don't know," she said, her voice was getting lower and the agitation was growing.

"How about we start off with the month?" Willow's words were gentle.

Sam took a deep breath before she spoke. "I said, I don't know."

She wasn't sure if she was mad at Willow or at herself for not being able to answer, but either way the tears started before she could do anything about it.

"Sam, take a deep breath."

Sam ignored the words. Her heart began to pound and though she was breathing, it felt like there was never enough oxygen. She closed her eyes in an attempt to calm down.

Sam wanted to have an answer. She hated not knowing and she didn't want this woman to keep asking questions.

"I need you to listen to me." When Sam heard the voice she knew it was too close. She opened her eyes to find Willow leaning close, her arm reached out for her shoulder.

"Don't touch me!" Sam yelled.

Her face was a scarlet red, and her voice hit a higher octave. When she screamed, it was hard to deceiver whether it was from fear or anger, but whatever emotion it was, it did not want to be quelled.

"Shhh," Willow said. She pulled her hand away, but failed to physically step aside. Sam's eyes darted around the room, always coming back to Willow to make sure she didn't come closer.

"Where's my doctor?" she asked, her voice shrill.

"He's with another patient right now," Willow said.

Again, her eyes roamed the room, looking for a sign that what Willow said was true. The call button sat next to Sam's bed and before Willow could follow her eyes, she pressed it. The feeling was lack-luster. There was no beep or flashing. For all she knew the button was unplugged.

A beeper went off on Willow. She looked away from Sam to turn it off.

"I'm right here, you don't need to hit the call button," she said.

"I want to see my doctor." In her mind, the words came out firm and brave, but when they lingered in the air, a hint of hysteria was here.

"He'll be coming in to check on you later."

Sam could hear Willow sigh as she put the notebook down and stepped over to the left side of the bed to check the IV. When Willow was walking over, Sam could see the pages of the small notebook, the writing much too unorganized for proper medical records. She could swear her name was etched all over the pages.

"I'll let Dr. Ash know you want to see him," she said, finishing with the IV. She left the room, and for a moment Sam felt like maybe she had won.

# Chapter 17

Shelly didn't protest when Avery stepped out the door with nothing but her purse and cell phone. She had just finished speaking to the fire department, and she knew Avery needed space to process the news — or lack of news. Shelly's lips turned down when she watched Avery climb into her car in the front yard.

"Don't come home late, and call if you need anything," Shelly said.

"I will, I love you!" Avery shouted across the driveway as she sat in the car and closed the door. She heard a muffed reply from Shelly as Avery put the car into gear and backed out of the driveway. The tears came after Shelly was out of sight, and they ran down her face in small streams.

Avery wasn't sure where she was going. She turned up the music in the car until the song on the radio blurred out her thoughts. The tank in the car was full, she could go anywhere, but all places far away meant driving by her parents' house.

She supposed she could have driven by fast, never giving a glance out the window, but as her car approached, she found herself slowing down to a halt. She turned the hazard lights on in her car and stepped out.

The entry to the house was the only thing that remained normal. The shutters, which has once been a muted tan, were now stained with black soot. The roof of her home was caving in from where the flames had started to eat away at it from the middle.

This was all that was left. Her home was in rubble. Soot was pouring out of the doorway and windows, begging to be released. The grass around the house was still dead, some of it singed away completely.

She walked until she was at the front door, caution tape safe-guarding her home. She stretched her hand under the tape until her fingers tightened around the doorknob and pushed open. She almost expected the metal to burn her fingers.

She slipped under the tape and shut the door behind herself.

It felt like she was looking at a ghost. Everything around her was charred and burnt. Layers of ash coated the walls, leaving everything black and brown. Ash was still floating in the air. Every step she took disturbed the dust and kicked it back into the air. The hardwood was coated and streaked with ghosts of flames. The carpet that was on the stairs was burnt and charred.

Avery walked up the stairs, testing each step as she went. Sam's room was the first one at the top of the stairs. The door was kicked down and laid off to the side in the room. Sam's belongings were unharmed, save for a small coating of ash.

Sam's bed was unmade, like at any moment she might come back to curl in for the night. Avery smiled when she saw a familiar face at the edge of Sam's pillow.

– – – – –

"Hey." Sam was the first one to speak when Avery stepped through the door.

"I brought you something," Avery said. She held a gift bag out to Sam as she walked into the room. Sam waited until Avery pulled a chair over to the side of the bed before she tried to sit up. The movements were slow and timid, but once she was seated Avery gave her the bag.

"Thank you," she said. She pulled the gift-basket onto her bed and pulled the tissue paper away. A little stuffed dog was inside. His floppy ears were worn and his fur was a little too textured to be new. Sam pulled the stuffed animal to her face and buried her nose in his fur. Smoke filled her nostrils and she pulled him away. If she looked close, she thought she could see bits of ash in his fur.

"Do you remember him?" Avery asked.

Sam looked over to Avery while she held the dog. She felt a vague familiarity when Avery spoke, but otherwise she didn't know what Avery was talking about.

"Dad bought you him after a trip to the dentist. It was the only way he could get you through the day. I went to the dentist that day too, but I didn't pitch a fit so I left empty-handed."

As Avery spoke, it was like puzzle pieces were being fit into place. Sam didn't have to struggle for an answer; Avery found it before she had to look.

"I was so mad you got a stuffed animal that day, so I kept complaining until Dad bought me one too." She laughed to herself and smiled. "You named the dog Arnold, right? I can't remember." The nostalgia of the moment didn't hide the dark circles under her eyes. Her body seemed barely able to hold itself up in the chair.

"Your guess is as good as mine." Sam barely recognized the little dog, though the story rang a bell. She held Arnold in her arms, feeling his fur, waiting for something else to click into place but it never came.

"How have you been feeling? Avery asked.

Sam looked into the plastic eyes of the dog, the sewn-in smile. "A little lost," she said.

"Me too." The words were heavy when Avery spoke. Whatever happiness she had found talking about the stuffed dog slipped through the air in just a handful of seconds. "I went back to our house," Avery said.

Sam put the dog on her lap to look at Avery. Her eyebrows furrowed together.

"They haven't really done much except block things off. There wasn't much to see."

Sam looked back at the little dog in her hands. The smell of smoke seemed more pungent on him than she had first noticed. She brushed away at his fur and small bits of soot floated in the air.

"When was the fire?" Sam asked.

Her eyes stayed on Arnold. She couldn't remember all the memories he held, but she could feel them. This wasn't just a little stuffed dog. He meant something. She imagined flames curling up and around Arnold's body, and she wondered how he had survived.

"Sam?" She lifted her head and saw Avery looking at her. She wore a deep frown, her eyes glossy. "You don't remember?" Avery said.

Sam shifted the dog in her hands. He was just barely the size of her palm, and his legs flopped in whatever direction you turned him, but looking at him could not lift Sam away from Avery's face. Her sister looked back at her stunned, anguish written all over her.

"I know there was a fire," Sam said. There were bright

flames of red streaking across her memory, the feeling of singed skin and lungs unable to breathe. "That's all I know."

The two girls were silent as the moment was held in the air. Neither could look at the other.

"Am I going to be okay?" Sam asked. She couldn't stop looking at the stuffed dog.

Avery looked at the tight grip Sam had on Arnold, and she placed her own hands over hers. Sam relaxed, but only enough to let her hands loosen.

"You'll be fine, it just takes time." As Avery said the words she knew how feeble they sounded.

"But it's not just the fire, it's everything," Sam said.

"Like what?"

"I don't know what month it is, never mind what day. The doctor keeps asking me these questions, and sometimes I don't know the answer. I should know. It's stupid things, simple things, but I don't know."

"It's March," Avery said. "March 19th. It's Saturday."

It was the most information anyone had given her. For so many days the doctor and nurses have been asking questions, without once giving her an answer. How was she ever supposed to know an answer if they always left her wondering? Sam stored the information away for later use.

"Did you come alone?" Sam asked.

"Yeah, after leaving our house I wanted to drop off Arnold."

"Oh," Sam said. Her eyes lingered on the stuffed dog. She pet his fur, searching for answers that couldn't be found. She felt like she was losing something that was in her grasp but was being pushed farther away.

"Avery?" Sam said when she hadn't gotten an answer.

Her voice wavered with panic as she spoke. The possibilities hung between them. For now, Sam lived in a world where their parents were still alive, but that world was about to be shattered.

Sam looked down at Arnold, the soot on his tail. "What happened with the fire?" she asked.

Avery wanted to speak and tell her the truth, but if she were Sam and could choose to live in ignorance for just a little while longer, she thought she would choose that. But there was always the fear that maybe Sam would ask again where their parents were, and lying twice seemed like too much.

"Avery," Sam said again. Her voice was dropping. She already knew something was wrong.

"Sam, our parents are dead." Avery said the words quickly. Someone who didn't know her might think that the words were too blunt, but for someone who knew Avery like Sam did, she knew that speaking the words were just as hard as Sam hearing them. The cold emotions threatened to grip Avery and take her under again as she let the tears erupt.

Sam wanted to react like Avery, to just let all the emotion lift and take her away, but instead she could feel herself becoming this numb, a lost figure in her own world.

"In the fire," Sam said.

Avery nodded her head after she took a deep breath. It was one of those moments where words would never fix anything. The gash in the heart was too deep to heal, though there was a hope that possibly time would stitch up the wound.

"Sam?" Avery said. She took another breath. "I'm going to go."

"I'm sorry I can't remember," Sam said.

Avery never said why she had to leave, but Sam knew it was because visiting her was like re-opening a wound. Avery couldn't heal if she had to keep re-living what had happened.

"It's okay, Sam. You just need time."

Avery left the room and Sam couldn't help but wonder what time would do. Bring back her memories? She wondered if she wanted the memories of the fire, or if she was better off pretending like it never happened. Would she soon adjust to a life without her parents, without having to question where they were or why they'd disappeared?

— — — — —

"Excuse me?" Avery's eyes were freshly dried, though still red-rimmed. Her hand lingered on a nurse's shoulder, and the woman turned to look at her. "Who do I talk to about my sister? She's in room 316?"

"That's Dr. Ash's patient. Would you like to speak with him?"

"If I could," she said.

"Let me see if he's busy," she said, putting some things down on a cart.

Avery stood in the hall outside Sam's room for so long she assumed the nurse had forgotten about her until she saw a man approaching her. He held himself with the type of confidence that only comes with years of experience in the field.

"You're Sam's sister, right?" he said, offering his hand out. "What's your name again?"

"Avery," she said, shaking his hand, but his grip was too tight. She stepped farther away.

"Have you seen her today?" He looked past Avery to the room Sam was in.

"I was just with her, and I had a few questions." Avery paused to take a breath. "She doesn't remember the fire or our parents dying. When I was here last week we had to tell her our parents died in the fire and just now…it was like we had never had that conversation. She completely forgot."

She waited for Dr. Ash to speak up, but something ignited in her and she continued on before he could speak. "Sam has told me over and over, something doesn't feel right. Isn't there anything we can do?"

Dr. Ash ran his hand through his hair and let out a sigh. In his mind he ran over Sam's records again, but of course nothing had changed. Still no abnormalities.

"The mind is a complex thing," he said, but even he couldn't stand his own excuse.

Avery wrapped her arms around her stomach and blinked. "Of course, it is," she said. "You think I don't know that? But there has to be something that we can do."

"All the tests I've run so far have come back normal. We can keep monitoring, but we don't want to start treating for something until we know what it is. She stable and she's awake and talking. As of right now, if you're just going off her charts, she's perfectly healthy. The IV that she's hooked up to is a precaution. She doesn't need it, but we're trying to do everything we can for her."

He backed away, knowing he only had so much time to talk to her, and that time was almost up. Avery didn't speak, so he began to turn.

"Dr. Ash," she said, once his back was to her. "Have you ever had to tell someone their parents are dead?"

He didn't turn to look at her because all he could picture was Willow on the side of the road with her father. The agony in her face was a permanent fixture in his mind that showed no signs of fading away.

"Imagine having to tell someone, every time you see them,

that their parents are dead, and you both have to re-live that moment every time. I know she doesn't seem sick or is in pain physically, but isn't mental anguish enough? Isn't that enough to want to figure out how she can remember things without having to learn over and over that some of the only family she's ever had is gone?"

Dr. Ash turned to see Avery holding her stance, but her arms were shaking, still wrapped around her stomach. Her face was stone, but her eyes were watering.

"I will do the best I can, Avery. I will always do the best I can." And with that, he walked away.

# Chapter 18

The sound of the MRI machine vibrated across the room. Sam's eyes were shut and her headphones blocked out only a small amount of the sound coming from the machine. When they first started putting her in the machine, she would count. She'd start from 100 and count her way down. Recently, it had become harder. She'd get the first few numbers and then something would slip. She wasn't sure if it was lack of concentration from all the noise, or just because whatever was wrong with her was getting worse. Even starting from one and counting her way up was becoming a problem. She could only get so far as twenty before something pulled her attention away or she just forget the sequence of numbers.

"Hold still," a nurse said.

Sam kept her eyes shut. She wanted to hum to the beat of the MRI machine, but the nurses always said that she was moving too much. Was she moving too much to breathe as well?

No one came to stand at the foot of the machine anymore. Avery came to visit, but only after going to school first and her grandparents came at least every other day, but her biggest visitors were the doctors and nurses. The days blurred together, and her sense of time was waning. She wasn't sure it was because she had been there a long time or if her memory was getting worse. One thing she was sure, there seemed to be little time she was alone. All these tests and yet the medical staff still stood baffled. Twelve days since the fire and still no answers.

"Okay, Sam."

The slim surface she was laying on was pulled out of the machine. The plastic contraption around her head was removed and a hand was placed behind her back to help her sit up.

There were two nurses helping Sam, talking amongst each other. Sam tried to catch their words, and at first she could, but the longer their conversation went on the more lost she began to feel. Their words simply flowed too fast. For all she knew, they might as well have been talking in another language.

"Sam," the nurse said. Her voice was firmer than usual, and Sam knew she must have been trying to speak to her for a while.

"We're going to send the results over to Dr. Ash, and he'll meet with you. Will your grandparents will be coming in today?"

The nurses always knew the answers to these questions. She was an impaired patient so information was never reliable. Yet, they always asked her in an attempt to make her feel more independent, but for Sam it always had the opposite effect.

"I don't know," Sam said. The last time Shelly and Paul came to visit they said they'd be back in two days. Sam wrote it down on the paper pad beside her bed that they had given her, but it wasn't a fool-proof plan. She'd write "Grandparents will be back on Tuesday," but that only worked for a little while. As the weeks went by and her memory grew worse she never knew what day of the week it was and never remembered to ask one of the nurses. Soon enough she gave up on trying to keep track of days. Instead, she wrote it was April so whenever Dr. Ash or the nurses came in, she could have at least one answer correct—until the next month came around that is.

"Well, let me walk to your room and we'll find out, okay?"

Sam was escorted out of the room, leaving only one other nurse who was sanitizing the equipment. Willow had been waiting outside the room while the MRI was being performed and once Sam was led away, she slipped in. She was thankful when the nurse working to clean it didn't look up when Willow took control at the machine.

She typed a code into the machine and pulled up Sam's scan. Dark splotches were scattered across the screen. It was frightening how much it looked like her father's scans. The peripheral of the brain showed cells dying. Twelve days since Sam had arrived in the hospital and the similarities of Alzheimer's disease in her brain were uncanny.

Willow pulled her small notebook out and began to write down notes. Where the spots were located, how much they'd changed since Sam's last MRI. The notes were quick but thorough. Finally, she slipped out her phone and took photos of the screen. Once she was done , she entered another code into the machine and deleted the file, replacing it with the first scan of Sam's brain before the serum had been injected. She finished by changing the date listed on the scan.

The switch was done in a matter of minutes. The first time Willow had to switch out the MRI scan, she panicked thinking there was no way she'd ever be able to pull it off, but practice proved perfect. Every week, as Sam declined more, she was sent in for another MRI. Each week, Willow made sure her shift was during Sam's MRI and that the technician never saw the real results before they loaded onto the screen. It was an act of being in the right place at the right time, and so far, it had worked. Willow was the only one to ever see the real results and she switched them out before anyone else got the opportunity.

"Is it all set?" the nurse who had been cleaning the instruments asked.

"Just sending it now."

With a few clicks of the mouse, Sam's information was gone.

— — — — —

"I don't get it."

Randy was in his office when Willow walked in. He was sitting at his computer and had Sam's file pulled up. The MRI of a healthy girl was on the screen.

"What is it?" Willow said. She had a coffee for him in her hand, but he didn't take it. His eyes were glued to the screen and there was nothing she could do to take him away from it.

"The MRI results. There's still nothing wrong. I don't know what else to do. When I talk to the girl, she's impaired. She can't remember things, she has a hard time concentrating. It's like she has," but he stopped himself, and it was not lost beyond Willow.

"You can say it," she said. "It's like she has Alzheimer's."

He stared up at her, waiting for her to show some sign of distress. For so long, any talk of the disease seemed to send her spiraling, but now she seemed calm. He tried to remember the last time she had a breakdown but pushed the thought away when he saw the MRI results in the corner of his eye.

"Every test, she passes. It can't be possible. I don't know what to do. I have grandparents who just want their grandchild back, but I can't even tell them what's wrong with her, never mind treat it."

He was quiet while he looked over the files again. Willow had never seen him so invested in a patient, then again he'd never encountered a patient he couldn't diagnose. She had considered once or twice, telling him what she had done, but she knew her husband. What she did, he would never approve of, and even more frightening, she wasn't sure if he'd ever forgive her.

She wondered if she could go back in time, if she would undo it. The moral part of her said yes, but the desperate part, the part that needed the cure, that feared she'd die from the same disease her father had, wished more and more to push the experiment further. She also needed to protect Randy from what she had done, and there was very little she could do.

"Maybe I should refer her somewhere else. There has to be some kind of technology or some other doctor out there that can pick up on whatever's wrong."

"No," Willow said, too quickly.

He looked up at her, confused at her reluctance. They referred patients out all the time.

"You've invested too much time into this already," she said, gripping on to some way she could keep Sam in her care. "Any other physician will be starting from scratch, and she doesn't have the time to start from scratch. She's been declining. We can all see it in front of our eyes, so we can't wait for another doctor to give their input."

Randy covered his face with his hands and sat back in his chair. He couldn't deny her logic, and yet he couldn't push away the sense of dread.

"This is my patient," he said. "I won't be able to live with it if I can't find out what's wrong with her. What if someone else can?"

Her throat began to close in on itself. He had no idea what

he would unearth. There was a part of her that frightened even herself, and at times she couldn't control it. She had to fix her mistakes before they put Randy at risk.

"There will always be a what if. What if another doctor does find what's wrong with her, but what if you could have found it sooner if you had just stuck it out one more day?"

"Willow, this is someone's health, maybe even life, on the line. I don't care about vanity. Whoever finds out what's wrong with her, finds it. I want her to be better. Her grandparents have already lost so much; they don't need to lose a grandchild as well."

She was afraid to talk. If there was one thing she loved about her husband, it was his dedication and compassion. When she compared herself to him she knew he was a much better person. He was meant to be in the health field, and often times she questioned whether she was. She wasn't willing to sacrifice her father to finding a cure, but she too easily put an innocent life at stake.

# Chapter 19

When Dr. Ash walked into the room, Sam was holding a small stuffed animal in her hands. "How are you feeling today, Sam?" he asked.

She looked up at him and smiled.

"This is my pup," she said. She held up the small dog for him to see, the stuffed animal's legs falling out to the sides.

"Can you put the dog down?" he asked. He's always asked, ever since she first received the toy, but she never let it go. She attached herself to it, and it became the only thing that was consistent to her. He caught her tending to the little dog, brushing hair that didn't exist, asking the nurses to bring him food. At first it started off as just a fondness for the toy. She would put it down but there was always a resistance to let it out of her sight. Now, she tended to it like a living thing.

"I can't."

Dr. Ash pulled his chair forward, keeping his notes in his lap.

"Do you know what month it is, Sam?" he asked.

For almost a week, Sam could answer the question correctly. He could see her eyes wandering around the room until it found the notepad beside her bed that had the month written down, but he let her cheating slide. With so many wrong answers, he always allowed this answer to be right.

"Umm," she said. Her eyes wandered the room but they don't find the notebook.

Dr. Ash looked over to the notebook where March was crossed off and replaced with April. The handwriting was too neat to be Sam's.

"Look at the notepad," Dr. Ash whispered. He pointed to the bedside table until Sam turned her head enough to read. She stared at the paper and bite her lip.

"April?" she finally said, but even reading it off the paper she sounded unsure.

Dr. Ash smiled and took out his own notepad. He wrote out a quick sentence in large script.

"Can you read this for me?" he asks.

Sam frowned and looked at the dog.

"Pup can't read."

"I want you to read. You can pretend you're reading to your pup." He tried to sound encouraging, but when he heard himself all he could hear was exhaustion.

Her fingers loosened from the dog's neck, and she shifted forward to read.

"The yellow," she paused. "House. Was down the road. From the green house."

She finished the sentence and turned back to the dog. She pet his hair and held him up to her face, giving him small kisses.

Dr. Ash wrote another sentence and held it up to Sam.

"What about this one?"

Sam didn't let the dog drop this time. She held it close to her face as she leaned forward to read. "The cat," this time a longer pause. She blinked before she could continue. "The cat danced all night long."

Her face contorted like she smelled something bad.

"I don't want to play anymore," she said.

"Then tell me about your dog," he said, trying to switch gears as fast as she could.

He didn't think she heard him at first. She kept the stuffed animal close to her, never once looking up or at Dr. Ash.

"His name is Pup," she said in a soft voice. "And he doesn't like it here."

"Why's that?"

"You're mean to him. He doesn't like it when you're mean to me."

All the while she refused to look at him. Her eyes were for Pup and Pup only.

"Why do you think that?" he said.

"You hurt me!" she said. The words are too loud for the small room. "You poke me and pinch me and put me in that big machine."

She turned to Dr. Ash with fire in her eyes. In her voice, he heard anger, but her eyes melted away to something deeper. He imagined a girl trapped inside her own body. Did she know what's happening to her? All the things she'd lost?

"I know it's scary here, Sam."

When she heard her name, her face twitched and whatever anger had been holding her together shattered.

"I want my mom," she said. It was like she transformed from a small child to a young girl in front of his eyes. Her voice had gone from belittling to a serious in a matter of seconds.

"I know," he said. She had been asking for her mom for days. As time wore on Dr. Ash contemplated not telling her that her parents died. He wanted to say, "She's on her way," or, "She'll be here tomorrow." Save the anguish and let her have that one moment of peace. But he was always afraid. Would that be the one thing she remembered? Would she wake up every day, still asking for her mom, knowing Dr. Ash said she was coming?

He was selfish. He didn't want to watch the child go through the realization that her mother was gone, so he let the moment pass and hoped she didn't ask for her mother again.

"Do you want to count backwards for me, starting from 100?" he asked.

She frowned and held the dog up in the air. She didn't look like the girl who had been transferred to the hospital weeks ago. Everything about the way she acted seemed unnatural. Her smile was too large and her frowns too deep. When she spoke, the words sometimes slurred, and yet other times her diction was perfect. Nothing was consistent except that week by week, she was fading away.

"Pup says he's hungry," Sam said.

"No, Sam." He stood up and took the dog from her hands. The stuffed animal was a ragged thing and flopped lifeless in his arms. Sam sat, watching in terror as Pup was ripped away from her. The reaction was slow, but it was also unexpected. Dr. Ash thought she would scream, throw a hissy-fit of some sort, but she just stared at him. Her eyes were more focused than he'd seen them in weeks. He tried to decipher if she was upset, but there was no emotion in her eyes.

"I need you to concentrate," he said.

She blinked. Her mouth was in a straight line, her face was flat.

"I can't," she said. And there it was. The flicker of her old self. The childlike Sam that was holding onto a dog was replaced with the Sam full of doubt. Was it this doubt that made her so sick? Could all this just be some large physiological mess, her way of protecting herself from her parents' deaths?

"Why?" he said. His voice was soft and he sat once again. He still held the small dog in his hands, terrified that if he gave it to her again that she might slip away.

She looked around the room as if she was seeing it for the first time. Her eyes roamed and lingered on the machines and he saw the question in her eyes. Why am I here?

"We're trying to help you," he said.

When she looked at him it was like she was looking past his physical being and to his soul.

"I don't feel safe here," she said. Her words were simple. They were more solid than anything she'd ever spoken before and never once did her eyes flicker away from Dr. Ash's face.

He opened his mouse to speak, but closed it again soon after. She kept her eye contact until he spoke.

"Why?"

"Can I have Pup?" Her eyes had lingered down to his hand and she was gone. Whatever focus had been holding her to the conversation was gone.

— — — — —

"Paul, he's supposed to be one of the best neurologists in the region. There's nowhere else to go that could be better." Shelly's voice was soft when she spoke.

"Best in the region, that's bullshit and you know it," Paul said, pacing in front of Sam's bed.

That was the first thing Dr. Ash heard as walked into Sam's room. When he saw her, she was staring off into space again. She had the small stuffed dog in her hand and even though her grandparents were visiting her, she didn't take notice.

"Good evening," he said. Paul and Shelly turned, and they

weren't happy. Shelly had the face of someone at a funeral — a look she seemed to be sporting ever since he met her — and Paul was seething. They'd seen Sam like this for a few days now, but each day they came in they asked more and more questions that Dr. Ash couldn't answer.

He knew what Paul was going to say before he opened his mouth.

"What the hell is the matter with her?"

Dr. Ash only knew what he was going to say because it was what he said to himself every time he looked at Sam's charts.

"Paul, Shelly, would you both please sit down?" He motioned for them each to take one of the plastic chairs that was in the corner of the room.

"Unfortunately, it appears Sam has been deteriorating more. She seems more impaired, but the exact cause is uncertain. All tests we've run come back normal. The MRI scans are that of a perfectly healthy sixteen-year-old girl. However, when I do cognitive tests, she continues to decline."

"So what does that mean?" Paul said. He sat in his chair, but just barely. He was one move away from storming out of the room.

Shelly reached out to grip his hand. He took it, though it did little to sooth him.

"It means, we still aren't sure what's wrong."

Paul rolled his eyes and sat back in his chair. Shelly looked over to Sam who was still in the room but completely oblivious to the conversation they were having.

"You've got to be kidding me. So what do we do? Wait again until she turns into a vegetable?" Paul said, pointing to his granddaughter.

"Paul." Shelly's voice cut through and she gave him a pointed look.

"I think it might be time to start considering other

avenues. I'd like to see Sam get a psychological evaluation."

Paul balked at his words. "Seriously? So you think she's crazy?"

Shelly cowered away at his voice. Sam was the only calm one in the room.

"I think that because nothing is showing up physically, that the only answer is that this might be psychological. Up until the fire, she'd never had problems, right?" Dr. Ash asked.

"Right," Shelly said. Paul looked at her quickly before turning to Dr. Ash again.

"So, what, you think the seizure was all psychological too?" Paul said.

"No, that could have been something completely different. But this," he pointed to Sam, "might be her way of protecting herself from the trauma of the fire."

"This is bullshit." Paul got up and took Shelly by the hand. She followed but the movements were slow and tentative. "I want my granddaughter out of this hospital."

"Sir," Dr. Ash raised his voice and the room was silenced. Paul turned around but the anger was still radiating off his shoulders. "I don't recommend moving her out of this hospital unless absolutely necessary. Any other hospital, or doctor for that matter, will treat Sam as a new patient. They won't have the same history of her as I do. From what I've seen, Sam's situation is becoming critical and at a rate we can't predict. The amount of time it will take a new doctor to observe Sam and learn everything they can about her isn't something she can afford. I'm searching for answers to the best of my ability."

Shelly looked at Dr. Ash, her eyes apologetic. Paul stood his ground as his eyebrows furrowed into a line.

"Don't you dare tell me what's best for my grand-daughter."

# Chapter 20

Willow was asleep on the small couch in the corner of Randy's office. Her hair was pulled back into a braid, but small strands stuck to the skin around her face. Her eyes were closed, relaxed.

"Willow?" Randy whispered, closing the door behind him as he walked in. Her lips twitched as she rolled onto her back. The small notebook that had been in her hands dropped to the floor.

The cover of the notebook fell to the side and exposed the pages. "Venom Trials" was printed in neat script.

When he started reading the notebook, he thought Willow had just made notes on the article that she had read on the experiment. A formula was written out, the exact measurements and how to mix the compounds covered the pages. His stomach dropped when he flipped past the chemical formulas and found notes referring to an unnamed patient.

*Took solution well, didn't wake up.*

*Showed signs of memory loss.*

*MRI scan shows significant deterioration.*

*Has begun to carry around a stuffed animal. Named him Pup.*

He almost dropped the notebook when he read the words. It wasn't until that point that he flipped through the pages faster, looking for some sort of sign that what he was thinking wasn't true. His thoughts were proven correct when he found her chart in the back of the notebook that Willow had been using to document vitals. It was eerily similar to the chart on Sam's records.

He slipped past the chart to another page. Another chemical formula was written across the pages, this one different than the last. The first one was perfected and written only as instructions on how to proceed. It was obvious by this second one that it was a work in progress. Formulas and measurements were written and crossed off over and over, no combination ever the same.

"Willow?" he said. He flipped through the pages, never once did she name her patient, but her name screamed loud in his head as if it were carved into the pages.

She was still asleep. He looked at the woman he loved and thought of how every night the two of them would crawl into bed and count down the hours until they had to go back to work. Willow had finally stopped asking Randy about his research on Alzheimer's. He thought that had meant she had moved on, but the notebook was proof that she had merely moved her focus elsewhere.

"Willow," he said again, this time louder. "Wake up."

She rolled back on her side.

"Wake up!" he said. His hand lowered. He still held the notebook in his hand, but he couldn't get himself to look at it anymore.

Willow stretched out before she opened her eyes. Her first thought when she woke up was that Randy was waking her up to get back to work after her lunch break, but then she saw Randy's face. His lips were drawn down and his eyes looked lifeless, like someone had shot him in the chest — or better yet, that he had just witnessed someone else shoot *her* in the chest. There was no anger as he stood over her, only heartbreak. He looked at her hoping she would be able to explain everything to him and that it would all just be a big mistake, but the feeling in his gut told him otherwise. The deepest part of him knew that each word in the notebook was exactly what it appeared to be.

"What's wrong?" she said, rolling up from the couch. Her eyes rolled down to the notebook in Randy's hand, and her stomach dropped.

"What is this?" He held the notebook out in his hands. The cover was worn from all the days Willow had carried it around in her pockets. There was so much research pouring into those pages, so much information that was never meant to be seen by anyone except Willow.

"Tell me what's written in this notebook," he said, his voice quiet. He wanted to be angry. He wanted to scream at Willow until she saw sense, but he couldn't help the tears that began to flow down his cheeks.

"It was an accident," Willow said. "I didn't mean for Sam to get sick."

"You put an unknown substance into her body with a syringe," he said, still holding the notebook out. "And then she woke up the next day and you continued to observe her like a lab experiment. And you did that every day."

Willow looked at her husband. As he spoke, he began to wilt. The notebook dropped to the floor. She wanted him to scream at her, hit her, do something that was less painful than watching him fall to pieces.

"For weeks," he said, his voice turned to a whisper. "For

weeks, I've been trying to understand this girl, to help her so she can go back to her family, and for all this time you've been working against me and letting her sink deeper and deeper into your game."

"It's not a game," Willow said.

"Of course, it's a game!" he said. "It's always been a game with you, and the prize is the cure. But did you ever think of this girl's life? She never chose this for herself. You did, all because you needed to find a cure."

Randy threw the notebook across the room, knocking a certificate off the wall. Willow didn't weep at his anger, she absorbed it.

"At least I'm trying," Willow said, her face reddening. "I've always been trying. I want to find a cure. Is that so wrong?" Her hands shook and through the anger she couldn't help but want to cross the room and take her notebook back before Randy could do anything else with it.

"Of course, I want to find a cure, but we have to do it correctly. You don't even know if injecting the mock disease will help aid in a cure."

"We won't know until we try, "she said. Willow's breathing shuttered and she took a moment to compose herself. Her body wanted to be elsewhere. She craved to have the notebook back in her hands.

"Where are Sam's real MRI scans?" Randy said. His voice was calm, but his body stood stiff.

"In the safe," she said. Her voice was quiet as she held her head down, only glancing up to spot the notebook still laying across the floor. The pages were splayed open and she wanted to close then contents tight.

Randy crossed the room and knelt to the ground in front

of his desk as he entered the combination on the safe. As the tumblers fell into place, Willow knew she was about to be exposed. She remained on the couch as Randy ruffed through the papers and pulled out Sam's files, her MRI scans printed out in full, never seen by anyone except Willow.

"Fuck."

Willow cringed as she heard Randy swear.

For a long time, Randy said nothing else. He never bothered to get up from the floor as he looked over the files. Instead, he laid everything out on his desk. He saw each scan in its entirety. He lined them up by date, watching as her brain cells began to die off one by one, slowly, until her real self was missing.

"Did you know her grandparents want to take her to another hospital?" he said.

Willow heard him shuffle the papers and bring it all to his desk as her stood. She couldn't speak.

"Because she hasn't been getting better, they want a second opinion, and I can't blame them. In fact, I wanted her to see a psychiatrist for their input, but now," he looked down at the desk. Dark blotches from the MRIs scarred back at him. "Now I don't know what to do."

"You're going to turn me in," Willow said. It wasn't a question. She knew Randy. When he took his oath to become a doctor, she knew he meant every word he said. Above all, do no harm.

"I need you to leave," he said. His voice found a resonated calm.

"Please don't turn me in." She got up from the couch and crossed the room to pick up the notebook. She slipped it into her pocket and she saw Randy turn his head to watch it disappear out of site. There were no more secrets she could keep from him.

"Go home, Willow," he said. He didn't look at her. They never left each other without kissing, hugging, touching, something, but now he couldn't even look at her.

She found her way to the door, looking back one last time to be sure he was still that, that she had really been exposed. The door closed with a soft click behind her.

Randy watched the door for a long time, expecting her to come through and beg for forgiveness. He could hear her soft footsteps as she walked away.

Randy buried his face in his hands. When he ran his fingers through his hair, he was tempted to pull it out. How could she have done this? He stared across the room to where the notebook had fallen on the floor. The only reminder that it had been there in the first place was his MBA diploma, the glass in the frame now cracked.

Before he could change his mind, he grabbed all the papers off his desk and locked them in the safe. The next door to be locked was his office as he rushed to Sam's room before anyone would advert his attention. He grabbed a wheelchair before entering.

"Hi," Sam said as Dr. Ash walked through the door. She smiled when she saw him, sitting up a bit straighter.

"Sam, we need to do some quick tests," Dr. Ash said. His voice was soft and he continued to look over his shoulder as he spoke. Nurses walked by in the halls but none ever bothered to look into the room. He was being watched, or at least he believed he was. He put Willow out his head as much as he could. He didn't want to believe what she had done, but he knew he wouldn't know for sure until he saw the results for himself.

Before Sam could protect or notice any difference in the usual routine, Dr. Ash scooped her up, wrapping his arms around the back of her legs and her back and placing her into the wheelchair. She stared off into her own world as he wheeled her down the hall and into the room with the MRI machine. He hadn't bothered to check the room's schedule before they entered so he was lucky when he stepped in and the room was empty.

"What are we doing?" Sam asked. It was an innocent question, one she asked all the time, but his confidence was shaken. He looked at the door like he had been caught, but no one was there. It was just the two of them in the room, Sam looking around, examining every square inch even though she received MRI scans on a regular basis.

"We're doing a test, Sam," Dr. Ash said.

Sam's face dropped. She didn't like tests. She failed too often and it always ended in disappointment.

Dr. Ash lifted her from her wheelchair once again and laid her across the hard, thin table of the MRI machine.

"Do I have to?" Sam said. Her eyes were wide, her body tense. She looked at the machine feeling a vague familiarity, but not sure why that was.

"It will just be a quick test," he said.

"I don't want to fail," she said.

She was laid out perfectly as Dr. Ash lowered the head piece over her forehead. She stared through the mirror to the empty room. The loneliness made her breathing pick up. What was he doing to her?

"Now just hold still," he said.

Sam heard his words, but she couldn't find where he was coming from. She began to squirm.

The machine began to hum and pulse. Sam hadn't realized it, but he had placed headphones over her ears. There was no one at her feet for comfort. When she looked through the mirror above her eyes, she was still utterly alone. Everything was too loud, but she couldn't lift her hands to cover her ears.

"Just lay still and we'll be done in no time," Dr. Ash said. His voice, normally calm and even, possessed a tone of doubt.

Sam took a breath and hummed to herself, waiting for the sounds to stop and to be let out of the machine. She closed her eyes, waiting for the panic to go away.

He was in a room aside from the MRI machine. As the machine pulsed he stood, waiting for confirmation that what Willow had done was all just a big ruse. He begged for her scans to come back as they always did: normal, utterly healthy. Within seconds, images began to pull up onto the screen and with it brought a certain dread.

The buzzing held the room when the results finally came in. Darkness clouded her scan. It was as if he was looking at one of the MRI scans Willow had printed out herself. A dark, large spot was in the center of Sam's brain. If he hadn't known any better, he could have thought he was looking at a scan of an elderly patient with dementia.

Dr. Ash blinked once, twice, and stood in front of the screen. Sam began to squirm in the MRI machine again, but it didn't matter. The results were already in. Nothing could undo what Dr. Ash had seen.

He walked back into the room with the machine and pulled Sam out. Her eyes were full of tears when she had the mirror headpiece pulled off.

"Where's my pup?" she said.

She sat up quickly and looked around the room. Nothing was important except finding her pup.

"Come on, Sam," he said, trying to get her to sit in the wheelchair once again.

She pulled away from him and ran to the door. Before she could understand how to open the door, Dr. Ash had his hand wrapped around her wrist.

"Let go!" she screamed. She pulled against him and fell to the floor in hopes he would release her.

"Samantha!" he said. His voice was firm, but she didn't budget.

"No!" She was a toddler on the floor, wrapping her arms around her legs so she shouldn't walk or move.

"Get up, now!" He spoke too loudly and she froze. He could feel the control slipping from him. He didn't know what to do. There was this girl in front of him. For days, she had been suffering from something unknown and now, all at once he knew. She was suffering from something all too similar to Alzheimer's. For so long, he had been wishing to know what was wrong so he could work closer to a cure, but now that he knew, he wished he had never found out.

Sam was still on the ground, but she had stopped protesting. She was looking up at Dr. Ash with a look of wonderment and confusion. He gripped her hand as she got off the ground and found her seat on her wheelchair.

He wheeled her through the halls, and she never spoke a word. Every possibility passed through his mind as he pushed her wheelchair. Sam needed help. Willow needed help. Both were very different forms of help, and he knew he couldn't find a solution that would leave both Willow and Sam safe.

"Hi, Dr. Ash." He jumped when a nurse passed him. She smiled as Dr. Ash walked by, and if she noticed that anything was off, she didn't say anything.

# Chapter 21

The pup was staring at her. That's what Sam was sure of. The pup had been sitting, perfectly still, without once needing to blink. She watched him, stunned by his resilience. How does he do it, she wondered. She mimicked him as he sat. Two hind legs out to the side, front legs perfectly straight in front of her. Head level, eyes unblinking. Getting the eyes right was the hardest. No matter how hard she tried, she always had to blink.

"Come on, Pup," she said. She begged him to blink, but he never did.

Pup had become her greatest companion. He was the only one that was always there. Sometimes nurses or doctors come in and took her out of the room for tests, but when she came back he was always there, waiting for her. She never remembered anyone's name, but she knew his: Pup. And that was all that she needed to know.

She knew Avery had brought her Pup. Avery came most days. She always sat at the edge of the bed and talked to her about her day. Lately, she had stopped asking how Sam was doing and instead told her how she was doing. Admittedly, Sam had a hard time understanding Avery. She spoke too fast for her to follow, but as long as Avery didn't know, she was okay with not catching the whole conversation.

Sam heard people walking by in the hall and she finally looked away from Pup. He could win the staring contest again, she supposed. She watched at the door, hoping Avery was going to peek through. She placed Pup on her lap so he could watch as well, but he didn't pay as much attention as her.

Two nurses walked by her door, talking about something she didn't care about. She held her breath, hoping Avery was close behind, but no one else came. The sounds of footsteps in the hall disappeared.

"Want to find Avery?" Sam asked Pup. She looked to Pup for his response, but he never barked or sniffled. She stood up and sat him on her bed pillow. "Watch my bed while I'm gone."

She strode from the room, Pup watching her back as she strode away. The hallway was mostly empty except for a few pieces of equipment the nurses rolled around. People were in the halls too, some dressed normally but a few had scrubs on, so Sam knew they were nurses. She liked her nurses, but they never let her explore the hallway, so she steered clear of them.

Sam tip-toed to each doorway, poking her head through the entry to see if Avery was within. For the most part, the rooms held only one or two people. Every now and then she would see a nurse and turn away before they heard her. Eventually, Sam came to a room full of people. The sound of laughter is what pulled her in.

"Ricky, look at this!"

A little boy was sitting in the hospital bed. A woman was holding out a baseball, and he was staring at it in wonder. Sam found herself being drawn into the room. Ricky's visitors slowly turned one-by-one as they each noticed the strange girl walking into the room. They looked at each other, but no one knew who she was. The woman who had given Ricky the baseball stepped away from his bed and came over to Sam.

"Are you lost?" she asked.

Sam gazed past her and to the baseball in Ricky's hand. His face was placid as he looked back at Sam. The smile he had a few seconds ago was gone.

"No," Sam said. She tried to walk past the woman but she wouldn't let her.

"Sweetie, this isn't your room. Let me go find a nurse." The woman reached for Sam's hand, but she pulled away, backing out of the room herself.

"No," she said again, this time louder. Everyone in the room was staring at her, this she knew, but she wanted to know what Ricky had. What was so special about a baseball?

"It's okay," the woman said. She walked closer to Sam and Sam backed away. She didn't want to be touched by this stranger.

She was about to turn around when she backed into someone. Whoever it was wrapped her hands around Sam's wrists.

"Come on, Sam," the voice said. A nurse with curly hair was pulling her out of the room gently. Sam pulled away in protest once she saw the nurse. She couldn't bring the nurse's name to mind, but a pinch in her gut dropped when she saw her. The nurse looked tired, and if she looked closely enough Sam could see smudges of mascara around her eyes.

Sam thought about protesting more, but the nurse's hands were still at her wrist, grasping a bit too firm. As she was pulled from the room, she looked back at the boy Ricky. He still held his baseball, but the excitement was gone. She was sorry to have ruined the moment.

"I need to find it," Sam said once she was pulled far from the boy's room. They were turning back in the direction she had come from. All the ground she had covered, all the time she had spent searching, wasted!

"Find what?" the nurse said. Her grip relaxed on Sam's hand, but her voice had an edge of exhaustion to it.

Sam paused at her question. She knew that she was looking for something, but she couldn't remember what it was. She hoped that if she did find it, she would know it when she saw that, but even that was questionable.

"I need to find it," she said again, but she followed the nurse anyways.

The nurse led her through the door of a room, and as soon as they stepped through, Sam saw Pup waiting for her. She leapt forward and wrapped her arms around him before he had a chance to run away.

"Pup," she whispered in his ear.

The nurse watched from behind as Sam sat on the bed with the little stuffed dog cradled in her hands.

"Was that what you were looking for?" Willow said.

She looked behind her to the doorway. She almost expected Randy to come through, ordering her to get away from Sam before she did any more harm. There were no footsteps in the hallway, so she stepped closer.

Sam paused to look at Pup. He didn't smile back at her. His little mouth was always in the same straight line. She was waiting for her memory to jog and remind her that Pup was what she had been looking for, but nothing ever clicked.

"I think so," she finally said.

Willow stood at her bed, silently watching as Sam ventured off into her own world. She was quiet on her bed, mumbling only loud enough for the little dog to hear.

Slowly, Willow backed out of the room. She watched Sam with every step, taking in her movement and her soft whispers. How quickly the girl had changed. The serum was potent and the effects were clear. The girl she used to be wasn't there anymore.

— — — — —

"Randy?" His office door was unlocked. When she looked in, she saw him sitting at his desk, face buried in his hands. Papers were strewn everywhere and a coffee mug was beside him.

"Is that coffee?" she asked.

He looked up, and she could tell he had been crying. It was something she saw only on rare occasions. The last time she had seen it was the night her father died. That night he was crying not for her farther, but for the pain Willow had to endure. Her pain was his pain, and that was never more evident than right now.

"Yes," he said. His voice was stiff. It had been two days since he discovered what she had done and while it was clear he thought about it every second, he refused to bring it up in subject.

"You don't drink coffee," she said. Willow came to his desk and took the coffee mug away. When she lifted it, she saw the print-outs of Sam's MRI scans. They stared back at her with a menace.

"I know," he said, gripping the mug back out of her hands. He did it gently, but the gesture still stung.

She looked at the papers in front of him. They were pages of his notes from all the past appointments with Sam. Notes from when he didn't know what was wrong with her. They had been nothing been pen scrapping but now they were glittered with highlights and notes in the margins.

"Willow, I need you to leave," he said. An edge of anger

was there. He refused to look at her, yet she couldn't stop looking at him.

"What are you going to do?" she asked.

He slammed his hands to the desk. The coffee he had taken out of her hands spilled onto the MRI scans and blurred the ink. When she saw the mess part of her felt relieved. One piece of evidence removed.

"I don't know," he said. He was finally looking at her again but knew her eyes were averted to the coffee stain. The smell of the black coffee filled the room. It wasn't a scent either of them was used to. "I *should* turn you in."

Willow looked up at her husband and her face dropped. She felt the tips of her fingers go numb, and she wasn't sure if she had heard him correctly. Turn her in?

His eyes teared up, and she never said a word. He hated himself for what he said.

"I should turn you in and forget any of this ever happened." His mouth turned into a hard line. "But that's not how it would work. If I turned you in, I'd be turning myself in. If I turned you in, I'd never be able to forget."

"But you didn't do anything," she said.

"I loved you," he said. "I loved you and I let you do this to yourself. I let you do this to a stranger, a girl who has already lost so much, but she doesn't even know it because she can't remember."

"Isn't it better that way?" Willow said. She tried not to let herself notice the fact that he said loved, not love. It was like a nit was biting away at her, urging her to pick at his words. She knew what she had done to him. She knew she didn't deserve his love or forgiveness but the words stung.

Randy paused to look at her. Was she joking?

Her eyes spoke something she couldn't get herself to say. They were searching for a solution, but most of all they were searching for a cure, and whoever got in her way was to pay the price.

"Do you hear yourself, Willow?" he said.

She blinked away and looked at the MRI scans again. With the combination of the coffee with the darkened cells, Willow felt like she was looking at an ink blot test. What did she see? The closer she looked the less she saw. There was nothing.

She sucked in a breath, terrified of what he might be thinking. In these quiet days, where she was left alone to think about what her husband might do, was he thinking about all the reasons she didn't deserve his love and mercy anymore? All the reasons he needed to turn her in?

He put his arm out to rest on Willow's shoulder. She knew he wanted her to look up, but she couldn't do it. Standing in this room, having everything so exposed, she felt raw. So much time spent healing and fixing, finding a cure to this disease, and here it was laid out in front of her. It was ripped from her hands. She felt crazed, desperate and raw with no way of healing.

There were still moments in the days where her memory lapsed and a pit in her stomach formed. She was becoming her father and she imagined herself in a few years sitting on a couch, her eyes just as vacant as her father's. Her fear is what fueled her, and it was a fear she couldn't admit to Randy. If she told him she thought she had Alzheimer's, what would he think? Would he be just as desperate to save her before she lost herself more than she already had?

"We could learn so much," she said. Her rationale for finding the cure was completely selfish. She let it guide her.

Randy couldn't speak. He let the air in his lungs release.

He looked at his wife, at the woman he loved, and wondered just how long ago he had lost her. Was it the day her father had died? Was this determination to find a cure stemmed from her loss, or did it go back farther than that?

"It's not ethical," Randy said.

"I found Sam in the halls today." She looked up at him. A spark was in her eye. There was excitement there, and when Randy looked at her he knew that this spark was what ignited her to act. "She was wandering, looking for something, but she wasn't sure what. She shows clear signs of Alzheimer's, but she's so young. Even her MRI scans are similar to those of Alzheimer's patients." She pointed to the scans but the gesture was futile.

"It's a tragedy," Randy said. He refused to let his eyes wander off her face.

She turned to him and her hopes diminished.

"But if we found a cure, it would be worth it."

Randy knew what she was saying and he knew exactly how she wanted to proceed with the experiment. But he kept picturing Sam in his mind, diving deeper and deeper into some place far beyond his reach. What if they did find a cure? Would it be worth it?

Willow smiled because she could see Randy was thinking. He was thinking of the possibilities, but in Willow's mind it wasn't just a possibility. If Randy let her proceed, she would make it a reality. She stood by, her nerves jumping, ready to do something, anything.

"I need to find a cure," she said. Her voice broke and her eyes diminished as some far-away emotion took over her body.

# Chapter 22

S helly was holding Paul's hand because he wanted nothing to do with being in the hospital. He was seething as they sat in the cold room with Sam. Today was a good day for her. She was quiet, and sometimes her being quiet made it easier to forget she was sick.

"I want her out of here," Paul said.

The two were sitting next to each other in fold-up chairs beside Sam's bed. Each time Paul spoke, Shelly tightened her grip on him. She was terrified that he might just run out of the room.

"I want to see what Dr. Ash has to say," she said.

"You heard what he had to say, he thinks Sam is crazy!" Already he was wound up, ready to blow up to whoever had the audacity to disagree with him.

"No, we didn't get to hear what he had to say because you stormed out of the room," she said.

"Of course, I—," he stopped talking.

Avery stepped into the room. Her pale skin seemed luminescent in the light of the hospital room.

"Sorry," she said. "I didn't know you guys were going to be here. I thought it would just be me and Sam today. I can come back later." She started to turn away, but she looked behind Shelly and Paul. Sam was on the bed, very much awake, staring out the window of the room.

"No, Avery, stay. I'm sure Sam would love to see you," Shelly said.

Sam was still looking out the window when Avery came over. All eyes were turned to Sam, and when she heard someone approaching, she looked up at Avery and smiled.

"Hi," Sam said.

"Where's the doctor?" Paul said. She stood up, letting go of Shelly's hand. "He's supposed to be here by now."

"Paul," Shelly said. He walked out of the room. "I'll be right back girls." Shelly followed behind him without another word.

Avery sat in Shelly's seat beside Sam once they left.

"Is everything okay?" Avery asked.

Sam smiled, just half of her face rising, and for a moment there was a spark of the old Sam. The crooked smile was Sam's signature. She was there for a moment, and then she was gone when she looked away and pulled Pup to her. She held onto him, not gingerly like a child might to their favorite toy, but with a loose, flopping grip. He was upside down when she held him.

"Sam?" she said. It was the first time she had visited Sam in a few days, but it was eerie how much she had changed. Everything about her was the same, but she held herself differently. She slouched forward and curled in on herself.

"You brought me Pup?" Her eyes were glossed over. She was looking at Avery, but to Avery it felt like she was looking past her to something else.

"Arnold," she said. She put her hand out to grab the dog. Sam let go of him as Avery put him on the side table, sitting right-side-up.

"Arnold," Sam repeated. Her eyebrows furled in. A small crease formed on her forehead. "Was that his name?"

Avery watched Sam. Puzzle pieces were clicking into place. Her glazed over eyes focused and everything in the room became clear.

"Sam?" Avery said. Something flittered in Sam's eyes. A change.

"Something's wrong," Sam whispered. Her heart began to race, and she looked around the room, searching for something. It wasn't the same mindless searching that she had been doing through the halls. This time she felt guided to something, but she wasn't sure what.

"What's wrong?" Avery said. She learned towards Sam. Her hand inched towards the call button, but she was terrified to let anyone else in the room. For a moment, Sam was present and as terrified as she might have been, she was there.

Sam looked at the IV in her hand and reached to take it out. As soon as Avery saw what she was doing, she pulled Sam's hand away. Sam wouldn't look at Avery. Her eyes never wavered from the needle.

"Sam?" Avery said.

"Get it out," she said. Tears were in her eyes. Her hand twitched as Avery held it down to the bed so she wouldn't rip the IV out. Avery adjusted her grip to hold her down with one hand and used the other to reach for the call button.

Sam's eyes darted to the button, and the small click echoed across the room.

"Get it out," she said again.

"Sam, it's okay." Avery covered Sam's arm with her other hand. Sam's skin was warm, a thin layer of sweat coating her arm.

"No." The words that came out of Sam's mouth were a whine. The word was barely audible, nothing more than a breath, but Avery heard the desperation there. Her eyes, tired and dark, watered as tears began to stream.

"What's wrong?" A nurse came into the room, and whatever had been holding Sam disappeared. It was like an elastic band snapping into place. For a moment, Sam was there, and then she was gone. Her muscles weakened as her body slumped and her eyes glazed. If a stranger was watching, they wouldn't have seen the difference, but Avery looked on in terror.

The nurse began working before Avery responded and calmed Sam until her heart rate slowed back to a normal pace. She replaced the IV bag, and Avery couldn't help but watch in horror as the IV bag was carried around the room. They began pumping her with a medication to sedate her: relax and cool the body.

"Sam?" she asked, standing up as the nurse began checking her vitals again.

"Where's Pup?" Sam asked. And in that moment it felt like she would never have her sister back.

— — — — —

"He cancelled?"

Paul was standing at the reception desk. Both hands were planted firmly to the counter, and Shelly was standing behind him, her arm outstretched to touch his arm. She was trying to reel him in, but the effort was a wasted one.

"I'm sorry, sir, but an emergency came up," the woman at the desk said.

"Am emergency? My granddaughter is an emergency. She's been here for weeks, and she's only gotten worse."

"Dr. Ash may be able to see you later today, but we don't know how long he will be," she said.

"No, I'm not waiting for him. We're leaving, and my granddaughter will be leaving as well."

"Sir, it says here that Dr. Ash wanted Sam to see a psychologist. Would you like to make an appointment? We have a few different psychologists located in this hospital. We may be able to squeeze you in today due to your situation."

Shelly looked over to Paul. She was already bracing herself for his response.

"Psychologist." He spit the words out. "I don't want my granddaughter anywhere near this hospital."

The woman at the desk took a moment to compose herself.

"I understand, sir, and we'd like to assist you in every way we can, but there are steps that need to be taken. If you'd like to take Sam out of this hospital then you'll have to let us know where she will be sent so we can forward her medical records. Have you contacted your insurance company yet?"

Paul looked at the women at the desk, shaking his head. He could feel Shelly staring at him from the corner of his eye. She wanted to walk away from this moment, but she also knew she was the only thing stopped him from losing it in public.

"Sir, if you'd like, we can make you a referral," the women said.

"Oh, fuck you," he said. He wanted to storm off, slam a door or two, but instead he walked away, hand-in-hand with his wife, resigned to the fact that his granddaughter was dying and the doctor wasn't doing a damn thing about it.

# Chapter 23

"Okay, Sam, I'm going to give you an address to remember," Dr. Ash said. He was in his chair at the foot of the bed while Shelley was in another chair at the head of the bed next to Sam. Paul was standing beside her, his arms crossed and one wrong word from storming out. He promised Shelly this one last appointment, then they would get whatever they needed to transfer Sam to a new hospital.

Shelley watched Sam like she might disappear if she looked away, but Paul never stopped glaring at Dr. Ash. He was two hours late to the appointment that he had asked his admin to cancel. Apparently, Paul and Shelly never got the note.

Sam smiled when she looked around to everyone that was in her room. She smiled because she didn't know what else to do. She looked around the room like there was a film over her eyes — she was only half there.

"15 Turn Street, Walkins, New Hampshire." He made up the address on the spot and wrote it down on his clipboard. Sam nodded and whispered the address to herself quietly. The stuffed dog was in her hands, clutched too tightly.

"Okay," she said, still whispering to herself.

Dr. Ash pulled cards out of a pocket of his jacket and held the first photo up. He felt all eyes in the room turn to him. The cards were simple. Perfect drawings of everyday objects, simple enough a small child could do it, but for someone with Alzheimer's, the answers would come slowly, if at all. He already knew how Sam would respond to the cards, but he hoped that his knowledge would fail him.

"15 Turn Street, Walkin, New Hampshire," Sam said. She didn't bother to look at the card.

"Sam, the address is for later. I'll ask you for it at the end of this session," he said.

"But I remember it now. I won't remember it later."

He wanted to say, that's the point, you have Alzheimer's. Instead, he said, "You might." He looked at the card in his hand. "Now tell me, what's this?" He pointed to the card.

"That's a dog!" she said. "Just like Pup!" Sam held up her stuffed dog.

"And this?" He switched the cards.

"How is this supposed to help?" Paul said, his voice cutting off Dr. Ash's. "Anyone can tell you what those are. She's not in first grade."

"It's just a test of her memory to see if she can put names to objects," Dr. Ash said. "Sam, can you tell me what this is?"

She had dropped Pup to her lap and stared at the photo. She bit the edge of her lip as she examined the drawing on the page. She knew what it was. She had seen the shape before, many times in fact, but the name escaped her.

"Sam, just tell him what it is," Paul said. His voice edged on anger and made Sam lose focus.

"Umm," she said. Wings. It had wings, so she knew it flew. Like a bird!

"Take your time, Sam," Dr. Ash said.

It was sorta like a bird, wasn't it?

"Sam?" Shelly said. Her voice cracked. Sam turned to her and saw there were little sparkles of tears in her eyes. Why was she crying?

Sam let go of Pup and reached out for Shelly's hand. She blinked, and a tear escaped.

"It's plane for Christ's sake," Paul said. He dropped his arms to his side and stepped closer to Sam's bed. Shelly closed her eyes and brought her hands to her lap. "Just tell him what it is so we can all move on and get your paperwork done."

"Paul, I need Sam to tell me. Interruptions will only make this harder for her. You can sit if you'd like." Dr. Ash pointed a second chair that was in the corner of the room.

Sam held her head down as Paul slid the chair across the floor and sat between Shelly and Dr. Ash. He didn't look at anyone, just the floor. He leaned forward, elbows on his knees.

"Sam?" Dr. Ash asked. He flipped to a new card.

She blinked once, twice, and smiled when she saw the feathers. "It's a bird!" she said.

Dr. Ash flipped the cards again. The room paused as Sam looked over the card. Shelly's eyes wandered back and forth between the cards and Sam. The picture was so simple.

*Rose*, Shelly thought to herself.

The room stayed quiet. Everyone feared interrupting Sam's train of thought. Paul stared straight ahead, trying to ignore the situation unfolding in front of him. The silence was thick in the room.

*Rose, Sam, a rose.* Shelly tried to push the thought into Sam's head. *Maybe flower would suffice...*

Dr. Ash watched Sam's face as her brows relaxed and her

gaze veered off. He flipped to the next card. Paul looked up, eyes ablaze.

"What the hell?" He stood up and Shelly cowered. "She was about to say what it was," he said.

"She wasn't," Dr. Ash said. He had hoped Sam would know the next card and maybe the card after that as well. He needed her to have an answer to ease the tension in the room.

"Can we do another test?" Shelly was the one to speak. She was caving in on herself. She reached her hand out to touch Sam's, and for now that seemed to be the only thing holding herself up-right.

Dr. Ash put the cards down and eased them back into his pocket. "Is that all right with you, Sam?"

She still held her head down. Her eyes would stray up, but only for a quick glance. Nothing more. She gave a small nod.

"Why don't you give me the months of the year," Dr. Ash said.

Sam's hand twitched in Shelly's grip. She took a few moments to compose herself, running through the months in her head. She didn't want to mess up. She had one chance to show everyone she was okay. She didn't want her grandfather to yell again.

Shelly held her breath the longest before Sam spoke.

"January, February, March, April, May, June, July." She spoke as she breathed, too scared the thought might leave if she paused. "August, September, October, November, December." Once the words were out of her mouth, she went through the months again in her head to be sure she was correct.

There was a release of breath from Shelly.

"Now tell me the months backwards, starting with December," Dr. Ash said.

Sam lifted her head to see if he was serious. She wanted him to be laughing when she looked at him, but his face was as placid as ever.

She sorted through the months in her head. When that didn't work, she whispered the months to herself again, trying to make note of the order, linking the names to each other so she could rattle off the months in the opposite order.

"December, November," she paused, said the correct order quickly in her head. "September, no, October then September." Again, running through the order. "August, July, June, May, March." She stopped herself. "Wait, not March. April then March." Shelly watched her as she whispered the orders to herself. "February, January."

Dr. Ash flipped a paper around on his clipboard and handed it over to Sam. The page was blank and he held out a pen.

"Now, why don't you write me a sentence about today's weather?" he asked.

"Aren't you going to correct her?" Paul said.

Sam had gripped onto the clipboard excited to write, but once she heard her grandfather's voice, her arms went slack and the clipboard well to the floor. She looked at her grandfather in the way a small child might look at their parents after they've been yelled at. If she were a dog, her tail would be tucked away.

"I only want positive enforcement, so we can encourage her as she takes these tests," Dr. Ash said.

Paul didn't say anything further while he looked around the room. Shelly bent forward in the silence and picked up the clipboard to hand to Sam. Her eyes were timid as she took the clipboard in her hands.

"I think it's time for you to go," Paul said. His voice was level as he spoke to Dr. Ash.

Dr. Ash thought about the serum that was running through Sam's veins. The moment Sam saw another doctor they would detect something was wrong. They'd trace it back to him, to Willow. He couldn't let them leave this hospital, but it seemed there was no more they could do. Would another doctor be able to find a cure for Sam? For Alzheimer's?

Paul didn't wait for Dr. Ash to step out of the room before he began making his phone calls. Paul escorted him out the room, his phone to his ear the entire time, and the moment Dr. Ash was out of the room he closed the door. He stood at the door, listening to Paul's mumbled voice through the walls before he walked away.

Randy walked by Willow as he went through the halls. She looked up from the nurses' station and smiled, trying to maintain some sense of normalcy. He looked back at her, but he turned away before she could have a chance to read into it.

"Randy?" she said. He continued to walk even though he felt her following him. "Is everything okay?"

He didn't want to walk away from her, but he couldn't look at her. Each time he looked at her, he could see that crazed piece of her staring back at him. There was a part, a strong and vital part of her he loved, but there was also a part of her that even she couldn't control.

"Willow," he said, his voice was rough, pained. His fingers twinned and trailed through hers before he walked away. He had other patients he needed see. It was a busy day—some appointments were overbooked—yet, here he was, retreating to his office. To do what? Sulk?

He stepped into his office, and Willow slid in as well. He shut the door behind her and sat on the couch as he buried his face in his hands.

"They would like to see another doctor," he said.

Willow looked at the ground as she thought. Randy glanced at her through his fingers and could see her working through the situation in her mind. All she had to do was exactly what she had done to Randy. Be the one to administer the tests and MRI scans. Let no one else get a moment to see what was going on in her brain. It would be hard, but she had done it for Randy, her own husband, how hard would it be for another doctor? She just had to find out who the new doctor would be. Her eyes darted from side to side as she thought.

"No, Willow," Randy said. She looked up. Her face was written in ideas. It didn't display the same type of fear that was painted across Randy's face. She was ready to continue with the experiment. "You can't keep doing this."

"But I can--,"

"Because they're transferring her to a different hospital. They don't trust me, or anyone else here. They want her care to come anyplace else but here. Sam will be transferred away, and everything you've been hiding will come to the surface."

Willow could only blink.

"They could sue," he said. "They *should* sue."

"Randy," she said. And there it was, that panicked look Randy felt like he had been hiding for so long. Now, Willow wore it. Her lower lip trembled the slightest bit as her eyes began to dart.

"If that was my daughter or granddaughter in that hospital bed, I would stop at nothing to find out what was wrong with her."

"Randy, please," she said. Tears were at the corners of her eyes. Before all this happened, he would have wrapped her in his arms until she stopped crying, but now he couldn't find it in himself to so much as offer a hand to her. He knew her tears. She was not crying for sympathy, she was crying because she got caught. But most of all, she was crying for herself. Her body jumped, begging to do something, to fight for the cure she was so close to grasping but about to lose. Her arms shook at her sides. She wanted to hold onto something, something that could hold her together.

"You realize I have to report this, don't you?" His voice was soft. She sat on the other end of the couch, away from Randy, and wrapped her arms around her knees.

She couldn't speak. She wanted to scream, but she didn't want to do that to Randy. He was the only thing she had left to hang onto.

He looked at her, her wide eyes and shaking body. Whatever world she knew had just shattered in front of her. The sobs came quickly afterwards. He wanted to be mad at her, to scream at her to at least try to knock some sense into her. He was confused as to what she had done, but most of all he was confused as to what he was supposed to do.

He left her in his office, locking the door so no one else could come in. She would be there, he knew, when his day was over and he reported the incident. Only a handful of times had he seen her give up, and that woman on the couch, that was it. She was defeated in the most infinite sense of the word.

# Chapter 24

He couldn't do it. He knew the measures and steps he needed to go through to report Willow. He knew that if he explained things clearly, he would be left out of harm's way once an investigation was conducted and he was deemed innocent. He also knew Willow's life and reputation would be ruined. What she had done was not something to be recovered from.

Willow was asleep again when Randy found her. This time, she was at the dining room table, paper littered around her. Her hair was pulled back in a braid, but small strands of hair escaped and curled. Her cheek was pressed into the crook of her elbow, the laptop open in front of her, though the screen had long fallen asleep.

He was careful to walk by quietly, taking small steps as he put his bags down for the day. The papers around her had long scripts of text and charts that he tried to ignore. He could already feel the word Alzheimer's floating off the pages. The words wanted to suck him in, but they were guarded by Willow body. With her eyes closed and face relaxed, she looked like she always had. He pulled a chair out from the table and sat across from her. If she woke up, would she return to her crazed fight for a cure?

He reached out and placed his hand over hers. Willow's fingers curled around his instinctively. She didn't need to be awake to know it was him. He thought he saw the corner of her lip rise.

He wanted to pretend there was only this. That was always his dream wasn't it? To fall in love and live the type of bliss you only saw at the end of movies. But then Tom got sick. Willow was strong, she could handle herself and her father, but when he eventually passed away, a piece of herself was cracked. Randy always imagined he could fix that crack by the research he was doing for Alzheimer's, but it hadn't been enough. The search for a cure only deepened the fissure.

He rubbed his thumb over the top of her hand and she mumbled as she woke up. These were his favorite moments. When the sleep was still heavy in her eyes and the weight of the world had yet to bear her down.

"What time is it?" she said as she pulled her head up.

He looked at the watch on his wrist. "9pm," he said.

The words worked to sober her, and slowly, Randy could see her stature change. As she woke up, worries pooled into her eyes. Wrinkles formed in the corners of her eyes. They were taking Sam away.

"Is she gone?" Willow asked.

Randy frowned when he heard the words.

"Not yet. Last I checked, her grandparents were fighting about where to send her. They started the paperwork for the transfer, but they can only do so much until they pick out a new hospital and doctor. It may be hard for them to find someone willing to take on her case."

"We still have time." She tapped the space bar on her laptop until it came back to life. She ruffled through a few papers while her browser was loading.

"Willow," he said. He let go of her hand and pulled away.

"See this?" she pushed an article towards him. It was on an experiment conduced in the last year that had recently come to a close. The abstract said the goal of the trial was to stop Alzheimer's in its tracks. The article was hefty, the papers about an inch thick printed, but as he read the first page he had to admit his intrigue.

*The solution was injected into mice to bring on the likeness of Alzheimer's. Because of the artificial form of Alzheimer's, scientists are now led to believe that the disease is caused by something present in the body that remains dormant until old age. Within days, symptoms of Alzheimer's began to surface in test group A of the mice. Scientists extracted cells from the mice in hopes of using their DNA for further research. With a dozen mice in test group A artificially infected with the disease, scientists were able to extract cells and use them to create a vaccine that was later injected to test group B of mice. After receiving the vaccine, test group B was administered the artificial disease, which had no effect. The second round of mice are thought to have immunities towards Alzheimer's disease, though further testing may prove otherwise.*

"Is this the serum that you gave to Sam?" he said.

"They haven't moved forward with human studies yet, but if they did, they might have a cure. They just need to take that next step."

Her body was rigid. Willow's focus was on the serum, and every move she made reflected around it. The longer Randy read the article, the more he was astonished by the research and also terrified of what Willow may be thinking.

"What happened to the first set of mice?" He flipped through the pages of the article. It went on, stating the benefits of the trial and the hope for future trials, but it wasn't until the very end that he saw the words: *Specimens from test group A were given the vaccine but could not be resuscitated.*

"Now that Sam is far enough into the disease, I can extract cells and do the same they had done and create a vaccine. I'll have to take as many samples as I can before she's transferred," she said.

"Willow," he said. She wasn't listening. How fast had she forgotten the legal ramifications of what she had done? It already seemed to be beyond her that another doctor from another hospital might discover what she had done before she had any hope of finding a cure.

"I'll just have to stay late, to use the lab."

"Willow," he said her name again. His voice was hard as he spoke. She looked up from her laptop. "The first set of mice died."

She didn't want to say anything, so instead she bit her lip. There was nothing that she could say.

"That was mice," she said.

"Yes, mice that are used and breed for experimentation. Sam is a human with a family that loves her."

"I won't say it's ethical," she said. "But I am saying it might be successful." Her face was stone. She had acted upon her will and it was too late to do anything about it.

"This is a child's life we're talking about," he said, his face twisting down.

She felt a twang in her stomach after he spoke. He was right, but she wanted to push forward and test the limits. The child had no parents and no memories. To her, it was the perfect situation.

"In the experiment they never tried the vaccine on the first round of mice. They were so preoccupied with test group B that it slipped by them until it was too late," she said. She held her head down as she spoke. It could work, she just needed Randy to believe it as well. "We could do good by Sam. We could find the cure and get her back to health."

"Consent." That was the only reply he had for Willow, and still, she never looked up.

Willow paused before she spoke. "She didn't give consent the first time. I've ready administered the serum once, so what harm could it be to do it a second time, especially if the second time could be to her benefit? All we know right now is what happens if nothing is administered. We don't know what will happen if the vaccine is given to her."

She lifted her head to look at him. Randy was looking up, above, and past her. He was staring off into some faraway place that she wasn't welcome anymore.

"It's not right," he said and stood up from the table. She let her eyes follow him as he walked out of the room

He went upstairs quietly, grabbing his bag from work as he walked by. He tiptoed across the house, and there wasn't a creek of a floorboard as he ascended the stairs. She supposed at some point he must have shut the door to their bedroom, but she never heard so much as a click of the knob. She would have preferred a loud slam to the silence. Anger was easier to deal with than his disappointment.

She would be invited into bed that night. Randy would crack open the door and leave it there for her to slink through. If she crawled into bed, he would reach out for her and the two of them could, at least for a moment, forget what she had done. But she couldn't bring herself to walk up those stairs. The confused and shocked look in Randy's eyes was etched into her mind, no matter how much she tried to shake the memory.

Willow slept on the coach, curled into a ball, knowing full well she'd wake up with a sore back and stiff neck. She imagined Randy would come down the stairs looking for her and kneel on the floor in front of her, whispering to come to bed. It was something they had always done after long work-days: bed patrol. If someone fell asleep on the couch or at the table, it was the other person's responsibility to wake them up and make sure they made it to bed.

Willow could almost feel his lips pressed to her forehead as she imagined Randy calling her upstairs. Her imagination took flight when she heard footsteps above her, and she tightened her lids to pretend to be asleep when Randy came down, but the footsteps never came closer. There was a squeak of a door, and she knew he was in the bathroom. A minute later, there was a squeak again and the footsteps faded far away back into the bedroom. He never shut the door.

Would the bed feel cold and empty without her?

She closed her eyes, pretending she was with him, Randy curled beside her, until her mind took her away in a light sleep.

— — — — —

She hadn't set an alarm, so Randy was the one who woke her up. He still had sleep in his eyes and stubble hadn't yet been shaved. She wanted to pretend it was a Saturday morning, just the two of them.

"You have to get ready," he said, and any thought of the weekend was dismissed.

He kissed her lightly, bristly, before turning way to make coffee in the kitchen. When she walked in, he already had her cup prepared.

"Sam won't be transferring." He said the words so smoothly, so coolly, she almost didn't catch them. She was about to bring the coffee to her lips but put the mug back on the counter.

"What?"

"My admin called last night. Left a message. She said Sam's grandparents have changed their minds. They've decided time is of the essence, and they can't waste any by starting over with a new doctor."

She wanted to be happy, but Randy was lost in some place far away. He ate his breakfast in small bites, his toast covered in butter but only one bite taken.

"I need you to fix this," he said, looking out the window. His shoulder sunk, and he was ready to give up. "Get Sam back to normal."

"With the vaccine?" She felt the lift in her voice when she spoke. There it was again, that hope that was always much too dangerous. She was on the edge of her seat, her senses ignited and ready to react the moment she was given the chance to take action.

He signed and put the toast in the trash and reached into the cabinet to get a mug, pouring himself a cup of coffee. He winced as he took a sip. He leaned against the counter for support. He didn't want any part of this.

"Do whatever it takes." He closed his eyes, swore under his breath so he could barely hear it. "Just don't let anyone else find out. Work quickly and efficiently, but most of all, make her better."

He said it, and that was all she needed. Her chin lifted, and she let her mind wander to what she could do the perfect the vaccine. She didn't have time to make mistakes. So much was on the line and it was time to risk it all.

# Chapter 25

"We just need to take some blood samples," Dr. Ash said. It wasn't the first time he had asked for blood samples, but this time it felt wrong. In the past, the samples were for finding out what ailed her, now it was for an experiment that might kill her.

Sam never looked away when the needle came to touch her skin. She winced as it went into her arm, but both she and Dr. Ash watched the bright red liquid fill the vials. Normally, he let his nurses do this step, but he couldn't let them know what the blood was being used for.

"You can relax," he said, letting her know to release the fist she had formed. The blood continued to flow fast and steady. He put the last vile into place and once it filled, pulled the needle away and replaced it with gauze.

"Hold this," he said.

Sam held the cotton in place in the crook of her elbow, staring at it like she was trying to memorize the patterns and folds of the gauze. He put the vials into a small baggy that had her name on it in fine, printed script. He tapped the gauze in place and slipped the bagged vials in his pocket.

"All right, that's all set." Sam watched him with full eyes. He had a habit of telling his patients every step he took, but this time he couldn't tell her. Was she waiting for him to say something? Tell her what was going to happen next?

"Do you need to take pup's blood?" she said. Her eyes were hesitant when she spoke. She had her stuffed dog on the bed next to her, but her arm hid him against the side of her body.

"Is he sick?" Dr. Ash asked.

Sam looked over to the stuffed dog to examine him. She lifted him onto her lap and pulled his paws out for a closer look. Dr. Ash leaned down next to her and looked over her shoulder at the stuffed patient.

"He seems limber," he said, testing the range of motion on his front leg. "And his eyes are clear. I'd say he's good to go, no need to take any blood samples."

Sam smiled and put the dog back by her side where he could nap the day away. She smiled to herself before Dr. Ash went out the door.

"Good morning, Dr. Ash."

He jumped at the sound of the voice and moved to hide the bag of vials in his pocket. Jenna smiled as she walked down the hall with a quick wave. Dr. Ash let his hand linger in his pocket, making sure the vials were still there.

— — — — —

The room was sterile, possibly the cleanest area in the hospital. There were signs everywhere, labels, biohazard waste baskets. For now, the lab was empty all except for Willow, but she knew that could change in an instant. There was a chart on the door with the lab's schedule so lab technicians could have their own space as they worked, but everyone also knew it was fair game any day the schedule was empty. Today was one of those days.

She had her scrubs on, a hair net, gloves. Only the skin around her face was exposed. She pulled everything she might need out in front of her and slipped the three vials Randy had given her out of her pocket. Also in the pocket was the article that detailed how the anti-venom was produced. It wasn't the full article, just the page on the formulation for the solution. She had done further research to double check the science behind the vaccine and was pleased when she saw, in theory, that it should work.

There were test tubes all around her as she worked. Her work was too fast and meticulous. She labeled everything falsely, under another patient's name. The test called for the vaccine to sit overnight, be tampered with further, and then allow to freeze. She had thought about doing the chemical work from home, but knew all the equipment she would need would be right there in the lab. Easier to hide the vaccine than to steal equipment that's used on a daily basis.

Her hands moved fast, and she didn't let a drop of Sam's blood go to waste. Only a small sample of blood was needed to create the vaccine — three vials went a long way. She could cure Sam and prove to the world she had found a vaccine for Alzheimer's.

A long list of side effects came to mind. The article had gone on and on about the adverse side effects that were seen in some of the mice. Some began vomiting, experienced weight loss, seizures, mania. The mice that overcame the side effects seemed cured. They could fight off Alzheimer's. Those that couldn't beat the side effects succumbed to them. Most died quickly after the vaccine was administered and the side effects appeared. A quarter of the mice died from the vaccine, but without the vaccine they would have died anyway.

With a drop of iodine, she was done for the night. The vials had been mixed with the correct chemicals, and now all she could do was wait until twenty-four hours passed. The schedule on the wall said the lab would still be free tomorrow, and she hoped it stayed that way. Willow used steady hands to label the vials under the name of Riley Rose. Anyone who came across the vials in passing would assume it was one of thousands of patients, and no one would blink an eye.

She left the lab, throwing her scrubs into the laundry basket and her gloves and hair net into the trash. She would be back tomorrow.

— — — — —

There was a man in the lab by the time Willow walked in. It was one of the new lab techs — she hadn't quit learned the man's name yet. He looked too young to be working with the lab equipment, but there he was, affixed above a petri dish. He looked up when she walked in.

"Hey," he said. His smile was quick and then he was back to his work. In a way, she was lucky. He was too new to know is she was a lab tech. To him, she was just another co-worker he hadn't met yet.

She had two options: tend to the vaccine as planned, or start over tomorrow when she had the lab to herself again. The solution called for a full 24-hour incubation period before the second round could be made, and she couldn't afford to take longer than necessary to make the serum.

"I'm Matthew, by the way." He put down a dropper he was holding and exchanged it for an empty test tube.

"Wendy," she said. Wendy was a woman who used to

work in the labs. She transferred to another hospital a few years ago.

"Nice to meet you," he said, turning back to the test tube and petri dish in front of him.

Willow worked her way across the room to where she had stored the test tube. She'd only have to add a few more chemicals, than freeze it, and she'd be done for another twenty-four hours.

She turned to the shelf with the test tube, but she continued to look over her shoulder at Matthew. His back was to her, but even if he was facing her directly, she suspected he was too engrossed in his work to notice what she was doing.

Her hands were rushed as she worked to get the proper supplies gathered around her. The vaccine had turned solid during the hours it set. Willow set up a Bunsen burner in front of her, making a sharp blue flame. She turned on the air vent on her head. On the bright side, Matthew wouldn't be able to hear what she was doing, on the down side, she would never know when he got up to get more supplies.

She kept looking over her shoulder as she used tongs to hold the test tube over the fire. A few seconds passed and the solid melted. She waited for the liquid to bubble and poured it into another test tube, letting it pass through a strainer on the way. The liquid that settled into the second test tube was pink. She used a dropper to add two dots of a bright blue liquid into the mixture. She stirred and it turned a dull purple. She grabbed another test tube and filled it with a clear liquid and gave it four drops of the purple solution.

Her forearm heated up, too close to the Bunsen burner, and she dropped the test tube.

"Shit," she said. The tube shattered across the table. She rushed to turn off the Bunsen burner before she tried to clean up the mess.

"You okay?" Matthew was standing next to her, wiping the liquid off the counter. She watched in horror as he dumped the shards of glass and strained paper towels into a bio-hazard waste basket. He looked over Willow's arms and hands for cuts, but there were none. There was a small browned area on her scrubs from where the Bunsen burner had almost caught her on fire.

"Make sure you turn that off once you're done with it. Even if you move it out of the way, it can be a hazard, but I guess I don't need to tell you that." His words are light, a joking effort, but Willow wished only to push him away. If it were up to her, she would have preserved every drop of the vaccine, but instead it was in the trash.

"Sorry," she said. "I must be too tired." Matthew was collecting all of the tools Willow had used and began putting them into a pile for sanitization. Everything she had done and accomplished was about to be bleached away.

"We all have those days. I hope that wasn't anything important."

"No," she said. "No, I'll just have to re-start. I hadn't gotten very far. It will be easy." But she was cursing herself. Nothing about this was easy. She wasn't a lab tech. Everything she knew was off assumption or research she had done online. Being a nurse didn't teach you how to make vaccines.

"Anything I can help with?" he said.

"No, I'm just going to take a break."

She put the Bunsen burner back on the high shelf with the others before walking out of the room. Matthew had cleaned her station. Any trace of Riley Rose was in the bio-hazard waste.

She thought she heard Matthew mutter something as she walked away, but she never stopped to listen. Once the door to the lab was closed ,she ripped her hairnet and face mask away and threw all her scrubs into the trash.

The way her heart began to race with her anxiety was starting to become a familiar feeling, but that did not make it comforting. Her body was anxious, not just her mind. She needed to do something, anything to make progress toward the goal of finding a cure, but for now she had no options. She was stripped and worn. Her efforts were useless.

Restart. She'd have to do this all over again tomorrow.

# Chapter 26

The skin was purple, almost black. It was the type of bruising that Avery sometimes saw in movies. In movies, it didn't seem realistic, like the dark splotches were too dramatic, but they weren't. The circle took over Sam's hand, fading out at the edges. Sam's hand was resting on her stomach, but Avery was left to wonder how much it hurt. Was it just when she bumped it, or did it hurt to move her hand as well? She told herself the bruise from the IV would fade soon enough.

"Hi Sam," she said.

Sam didn't smile when she walked into the room. She had a lot of off days, but even then, she was able to smile. Today, she laid in her bed, more tired than usual. The stuffed dog that Avery brought her was tucked in the crook of the arm that was resting on her stomach.

"I don't feel good," Sam said.

Avery pulled her chair up and sat by her. It was 4:35pm. She promised herself she'd stay for at least an hour today. Long enough to ease the guilt of not visiting enough.

"What's wrong?" she said. She pulled her backpack off. Inside, she had packed away an adult coloring book that Sam loved, but part of her wondered that it may be too advanced for her now. Should she have brought a children's coloring book just in case?

Sam looked at her hand on her stomach and lifted it. The stuffed dog that had been pinned in place fell to the floor. Avery picked it up and replaced it.

"Does your stomach hurt?" she said.

Sam's face dropped and her eyes were for the dog. The corner of her lip rose and she lifted for hand to take him.

"He's so cute."

"Sam," Avery said. "Does your stomach hurt?"

Sam lifted her eyes but tucked the dog back into her chest. She frowned.

"No?" she said, but the words came out as a question.

"Then what hurts?" Avery asked, but Sam had already let her attention be taken away. She was staring at the bruise on her hand, and although that was the direction of her eyes, Avery could tell her mind was somewhere far off. Not once did Sam blink. Her eyes were open, moving just slightly, but never enough for her to need to turn her head. Her lower lip hung just a bit.

"Sam?" Avery said.

"I don't feel good," she said. Her head stayed level. She was in a trance, and Avery was terrified to break it. As odd as it was, it was during spells like this Avery recognized Sam the most. With all emotion gone from her face, she could imagine the Sam she used to know.

Avery waited for Sam to speak.

"Something's wrong," she said. "But I don't know what."

Avery waited again, for more words to come or for her sister to surface, but she never did. Sam blinked and Avery could tell whatever trance it was, it was about to be broken.

"Do you remember the campfires we used to have?" Avery asked.

Sam turned to look at her and smiled. The gesture was real and there was Sam. Bright as day. There was no mistake that she was in the room.

"We'd roast marshmallows, and they'd fall into the fire," she said. "We'd never get to eat any because they always fell off."

"Yours fell off, mine caught on fire," Avery said. She laughed, but Sam frowned. She was still there, no matter how dull the spark, Sam was still present and aware. She didn't close her eyes; she stared straight at the ceiling. Avery followed and saw the plain, pale white tiles.

"Is that what you look at all day?"

"I get lost," Sam said. "It's been happening a lot these days."

"I bet," Avery said, though the words came out harsher then she intended.

"I forget it's there sometimes."

"What do you mean?"

Sam stared but made no move to answer. She was unblinking, and it was this staring that scared Avery. When she looked out into space like that, her body seemed inhabited. She supposed it was like that sometimes with Sam. She was there physically, but her spirit had long floated away. It came back sometimes, but only for fleeting moments that were always too short.

She never answered, but Avery saw her eyes gloss over. What was she thinking about?

"Sam?" she said.

Sam turned and smiled, but it was just her body going through the motions. The switch had been flipped, and she was gone again. It was odd, sometimes, how just by looking, Avery could see if Sam was all there. There was just a stranger laying in the bed smiling back at her, a stuffed dog she called Pup in her hands.

# Chapter 27

Willow was scrubbing her hands down before she entered the lab for the third time. By now, she could get into the lab without issue. She rushed away with Randy's badge and returned without anyone ever noticing. She had come back to fix her mistakes after she had dropped the beaker, and now she was ready to continue the next set of steps that would bring her closer to what could cure Sam and possibly anyone else with Alzheimer's. Her scrubs were fresh, and her hair was tied back and secured with a hairnet. She wore the full scrubs, covering all but her eyes. The schedule said the lab was going to be empty, but since her run-in with Matthew she wanted to keep risk at a minimum. The door to the lab was still locked when she turned the knob.

The room was cold, and when she flipped the light switch on it glowed. Instruments were lined up perfectly on the counter, and tools were placed on their shelves according to the labels that were scattered on everything imaginable. In the far end of the room was the fridge.

Willow pulled the door open. She was afraid of so many things. Someone could have taken her test tube, or broken it, or misplaced it. The lab had a system, but she was invading it. Even though she was following all the rules, she knew at any moment someone could catch on and take her vaccine away with it.

It was still sitting on the shelf when she opened the cabinet door. The test tube was latched onto a holder and a printed label said Riley Rose. Everything was exactly as she had left it.

She had gone in the day before and begun the vaccine from scratch with leftovers of Sam's blood that she hadn't used to make up for the test tube she had dropped.

She picked up the test tube and began to set up her station. It would be simple again today. Beaker, Bunsen burner, more chemicals — all these things that she had little to no contact with in her position as a nurse.

She lit the match and turned the knob of the Bunsen burner to release the gas. As soon as she held the match over the tip of the Bunsen burner it caught fire. It burned an uncontrolled orange until she adjusted it to a thin blue. Holding the test tube over the fire, it bubbled and turned the dull purple bright and vibrant. It took only a few seconds for the colors to shift, and soon enough, it was time to take it away from the fire and rest it in the holster. She turned off the Bunsen burner and pushed it away from her work space.

It was with careful breath that she used an eye-dropper to take samples of purple solution and drop them into the test tube full of clear liquid. One, two, three, four drops and she was done.

There was nothing spectacular about it. The vaccine neither bubbled nor simmered. She watched as the purple drops spread out through the clear liquid, muting the purple tone until it stood flat and clear with only a small hue of purple. She slid a small jar across the counter. The label read *steroid induced glutamine*. It was the only part of the solution that wasn't in the instructions. It was an ingredient the original creator of the mixture had thought of, but never implemented. It's unstable when used incorrectly, but it helps promote the production of nerve cells. She put two drops into the test tube.

The recipe didn't call for mixing; only dropping. The chemicals would react with one another, and that would be that.

She let the test tube stand for the allotted ten minutes, cooling itself. When the time was up, she used the tongs to grasp the test tube and open the fridge. It felt too simple as she placed the tube into one of the holsters.

She would come to think of the vaccine all night, wondering what it was doing in the fridge, how the two chemicals were reacting to each other that caused them to manifest a vaccine for a disease that stumped scientists for so long. Another twenty-four hours was all it would take to bring a cure to the surface.

Willow wasn't there the next morning when the lab techs were going through the fridge. Every Friday morning, they made it a habit to clean the lab from top to bottom. The goal was to get rid of any residue that may have accumulated on equipment and shelves, but it was also to take inventory and throw out any abandoned specimens.

It was a team of two that were going through the lab. They were students for the medical school across the street. Julie and Lucas worked together to log everything and scrub each surface they touched. Julie started on the left side of the room and Lucas on the right.

"Hey, Julie, all the samples have to be logged right?" Lucas was at the fridge. He was checking each sample as he moved it to clean the shelf.

"Yeah," Julie said. She was elbow deep in samples that were sitting on the shelf, but her notes still read clear.

"This one has a patient ID, but the lab tech's name isn't written on it."

Julie put her clipboard down and crossed over to Lucas. He held out the small test tube. The contents were clear with a tint of purple. Nothing floating, no bubbles. Julie took the tube from his hand.

"Riley Rose," she said. She looked closer to find a lab tech name on the tube, but there was none. She walked back to her clipboard and lifted the pages.

"What are you looking for?" Lucas asked.

"Sometimes when the lab techs reserve the lab, they'll write down what they're working on, but I don't see the patient's name in here anywhere. I'll write down the information on the bottle so we can look it up in the system when we get back."

Julie found a blank piece of paper at the back of her clipboard and copied the patient's name off the tube before handing it back to Lucas. He placed it back on the original shelf after he had finished cleaning it, and by the time the two students left, it was like they had never been in the lab in the first place. The only tell was the sharp smell of bleach that hung in the air.

Willow slipped through the door at the twenty-four-hour mark. As soon as she opened the fridge door, she knew something was off. She tried to remember how the test tube was placed when she had been in the lab previously. Hadn't she left the label facing out? She looked around the lab and everything seemed a bit off. It was all too neat. The lab was always neat, but now everything seemed perfect, untouched. But the vile, Riley Rose, had been touched.

Her breath hitched. Could someone know, just by picking it up, that the vile wasn't supposed to be there? She had placed the false label on it to make it blend in, but she had never checked to see if there was a patient named Riley Rose.

The vaccine was done. Everything was exactly as it should be. The glass was crystal clear through the tinted sign. It settled into the vial perfectly smooth. All it would take now was a simple application with a syringe.

The door opened and a lab tech walked in. Willow jumped when he stepped through the door and the tube almost felt out of her hands. She slipped it into her pocket before the man had a chance to see her.

"Good morning," he said. He was suited up, but the ID on his scrubs had the medical school's logo. His name was Lucas.

Willow stepped away from the fridge and made herself busy by looking through one of the drawers with all the freshly sanitized tools. She listened to Lucas as he made his way across the room and opened the fridge door. His hand settled on the shelf the Riley Rose vile had been resting. Willow tried to ignore the way her blood pressure seemed to sky-rocket.

"Hey, you didn't happen to see a vial with the patient's name, Riley Rose, on it did you?" he asked.

He still had the fridge door opened when he turned to Willow. Her body went rigid when she heard his words. She wanted to run out of the room, but he didn't know she had it, not yet at least.

"No, I'm just checking things for Dr. Florence." She was thankful for the name once she thought of it. He was the department chair. Odds were Lucas knew who he was, but had never met him officially. There was no way he could fact check her.

Lucas pursed his lips and turned back to the fridge, moving some test tubes around to see if maybe he had missed the vile.

"Why?" she asked.

It was probably the last thing she should be saying. Keep your nose out of it, that was the best way to proceed without anyone finding out what she was doing, but she had to know what he knew about Riley Rose.

"Well, we did inventory today and came across a vile labeled Riley Rose, but there's no patient with that name in this hospital."

"Maybe another lab tech came and took it already," she suggested.

"Yeah, maybe. Or I could have just misread it." He laughed to himself quietly. "Certainly wouldn't be the first time."

Willow tried to let out a gentle laugh herself, but it came out forced.

"Huh," he said. He was still looking through the fridge. The vial was still in Willow's pocket, weighing more by the second. She imagined it was a huge bulk in her scrubs, that at any moment he could look over and see it there and he'd know she was hiding something.

Lucas was empty handed and confused by the time he left the lab. Willow pulled the vial out of her pocket and saw the name Riley Rose stare back at her. She buried it back in her scrubs and left the room, terrified and excited, all at once.

Here it was, what could be the cure to Alzheimer's, and it was in her pocket. Something so powerful and potent, and it could fit in the palm of her hand.

She could hear Randy as she walked down the hall. He was already in Sam's room, and he was the first thing she saw as she walked into the room.

"Look," Willow said. It was just the two of them and Sam. Sam had the stuffed dog in her hand, cradling it like a baby.

Willow pulled the vial out of her pocket and took her husband's fingers and curled them around it.

His face was confused at first. He turned it over until he could read the label.

"Riley Rose?" he said.

"It's fake," she whispered. "That's the vaccine, that's what I've been working on."

His face changed. Confusion turned to terror before he grabbed Willow by the arm and pulled her out of the room.

"I'll be back, Sam," he said, but she never looked up from the stuffed dog.

"Randy," Willow said, but he walked in a silent march as they both made their way to his office. He tried to appear normal to anyone passing by. He loosened his grip on Willow's arms and let his hand wander into hers until their fingers were intertwined. They walked down the hall like that. Anyone watching them would think they were both just taking their lunch break together.

They reached his office and locked the door behind him.

"Sit, please," he said.

He checked the watch on his wrist and let a breath out.

"It's the cure," Willow said. She had the vile in her hand again. It seemed too small to be so significant, but after years in the medical field, Randy knew otherwise.

"Don't say that," he said.

"But it is."

"You don't know that. Do you even know if that's what they had done in the original experiment?"

Her face dropped and her arms came to rest in her lap. "I had to make a few adjustments."

"And just because it worked on mice doesn't mean it will work on humans. It will need to be modified most likely."

"I did modify it," she said.

"But you can't test it first. Willow, do you realize how much testing a single vaccine gets before the thought of using it on humans is entertained?"

He realized now, just how much trouble they were in. Of course there was no way she could test the vaccine properly, everything about what they were doing was illegal.

Willow sank into the couch, but the vial was still firm in her grasp. She turned it over in her hands, watching the liquid turn in shift.

"Willow," he said. The frustration was there, loud and clear. She looked up, her eyes clear and sharp.

"Stop," she said. "Stop treating me like I don't know. I know what goes into creating a vaccine. I've been researching this disease for years. I've lived and breathed this disease. I've seen my father suffer from it. I've seen him die because of it, and now I can feel it! I can feel myself forgetting and losing myself just like I watched my father lose himself." The words rushed out of her mouth before she had time to stop them. His face was still tight when he looked at her, but he began to soften. He wanted to yell, but he couldn't. He saw the fever in her eyes, bright and clear. She held each muscle in her body taut, ready to run.

"What?" he said. He reached out for her hand, but she pulled it away. His attention made her feel like a child. She couldn't stand having him look at her like this, like she was broken and needed to be fixed.

"It will work," she said.

"Willow, have you been having issues with your memory?" He tried to think back to their nights at home, whether she wandered or had a hard time with conversations. They were both so tied at the end of the day, he couldn't think of what they normally talked about over dinner. Dinners were always the finale of the day, the last task you had to complete before going to bed. If she had been showing symptoms of Alzheimer's, she never let it show.

"I'm fine," she said. "The vaccine will work for Sam." She couldn't look at Randy. His eyes were probing, like he was scanning her for signs of the disease. She could almost see him tracing backwards in his mind to their past conversations, looking for clues. Had her memory been bad in front of him? She forgot things, but Randy would never think of it as early-onset Alzheimer's. He would have accounted it to stress.

At some point, he gave up. "Even if the vaccine does work, it will only prevent the disease from getting worse; it won't give Sam her memory back."

"It's possible it might."

She was contemplative. Her eyes were in a tight line as she looked across the room. The vile was still in her hand. She wasn't holding it out to him anymore, but now he eyed it with curiosity.

"What do you mean?" Randy said. He wanted more information, but was afraid to believe any of it. With discoveries such as the one Willow was hoping for, it was easy to jump to false conclusions before the science caught up with reality.

"The adjustments I made," Willow said. "They were to add a steroid induced glutamine protein, which reacts with the rest of the ingredients in the vaccine to cause speeded growth in nerve cells. It's been recreated in some of the same studies the mice were in. I was looking closer into the author of the article, and he had another finding, and that was using the protein to create nerve cell growth. He was going to combine the two experiments — the vaccine and the protein — but the article isn't published yet."

Randy was torn, that much was clear. He was watching

Willow with anxious eyes, but his body seemed to bounce with excitement as she spoke. There was a cure on the horizon and he knew it. How soon the cure surfaced was dependent on how much Randy let ethics stop her from administering the new vaccine into Sam.

"But you can't regenerate lost tissue. The memories that Sam had are gone forever."

"They are," she admitted. "But that doesn't mean they can't be found. Alzheimer's patients don't remember things because they've lost the tissue to hold in the information, but if the tissue was regenerated, in theory, they should be able to re-learn things. Similar —"

"To some cases of amnesia." He finished the thought.

Willow smiled as she watched him process everything. He was silent in his thinking and she didn't dare speak. He was methodical as he thought, and Willow knew that it would work to her advantage for once.

He eyed the vial and looked back to Willow.

"It could work," he said. "But what if it needs to be continually administered for the rest of her life? Alzheimer's isn't just one cell dying, it's a constant cycle of cell death."

"Then that's what we'll do. A cure is a cure."

"Her family will know. Eventually, they'll find out."

She looked back at Randy before responding. "Yes," she said. Her tone was serious.

"They could still sue. They'd win."

"We'd have the cure." She was much too confident in the cure. There were always repercussions of her actions, but she pushed the thoughts aside, focused only on the goal that lie ahead. She was counting on the success of finding a cure overshadowing the life she had put in danger — her bets were waged high.

"Willow," he said, because there was nothing else to say. He wanted to go back in time, to the day she had injected Sam with the serum and take it all back. No matter what they did, he could see the both of them losing their license to practice soon — more than that. Even if they did find the cure for Alzheimer's, would the medical world ever let them show their faces again? Or would they go down in history as the people who let their desperation get in the way of their ethics?

"Randy, we have no other choice," she said. He heard her words and knew just how painfully true they were. She put her arm out for him, and he sat next to her on the couch. They held hands, her grip firm and sure, and his weak and confused. The possibilities were in front of him, and neither option was ideal. Only one held any sort of hope, and it was slim.

"I know," he said.

She took a breath and let her hand slip out of his. She stood from the couch, placing the vaccine back in the pocket of her scrubs. When she turned to him his eyes were glass. Randy was a man who'd seen his fair share in the medical field. After years of being a doctor, this was the first time she'd seen him cry.

"I'll be back," she said. She kissed him on the forehead before she turned away. The door clicked shut behind her. He knew she'd step into Sam's room soon. Sam would be alone for another hour or two before she got her first round of visitors, but before that Willow would take the small needle to her arm and let the vaccine work its way through Sam's body. Whether or not it would work, Randy was still painfully unsure.

# Chapter 28

"I don't want another shot," Sam said. Her eyebrows were in a firm line, and she had her sight set on the syringe in Willow's hand. She shut the door behind herself when she walked into Sam's room, but now she eyed it again to be sure no one would be able to hear.

"I know it hurts," she said. She put the syringe down on a rolling tray that also had the antiseptic she needed to administer the shot.

Sam began backing away in her bed. Willow reached out for her arm as lightly as she could without scarring Sam. Her eyes grew wide once Willow's hand touched hers.

"No!" she said. She tried to tug her arm away but Willow's grip didn't loosen. She began to use her other hand to pry Willow's fingers off one by one. Willow let go and put the syringe down.

"Sam," she said. Her voice was firm, her eyes steady. Willow had patience. She watched Sam and Sam looked back, her wide, not sure what to do. At first she began to lean away again, but when she saw Willow wasn't reaching out for her anymore she let herself relax—she watched Willow's hands.

"Why do I need another shot?" Sam's voice was careful when she spoke. She never remembered the faces of all the people that came in to see her, but there was always one woman, the one that stood in front of her now, that made her sit on edge.

"This is going to make you feel better," Willow said.

Sam was watching Willow's hands. They were in her lap, resting, no sign of coming out to grab her.

"What's wrong with me?" she said. Her eyes remained on Willow's hands waiting for them to attack her.

Willow watched as Sam turned shallow and pale. It was like she wanted to cry, but her body didn't have the strength to. Instead, she laid her head to the back of the bed, her body propped up, and breathed in deep raged breaths, crying without tears.

Sam closed her eyes as she cried, and Willow picked up the disinfectant from the tray next to her. She swiped a dampened towelette across the top of Sam's arm. By the time Sam opened her eyes and looked over to Willow, she already had the needle braced and in place.

Sam's eyes were wide as she watched the needle plunge into her skin. Willow tried to be as delicate and quick as possible, but Sam still let out a shriek as the vaccine was injected into her skin.

"No!" Sam screamed.

Once the vaccine was emptied from the syringe she pulled it away from Sam and tossed it into the biohazard container in the room. Willow held gauze to Sam's arm to stop any bleeding. Sam cowered away, moaning softly as she looked at the spot where Willow had given her the shot. Willow held the gauze in place for a few minutes to let the blood clot so she wouldn't need a band-aid. When Willow finally pulled her hand away, she noticed she was shaking.

Sam was still stifling a cry as Willow cleaned up any evidence of the vaccine. As she walked out of the room, she took the biohazard trash with her to be emptied.

She hadn't anticipated Sam resisting. She had planned for an easy injection like she had done before, but there was a spark in Sam that she hadn't expected. She'd never seen her fight so strong for something she didn't want. If she had known Sam was going to put up a fight, she would have waited a few hours, until after her grandparents came and left. Now their visit was in less than hour and Willow's only hope was that Sam would have forgotten the incident by then, or that if she did remember, her grandparents might dismiss it as one of the odd stories she liked to tell.

As she walked back to Randy's office, she tried to compose herself. She still had the trash in her hand and found the dumping station on the way. She supposed she should have felt better, having the evidence hidden away, but knowing that she had evidence to hide made her all the more wary.

When she got to the office, the door was locked. She knocked, but Randy didn't answer. She knocked again, putting her ear to the door afterwards. She thought the room was empty at first because she couldn't hear anything, but after holding her breath she could hear him within, quietly crying. His hitched breath seemed to reverberate through the wooden door.

She moved away from the door, assuming the only place to go was home, but as she turned away she could hear the door creak open. She turned and saw Randy's face, and for once they were mirror images. She looked at him, horror, shock, but mostly just shame.

Neither spoke to the other. In his mind, Randy was wondering if the vaccine was administered, but he was too afraid to ask while Willow was too scared to hear him speak. Was he mad at her for going through with it?

"Is it time to go home?" she said. Her voice wavered and that was all Randy needed to hear to know that, yes, she had administered the vaccine.

"Yeah," he said, and the two walked out the door of the hospital and went home. He told his team he was feeling sick and to have another doctor fill or change the rest of his appointments for the day. None one questioned him after they saw the dead, vacant look in his eyes.

— — — — —

Paul and Shelly were late. Dover Memorial Hospital was about forty-five minutes away, and by the time they hit the road they were already a half an hour behind. Neither of them talked much on the ride as Paul glowered at the road and Shelley stared out the window at the trees as they passed by. The murmurs of songs coming from the radio was the only buffer for the moment.

"What the hell," Paul said, his knuckles going white against the steering wheel. They had pulled onto the highway and already they were bumper to bumper.

Shelly leaned forward and switched on the station on the radio.

"A three-car crash on I-90 East has resulted in a backup going all the way into—" Paul leaned forward and shut off the radio.

"Why'd you do that?" Shelly asked.

"I'm in the traffic right now, I don't need to be told about it."

"Maybe there's a back road we can take?"

"A back road would take even longer," he said. "It's not like Sam will know if we're late anyways."

Shelly wanted to say something in Sam's defense, but she

knew it was true. It was after a long half hour that they got through all the traffic and pulled into the parking garage of the hospital.

"We're here to see Samantha Ellison," Shelly said. They were at the front desk of the inpatient hospital wing. The woman at the desk smiled and reached over for the clipboard guests were required to sign into each time they came to visit. Once they had their visitor passes, they went down the hall to Sam's room like they have so many times in the past month.

"Good morning, Sammy," Shelly said as she walked in. Paul followed close behind, but he didn't speak — the anger from the drive over was still spilling off him.

Sam was in her bed, propped up, but fast asleep. Her head was lulled off to the side, her mouth slightly open.

"Sam," Shelly said. She touched the top of her arm and Sam bolted awake.

"No!" she said.

Shelly pulled her arm away but leaned in next to Sam. "It's okay, sweetie, it was just a dream," she whispered.

Sam calmed at the sight of Shelly, but her body was still rigid. Shelly reached out to hold her hand. Sam pulled away at first, but eventually she let Shelly comfort her. She looked around the room, past Shelly to Paul. He was watching her, but soon enough he turned away to grab a seat to pull forward.

"It's okay, sweetie," Shelly said.

Sam's eyes were darting around the room and finally came to rest on the door that was left open. She was waiting for someone else to walk in. Paul followed her gaze and got up to close the door. It took only seconds after that for her body to relax.

Shelly was still holding her hand when she put her hand out and touched a sore spot on the top of her arm. She rubbed it like you would a fresh bruise to see if it really did hurt.

"Are you okay?" Shelly asked.

The corners of Sam's lips turned down and she covered her arm with her hand. "It hurts."

Shelly moved Sam's hand out of the way and looked closer. She thought she saw a speck of blood if she looked closely, but she wasn't sure if her eyes were playing tricks on her or not. She ran her finger over the small speck and looked over to Paul.

"Do you think I should call a nurse?"

"Is there any bruising?" he asked.

"I don't think so."

"Just wait until the nurse comes in later, they'll come to check on her soon enough. Maybe she was laying on it weird."

Shelly turned back to Sam and watched her squirm as she was laying down. Her face was flushed and Shelly put her hand to Sam's forehead. She was hot, overly hot.

"Paul?" she said. She heard him grunt as he got up from his chair and stood beside her. "Does she feel hot to you?"

He put the back of her hand to her forehead. Maybe she was a little hot.

Sam squirmed again, unable to get comfortable. She turned to her side, away from Shelly, and sat up.

"Sam, you okay?"

Before Shelly could say anything, Sam leaned over the edge of her bed and began coughing.

"Sam!" Paul said. He rushed forward and gripped her shoulders as she slumped her body over the edge. Her coughing continued until the vomit followed shortly after. Shelly stepped back from the scene and hit the call button by Sam's bed.

# Chapter 29

A nurse was holding a small disposable pan in front of Sam. Her cheeks were red, and she was leaning forward, gripping the bucket as if it were the only thing holding her up. Shelly was standing behind her, braiding her hair to keep it out of the way.

When the nurse first came in, she called in housekeeping and another nurse to help clean up the mess, but now it was just her. She said her name was Jamie.

"How are you feeling?" she said. She was gripping the bucket into place. Behind Sam, Shelly finished tying off the braid and stepped to the side.

Sam shook her hand and leaned forward a bit more.

"How bad is her fever?" Shelley asked.

"Not terrible. It's at 100.3 right now, but we'd prefer her not to have a fever at all. We've given her some medication to help lower it. She should be feeling better in a bit."

"What do you think is causing her to be sick?"

"It could be anything really. We've been monitoring her food intake and nothing has changed, so it's most likely not that. It could be a hospital acquired infection, but her symptoms aren't bad enough, and she also isn't hooked up to any equipment that would cause that."

"And what if it is?" Paul spoke up now. Their fight as to whether they wanted Sam to stay at this hospital was said and done, but Shelly could hear the conversation surfacing all over again.

"Our priority is to find the cause of what's making her sick, no matter what it might be, and cure it. Sam is already a tricky patient, and her being sick will only make her recovery harder." Jamie wanted to say more, that the fever and vomiting might be caused by whatever has been affecting Sam's memory, but she didn't want to add to their stress until Dr. Ash had his opinion on the matter, and he wasn't going to be in for another hour or so.

Sam began coughing again, and Jamie tightened her grip on the bucket. Her cough was loud, but she'd worked with patients long enough to know that vomit was not going to be associated with this cough.

"It's okay," she said. Sam's cough lightened, and she leaned back into her bed.

Jamie put the bucket beside Sam's hip and checked her IV. Medication had been slipped into the IV to help with the nausea while also keeping Sam hydrated.

"Dr. Ash will be here in the next hour to speak with both of you. We've been logging her vitals, and we're hoping by the time he gets here, Sam will be feeling better. We also want to figure out what's making her sick."

"Hour?" Paul asked. They were used to their visits by now, and it wasn't that he didn't want to spend time with his granddaughter, but it seemed ridiculous to spend so much time waiting for a doctor who may not have a solution.

"As soon as he steps through the door, I'll send him to you," Jamie said.

Paul didn't say anything, which Jamie took as an okay and walked out of the room.

In the hour it took for Dr. Ash arrive, Sam fell asleep again, hugging her stomach. Every now and then, Shelly would step forward and hold her hand to her cheek or forehead to check her temperature. Eventually, Sam's temperature dropped to normal and Shelly could relax a little more.

There was a quiet knock at the door even though it had been left open. Shelly and Paul both sat up in their seats as Dr. Ash stepped into the room. His eyes were shaded with dark circles.

"Good evening," he said. He smiled with his shoulders held back in an attempt to hide his unease as he crossed to where Shelly and Paul sat. He smiled in his usual way, but people who knew him closely could see the look of dread in his face as he walked into Sam's room.

Shelly was waiting for Paul to say something, but he kept himself seated in his chair. He had given up on Dr. Ash a long time ago. It was Shelly who spoke first.

"Do you know what's wrong with Sam?" she said.

Dr. Ash had looked over her vitals when he came in, but nothing was alarming about her results. Randy hadn't spoken to Willow after she injected Sam with the vaccine. He had looked at her and known she had carried through with it, but the vacant look in her eyes made him realize something must have gone wrong. He wanted to ask, but knowing he had to face Paul and Shelly, he wanted to play ignorance, even if it was for just a day.

"Her fever has lowered; she's back down to 98.9. We're going to keep monitoring her and run a few more tests, but I think she's going to be okay."

From afar, he thought he saw a bruise forming on the top of Sam's arm. Was that where Willow administered the shot? He blinked, and when he looked at her arm again it was the pale pink it had always been.

"Can I go home?" Sam said. Until now she had been quietly laying back in her bed. Her hair was pulled back into a braid and while just a few hours ago she had been vomiting, her eyes were bright.

"Sweetie," Shelly said. She stood up and came to Sam's side, holding her hand. Sam frowned when she touched her. "You have to stay here until you're better."

"What's wrong with me?" Shelly's eyes dropped to the ground when Sam looked at her.

"That's what we're here to find out." She looked from Sam to Dr. Ash and smiled. He wanted to give her something hopeful to hang onto, but it felt like it would be a false hope. "Doctor, is there anything else we need to discuss today? It's been a long day for all of us, and I think we'd all like to get some rest."

He looked down at his chart, mostly for an excuse to look away. "Not at this time," he said.

Shelly nodded and leaned forward to kiss Sam on the forehead. Sam felt a lingering feeling that she didn't want to be alone, but she didn't speak up for Shelly to stay. Paul got up from his chair and kissed her on the cheek. Sam reached to where her Pup had been sitting on the table and held him close.

"See you soon, kid." He squeezed her hand and gave her a smile.

Two days passed for Sam. She never vomited again after the first spell, but she did continue to have a slight fever that came and went. Every now and then, a nurse would observe her and find a rash on her stomach and arm, but by the time they started to think it might be serious, it began to go away on its own before anyone could make anything of it.

"Try not to itch it, okay?" Jamie said. She had become Sam's regular nurse. Willow had stopped coming after the last shot, and although Sam couldn't remember the name or face of the woman that had given her the shot, she knew that if she ever walked in the room to touch her again, she would know.

"It itches," Sam said. She was holding her arm out and Jamie was rubbing a cream in. Sam's arm was speckled with small red dots, like an allergic reaction, but with all the tests they had run, they hadn't discovered what she was allergic to yet—or if allergies were even the cause. Willow and Randy made sure to interfere with each test, working closely and carefully to hide any signs of abnormalities in her test samples.

"I know, we're working on it," Jamie said. Sam smiled and held out her other arm. It had been red and irritated the other day, but it was starting to heal while the other was beginning to flare.

"What does my blood look like?" Sam asked.

Jamie was looking closely at Sam's arm before she put more cream on it.

"It's red," she said, and Sam rolled her eyes. "But details beyond that? You'll have to ask Dr. Ash. He's the one who looked really close at your blood."

She finished the cream, and Sam pulled her arm back to her side. She liked the feel of the cream against her skin. Whenever she got the rash, the cream was the only way to calm the itching.

"Who's that?" Jamie asked. She was pointing to the little stuffed dog that was on the side table of Sam's bed.

Sam looked over at the stuffed dog while Jamie cleaned up the cream and put things away.

"That's Pup," she said, placing him back in her lap. The

fur on his body was stained, the tips of his fur bunching together. A bit of the cream that was on Sam's skin was already crusted into his fur.

"He's cute," Jamie said. "I'll be back later today to check on you, okay?"

"Okay," Sam said.

Sam kept her hand on Pup after Jaime left the room. He was her only constant. When everyone else came and went, Pup always stayed. She pet his head, running her fingers through his floppy ears.

"Good morning, Sam," the woman said. Sam turned to look and saw the woman who had given her the shot. Her throat felt like it closed, making it hard to breathe, but she wasn't sure if it was because she was scared, or because she was having another allergic reaction to some unknown cause.

"Don't touch me," she said. The words were meant to come out fierce, but instead her voice was feeble, fading.

Willow froze for a moment. She hadn't expected Sam to recognize her. She always had a feeling that Sam didn't trust her fully, but remembering Willow the second she walked into the room was a first for Sam. She panicked at first, knowing how much harder this would make monitoring the effects of the vaccine, but then she realized that this might mean the vaccine was in effect and working.

"I won't," she said. Willow had to be careful now. Before, she could do almost any examinations to Sam without having to worry about her talking about it to other nurses. Sam would forget things as soon as the subject was over, but what if Willow left the room and Sam told the next nurse that walked in that Willow had been giving her shots or asking weird questions.

Sam didn't relax. She had the stuffed dog clutched in her

hands and watched Willow closely as she walked into the room. The only thing that kept Sam calm was the fact that the only thing in her hand was a clipboard, and she wasn't reaching forward for any tools that were hidden away in drawers of the room.

"I just want to ask you a few questions," Willow said. "Actually, I want you to draw something for me."

Sam eyed her as she stepped forward to hand her a clipboard and pen.

"Just draw a few shapes for me," she said.

Sam took it and Willow held up a card with a square on it. Sam drew it almost effortlessly onto the page. Willow smiled and held up another card, this time with a triangle. Sam drew all the basic shapes that were held up, and eventually, Willow held up harder things to draw, like a boat or house. It took longer, and Sam had to concentrate a little harder, but she was still able to draw them.

"Good," Willow said once they had gone through all the cards. She took the clipboard and pen from Sam. "Can you tell me what time it is?" She pointed to the clock that was on the wall opposite Sam.

She looked at the clock, with all its ticks and numbers, and tried to find the place in her memory that told her how to tell time on the clock. The clock had three hands, the hour, the minute, the third one was for seconds, wasn't it?

"It's two," she looked closer to the minute hand. "Twenty-five."

"Can you tell me the months of the year?" she asked.

She thought for a moment and began to name them off one by one. "January. February. March. April. May. June. July. August. September. October. November. December."

"And now backwards."

Sam could feel her eyes widen in surprise. The questions were getting harder. She took a breath and recited them. "December. November. October. September. August. July. June." She paused. "May. April. March. February. January."

Willow didn't know how to respond. She wrote some notes quickly in her notebook, but she knew she wouldn't have to look back at it to remember how well Sam had done. Sam looked back at Willow, her eyes attentive but calm, having no idea how much she had progressed in such a short amount of time.

"Okay, just one last test." She pulled a small keychain light out of her pocket. Sam braced herself when she took it out, but once she saw that it was nothing more than a small light she relaxed into the bed again. "Just follow the light with your eyes."

She put a finger hovering in front of Sam's nose and moved the light from side to side. She was worried that along with the fever, vomiting, and rash, that the vaccine would have some effect on Sam's cognitive abilities, but her eyes followed the light perfectly. She wanted to ask Sam to stand and walk in a straight line as well, but she didn't want to do anything out of the ordinary that would cause Sam to talk about the tests later with the other nurses.

"Okay, you're all set," she said.

"Oh," Sam said. She was surprised the test was over. It was quick and seemed a bit pointless, but she felt like she had done well. She had answered all the questions correctly, hadn't she?

"Did I do okay?" Sam asked.

"You did very well." Willow smiled and left the room.

# Chapter 30

Randy wasn't in his office. It was just Willow, her notes, and the vaccine. She had produced more of the vaccine with the blood samples she had taken from Sam and now she had plenty of vaccine to administer to Sam when and if the first dose showed signs of wearing off.

She was looking over the notes she had taken when testing Sam's memory. It didn't seem possible for Sam to progress so quickly. Just a week ago, she could barely remember events of the day before. Willow kicked herself, because she forgot to do the most basic memory test with Sam. She was supposed to tell her an address at the beginning of the session and ask for Sam to repeat it back to her at the end of the session. Of all the tests Sam had taken, that was the one that she'd never been able to pass.

Willow took the vial of the vaccine out of the safe that was hidden under Randy's desk and held it in her hands until the glass became warm from her touch. When she looked into the clear-tinted liquid in her hands, she could feel her father looking back at her. She wished she had found this for him years earlier. Could it have saved him?

All the years of him losing his memory, fading into the

background. In the days he lived with her, it felt as if she woke up expecting to see her father but realizing he wasn't there. She would watch him in the morning, gazing out the window. She could love who he was in those silent moments, but when she spoke to him, he wasn't there. His mind was elsewhere, daydreaming, lost in reality.

Could that be her someday? Would her family be forced to love her, just an empty shell of a person? Would she look back at her husband one day and wonder who he was? Would she have that same lost gaze her father had?

As she aged, she felt like she was losing herself. There were moments she would be acting normal and then just…forget. She would forget why she was there and where she was supposed to be. Randy never said anything about her memory or anything else seeming off, but he was always too busy to notice such subtle changes. That was how it always started, wasn't it? Small differences, too small to ever make note of, but eventually all the small changes added up to larger changes. Was she already at that the point? Were there things about her that had already begun to change without her realizing it?

She rolled the vial across her palm. The glass was smooth, warm against her skin.

It could be so simple. She could inject the vaccine. It would run through her bloodstream and stop the Alzheimer's in its track. It was already making its way through her neurons, she was sure of it. It would be simple. A small injection. That's what vaccines were for after all: preventative measures. Children got dozens of vaccines in a lifetime to save them from ever having to deal with diseases. Why should a vaccine for Alzheimer's be any different?

She took the vial and hide it away in her pocket. She would only need a small bit.

She was running on autopilot when she left the office. She wasn't thinking of the effects of the serum or how it may have helped Sam and could kill her. She only thought of how it could cure her before the disease ever got its hold on her.

She riffled through the drawers of the nurse's cart out in the hall and pulled out a fresh syringe, slipping into an empty patient room before someone could notice her. She inserted the needle into top of the vial and pulled out a single milliliter. That was all it was going to take. Such a small, almost a miniscule amount, and it could defeat her Alzheimer's, whether or not it had begun.

She sanitized the top of her arm off and inserted the needle. It stung, more than she expected it to, but administered the vaccine with a steady hand. It was after she put the syringe down that her hands began to shake, just in the way they had when she administered it to Sam.

Even after the needle left her skin she felt a burn in her arm. Is that why Sam had protested so much?

Willow threw the syringe into the bio-waste trash, removing any evidence she was there, and left the room.

"Willow." She heard someone call her name as she walked down the hall. She turned, but there was no one there. She stood for a moment, waiting for someone to come around the corner, but they never did. When she turned back to where she had come from, her head began to spin. She took a moment to steady herself but lightheadedness began to take over. Willow took careful steps, but she could feel herself swaying in the hallway.

"Willow, you okay?" It was Jenna. Her eyes were roaming over Willow, looking for some sign of distress. She held out her arms in case Willow fell but for now at least, she stayed rooted in place.

"Yeah, I'm fine," she said. Willow took another step and felt her stomach drop. She was swaying on her feet and Jenna took her arm and walked to a break room.

"Is she okay?" It was Jamie. Willow could hear someone pull out a seat. "Here." Her voice was closer and Willow was being guided to sit in one of the hard metal chairs.

"What happened?" Jaime said.

"I don't know. I saw her walking, and it looked like she was about to fall."

A hand touched her forehead.

"She's burning up," Jamie said. "Let me go call Dr. Ash."

"No!" Willow said, too loudly. She blinked, her vision cleared, though she had never realized she had lost it in the first place. "I'm fine. You don't need to disrupt him for this. I'll just sit for a bit."

Her voice was calmer and Jamie walked away.

"You sure?" Jenna was kneeling next to her. Jenna knew her well, but she hoped that Jenna didn't know her so well that she could see through the unease that Willow was trying so desperately to hide. She could feel a sweat on her eyebrow and knew Jenna noticed. She smiled it away.

"I'm sure."

"I'll be back in a little bit to go check on you. I'll let Randy know you're in here." She gave Willow a soft squeeze on the shoulder.

Once she was alone, Willow leaned forward, using her arms to cradle her stomach. She put her head on the table and tried to let the nausea pass. Instead, her stomach took another flip.

"Willow?" She lifted her head, and the motion was too fast. She could feel herself tipping, but she could also feel something much worse about to come to the surface.

Arms around her waist. They were familiar, and Willow was happy and horrified that Randy was there. He helped lift her from the chair and guide her to the waste bin. She vomited shortly after.

"It's okay," he said. He had one arm across her chest holding her up, while the other was on her back, holding her steady. He murmured to her every few seconds, saying over and over, "It's okay."

Sweat was gathering at her eyebrows, but she felt chilled. She coughed a low guttural cough, but nothing came up. Randy pushed loose strands of hair out of her face and tucked them behind her ear.

"Did you eat something?" he said.

The top of her arm stung. Randy's fingers were pushing into the tender skin, but she was too afraid he'd notice the similarities between herself and Sam to point out the pain.

"Yeah, I think I just ate too fast or something."

She wrapped her arms around her stomach and lowered herself to the floor. Randy tightened his grip and walked her back to the table to sit.

"Do you feel any better now?" he asked.

She was tempted to say she did and go back to work without a problem, but the truth was she wasn't sure if she could stand. At least when Sam got the vaccine she could just lay in bed.

"Randy, you should go back to work."

"No, not until I know you're okay." She was sitting, just barely as he grasped her shoulder to hold her steady.

"I'm fine, like I said, I just ate too fast."

She was looking at the surface of the table, but she could tell Randy was giving her the look that said he didn't believe a word she said.

"I'm taking you back to my office."

He leaned down until they were shoulder to shoulder, and ducked under her arm until it was draped around his shoulder. He used his own arm to hold onto her torso and began to lift her. A cramp ran down her ribs and into her stomach, and she had to bite her lip to stifle the whimper.

"Randy," she said once she was standing. The words came out as a gasp but she pulled away from him and stood on her own. Standing straight felt like she was tearing herself apart, but she tried to compose herself enough to allow Randy to walk away. She was terrified to be in his office with him, that maybe he already had a hunch of what she had done, but he would never dare speak of the vaccine out in the open like this.

"I'm fine," she said again. She stood a little straighter but breathed a bit deeper. Her body groaned in protest and begged to turn back into a ball. Out of the corner of her eye, she saw the hard linoleum floor and it looked more and more inviting as the seconds passed by.

"You're not fine," he said. She was afraid he would force her out of the room as he wrapped his arms around her again, but instead he gently lowered her to the table and sat her down in a chair. He kneeled in front of her as he quickly, almost dismissively, took her vitals.

"I'll be okay," she told him. Her voice was soft, swollen almost. For a moment, it was like she couldn't breathe, and she realized it was because there were tears straining their way through. She wanted to swallow them down, but they came to the surface anyways.

Randy looked up to her and cupped her cheek. Small tears ran over his fingers.

"What's wrong?" he said.

His eyes were soft. He wasn't looking for the lie she had just told or the lies she was about to tell. In that moment, he could forget everything that she had done because he only wanted her to be safe. The way he touched her was more than she deserved. She wanted to say how terrified she was that every day, she was becoming more and more like her father. She could feel things— ideas, memories, these small little treasures—slipping away from her. How could she ever tell him all this? How could she tell him that he would have to go through what she went through with her father? How could she expect Randy to love her when her life was stripped away?

Worst of all, she knew Randy would love her through it all. He would stay by her side, bring her to every doctor appointment and do everything in his power to keep her whole. He deserved better than to love a woman slipping away. She had rather he leave her and let her fall into an ignorant bliss without pulling him down with her.

She opened her mouth to speak, but something broke. Randy wrapped his arms around her until she buried her face in the groove between his neck and shoulder.

He never said anything as she cried. He never asked for an explanation. He just held her there until she emptied herself. Willow was clutched into a knot. She was holding onto Randy, but she was also holding onto herself. She was terrified to let go.

"Willow," he said.

By now, her body had stilled and her tears had dried, but she still failed to pry open her body to the world once again.

"I have to go back to work," Randy said. His voice was soft and his arms were gentle. He was kinder than what she deserved. "I'll be back later."

Willow began to untangle herself from him. She couldn't

find it in herself to look at him. The cramps in her ribs were there, but now they were just small reminders of what she had injected into herself. The top of her shoulder still stung loud and clear.

"I'll see you in a little bit," she said. She was pushing in the chair when she said it, an excuse to look away.

"Lay down if you need to." He stepped forward and took her hand while he kissed the top of her forehead. Under his touch, her body felt rigid. "I love you," he said.

She looked up at him and saw the truth in his words. She memorized his face, but his eyes looked too tired. She hadn't remembered him looking so exhausted before. It made her stomach twist to think she had done this to him. "I love you, too," she said. Her voice shook as she spoke.

He walked away, leaving her in the wake of her own sickness.

# Chapter 31

Paul eyed the red skin around Sam's eye. The skin shined at him with a gleam of oil. The rash came and went, but no one seemed to know what it was, or how to prevent it. Sam did her best not to itch it, but Paul could see her thinking about it, lifting a hand only to put it back down.

"How's it feeling today?" he asked.

"Can I sit up?"

Shelly stepped into the room with some banana bread from the cafeteria. It was one of Sam's favorite snacks, so she put it on her bedside table, still wrapped in plastic.

"Sure," he said, pushing the button on her bed to pull the mattress up. She was already sitting up, but he pushed the bed as far as it could go until the mattress met with her back.

"No, I mean, sit-sit."

"Sweetheart, why don't you eat your banana bread first and then you can sit."

Sam frowned, but she took the bread anyways. Her stomach still churned every few hours, but for right now, she could eat. The bread was moist and fresh, with small chunks of almond mixed in.

"Thank you," she said. Sam moved her feet off the side of the bed and pulled herself up. She was careful not to knock her IV out as she did so, but when her feet finally touched the ground it was like she was finally getting a part of her life back.

"You seem to be feeling better," Paul said. He was eying Sam and watched her steady herself to a sitting position. A smile was painted across her face, and he felt like he was looking at his granddaughter again for the first time. He had just seen her the other day, and now it was like she was herself again, or at least on the mend. Her smile was the tell-tale sign that she was improving. He hadn't seen her smile in weeks.

"I haven't been throwing up anymore. I still feel a little queasy every now and then though." She skimmed her fingers across the paper-thin johnnie and wondered when it might be time to go home. Surely the doctor would discharge her soon.

"It's more than that," Paul said. He wanted to tell her it was like she had left them, that her spirit had floated away in the fire and was never coming back.

Shelly was silent in the corner of the room. She was scared to talk, afraid it might break the spell that Sam was under. After so many weeks of suffering and sickness, could she really be back, without any aid from the doctors?

"What do you mean?" Sam asked.

Her face was flushed, skin glossy, but her eyes were bright with a light they hadn't seen in weeks.

Sam turned to Shelly and frowned. "What's wrong?" she asked.

Shelly turned to Paul. Her eyes were tearing up, but a smile was erupting. She crept over to Paul's side and clutched his arm.

"Sam, you were so sick," Shelly said.

"Where's my parents?" Shelly's shoulders dropped. She could feel Paul's hand go limp in hers. But Sam was there. She was Sam, but she still had no relocation of what had happened.

Sam was looking at Shelly clutching Paul's hand. Why were they here and not her parents?

"Sam, there was a fire, and your mom and Daniel didn't make it," Paul said. Shelly was turning towards him for support, but he could barely hold himself up. He hoped this was the last time she would ever have to tell Sam, but the hope felt feeble.

"What?" Sam said. Her voice came out as a squeak and she could feel the nausea returning.

"After your mom died, you had a seizure, and ever since then you've been acting strange. You haven't been able to remember anything."

She was looking at Paul. Would she remember this conversation?

"What?" she said it again. Her voice wavered and she bit her lip. She had been in the hospital for a long time, that much she was sure of. She had vague memories of being in this bed with nurses coming in and out, but she was never sure why.

"You can come live with us," Shelly said. Her voice was rushed, stumbling into each other.

"What about Avery?" she asked. Her hand was shaking, and she pulled it into her chest to try to conceal the movements. Shelly eyed her but didn't say anything.

"Avery's okay. She's been visiting you as much as she could."

The information came crashing down. Not one by one like waves, but all at once like a monsoon.

"Sam?" Paul let go of Shelly's and walked towards her.

"My parents are gone?" she said. She took a breath. "And I

don't remember."

She was holding the tears in. They screamed to be let out and to run free, but not once did she blink and let them go. Shelly looked on in horror and cried for her. She lost her daughter, and still every day it was like she lost her granddaughter. Today, she had her granddaughter, but with it came its own bought of pain.

Paul leaned down to Sam and wrapped her in his arms. She hugged him back, but she couldn't stop herself from shaking. She couldn't breathe, but she let Paul's breath guide her. He smelled familiar, like oats, and she rested her chin on his shoulder. She clutched onto her grandfather; he was her guide.

"They're gone," she said.

Paul pulled away and Shelly stepped forward. Her arms were wrapped around herself, but Sam stood up from the bed and threw herself into Shelly's arms.

"They're both gone," Sam said into the crook of Shelly's shoulder. The tears flowed mighty and loud. With each blink and breath, Sam could feel them coming to surface. She wanted to pull away, to hide her tears from the world, but once one tear came, they all followed.

No one said anything as she cried. They didn't say things would be okay, because they weren't. "Sam?" The voice made them all lift their heads. Sam wiped her eyes when she turned to face the door, and there was Avery. Her figure was slight, and she held herself like she might fall at any moment, but she was there.

Sam took tentative steps forward but was stopped when she felt a tug on her IV—she'd reached the end of her line. Avery stepped closer until she was just an arm's length away. Sam's eyes were still wet with tears, but Avery's were dry. She was dazed as she looked at Sam. Confused in the sort of way that came with waking up from a dream.

"You're okay?" Sam said. She wanted to reach out and touch her to be sure, but the IV was like a leash.

Avery looked from Sam to Paul to Shelly. Shelly had her hand over her heart, like it was the only thing she could do to keep it still, while Paul had a tear running down his cheek, just for a moment before he was able to brush it away.

"What happened?" Avery asked, but she didn't look at Sam. One glance at her and she knew something had shifted. The vacant look in her eyes was gone. Avery was waiting for Paul and Shelly to respond, but neither of them could find the words.

"Avery?" Sam said. She wanted to step closer to her, but she backed away slightly.

"She seems okay," Avery said.

Sam turned to look at Shelly and Paul, but they were both looking at each other, searching for words. No one would talk to her, but there she was, standing in the middle of the room. Her arms began to itch. She rubbed the palm of her hand across the top of her arm.

"Don't do that, Sam." Shelly stepped forward and pulled her arm away. She was examining the skin, but for now nothing had changed. Her skin was still dotted red.

"What's wrong with her skin?" Avery asked, seeing the familiar red splotches on her arm.

"We aren't sure," Shelly said. She reached out to the bedside table. One of the nurses had left a jar of the cream they used on Sam's arm. Shelly rubbed a small dab into Sam's skin.

Avery looked on with curious eyes, but in all honesty, she wasn't prepared to see Sam like this. She was ready to see the Sam that laid in bed and had small conversations with herself. She was ready for the Sam that listened to her talk and only interrupted to ask the same questions over and over. She wasn't ready for someone who could really hear her. Coming once a week to someone who was physically there, but not mentally, became part of her routine. Come visit, pull up a chair. Talk and have Sam talk back but with her own conversation that didn't make sense. Talk about stupid things that Avery knew Sam would forget as soon as she left the room. She'd time the visits to one hour exactly. Once the hour was up, she left, wondering only if Sam would remember she came to visit at all.

Avery didn't have a hope. When her parents died she told herself Sam had as well. When she first began her visits, Avery looked for any sign of the old Sam, but eventually she came to think of Sam as another person. A friend that she made and felt obligated to visit but wasn't quite sure why. If she was honest with herself, Avery had thought about stopping her visits. When she came to see Sam, she didn't know who Avery was, so why put herself through visits that only end in heartbreak? Each time she stepped through the door she hoped Sam would recognize her, but she never did.

"Avery," Sam said. She reached her fingers out and brushed them down Avery's arm. She felt goosebumps across her skin as Sam touched her. It was like she was looking at a ghost.

Sam wanted to step closer, to close the distance between the two of them, but Avery held her ground and Sam was leashed in with her IV.

"What's wrong?" Sam said.

Avery hadn't realized her lip had started to quiver. Weeks ago, if the old Avery was standing there, she would have run into Sam's arms, cried until she was out of tears, but instead this was the new Avery. This was the Avery with the dead parents. She had a sister that had disappeared and left her body behind, but now, seeing Sam standing in front of her—the real Sam—she knew she had come to think of Sam as dead as well.

"How?" Avery said. Her voice was shallow and she took another step away from Sam. Cry. She could cry, but she felt like it would be anything but happiness. She didn't feel in control of herself anymore. She wanted to run at Sam, to scream at Sam. After all these weeks in the hospital, she was okay? It didn't seem possible, couldn't be possible, but there she was. How could she leave her alone for so long, to grieve without her, only to take all those emotions back weeks later?

Sam's mouth hung open for a bit before she could respond. "I don't know." Her words came out shy, afraid. Avery's voice was harsh, like she was accusing Sam of something, but she wasn't sure what. She could see Avery folding in on herself and Sam watched on, unsure of how to help. Avery's eyes spoke what her words could not. She looked in every direction of the room, like she was ready to run away the moment someone so much as brushed lint off their sleeve.

Paul looked up at Shelly and saw her frowning. It wasn't the reunion they had hoped for. Sam backed away from Avery and came closer to them.

"I'm so sorry," Sam said, but she wasn't sure what she was apologizing for. Her voice was still timid, but it held a note of confidence that morphed into fear. Her heart broke for Avery, but it broke even more for herself, and for that she was ashamed.

"Why are you okay?" Avery said. The words snapped from her lips before she could think them through. She wanted to take them back, but another, larger part wanted to know why.

"I told you." But Avery stopped her.

"No. Why are you okay? After all these months of losing person after person, why have you finally come back? I told myself you were gone. That was it. That girl in the hospital bed? That wasn't you. But I still came back every week. I listened to you talk, and you listened to me, and none of it meant anything because the next time I saw you we'd be starting all over again.

"But I came back every week, and I knew you'd never be better and I was okay with that. I've been okay with our parents dying, and now I live with our grandparents and I'm okay. But now, now you're okay and I have to do this all over again?"

She stopped because Shelly came up next to her and tried to put an arm around her. Avery pulled away and stepped closer to the door of the room.

"I'm not doing this again," Avery said. "You're okay now, but what happens if you disappear again. I've watched you come and go, like your body was sometimes occupied or vacant, and I don't want to do it anymore."

Sam couldn't say anything. She was looking over Avery and how her hair was grown out almost to her elbows. Hadn't she just gotten a haircut? Had much time had passed without her?

"What can I do?" Sam said, because there was nothing else she could say. How long had Avery been crying without her, for her?

There was a lost, empty feeling in Sam's stomach. She was missing something, but she wasn't sure what. Time had passed, and she wasn't sure how much, but the world went on without her for too long. Damage had been done and she only hoped that her life could be pieced back together.

Avery looked at Sam and frowned. She wanted to have her sister back, to touch her and make sure she was really there, but every part of her told her not to believe it. Just because she was there now didn't mean she would be there again tomorrow. All Avery could think about was coming in the hospital again next week and finding Sam lying in bed all over again, asking where their parents were because she couldn't remember.

# Chapter 32

It had become a habit for Randy to slip into Sam's room at the end of his shifts. Sam would normally be asleep by the time he stepped into the room, but ever since Willow had injected her with the vaccine she'd been awake, almost always sick in some form. Not in any serious way, but enough that a nurse always seemed to be close by in case she needed medication to lower a fever or to put cream on a rash.

Jamie was at Sam's bedside when he stood in the doorway.

"How is she?" he asked.

Jamie had her fingers wrapped around Sam's forearm, brushing the skin lightly.

"Very well, actually," Jamie said. She stepped to the side when Randy came in.

He lifted her arm and leaned down for a closer look. Sam's skin was a smooth, a flushed pink. She would heal without scarring. There was a scratch closer to her elbow, but he was sure that would heal on its own as well.

"Now if only your grandparents were here to see this," he said to Sam. She smiled back, watching Dr. Ash as he lowered her arm back to the bed and stepped away.

"Can I get up?" she asked. She wanted to get out of bed and stretch. She spent too much time lying in bed; it was starting to feel like an extension of her body, but they never let her go for walks down the halls.

"Not right now," Jamie told her. It was the same response she always got when she asked to get up. She never said why or when she may be able to go for a walk, so Sam always made it a point to keep asking.

"If I can't go for a walk on my own, can you go with me?" Jamie smiled but Sam could tell she was getting ready to give her some excuse as to why she still couldn't leave her room.

"Actually, Sam, Jamie will be on her way out soon. Why don't you take a walk with me?"

"I'll see you tomorrow," Jamie said, giving her a small wave before she went out the door. Sam watched after her before sitting up in bed.

"So, do you know why you haven't been able to go for walks yet?" Dr. Ash asked.

"No," Sam said. The nurses had been coming in to help her stretch, but it was rare she got to leave much farther than her room.

She didn't have any shoes but she didn't care. The socks on her feet were enough to keep her toes warm. She just knew she was ready to move and get away from her room for a while.

"There were a lot of reasons, but most of all we just didn't know what to predict out of you. We had rather played it safe than sorry." He pulled up her files from a clipboard that she hadn't noticed had been resting on the table next to her bed. "But it looks like in the last twenty-four hours at least, you've been doing pretty good. How do you feel right now?"

"Cooped up," she said.

Dr. Ash laughed and put the chart back down and disconnected the tubing from the IV bag that was hanging beside her bed.

"If you were well enough, we could have you walk with your IV." He took Sam's hand, wrapped delicately in tape, connecting the IV to her skin. "But we weren't sure, with you being sick so suddenly and so easily, if you'd make it very far until you had to be brought back to your room." He pulled the tape from her skin as painlessly as he could. "But today is your lucky day to get outside." He pointed to the window across from Sam's bed and as soon as she looked away he pulled the small flexible tubing from her skin, and just like that, she was free. He worked quickly to bandage her.

"We're going outside?" Sam asked. She looked at Dr. Ash for confirmation before turning back to the window. She wasn't sure what floor of the hospital she was on, but she was high enough that her only company was the tops of buildings and small puffs of clouds.

"Do you think you're up for it?" he asked.

Sam was already halfway out of her bed, her socks on the floor and hospital gown exposing her backside. Her feet, which wore the socks with grips pads on the bottom, touched the floor. The fabric did little to protect her from the laminate, but she was thankful for that cold feeling at her feet.

"I want to walk," she said.

He held his arm out for support, but she didn't reach for it. They stood side by side as they walked down the hall.

"Are we really going outside?" she asked. Her eyes were full, and there was a spark of life there that he hadn't seen before.

Dr. Ash looked down at her feet at the socks. Sam's eyes

followed his and she frowned.

"Sort of," he said and the two of them walked down the hall and entered an elevator.

"What day is it? Sam said.

"May 2nd. Tuesday."

She had hoped once he said the date the information would cause things to fall in place, but it didn't. She wanted to ask the date she was admitted in the hospital, but she was too afraid to hear the answer.

"How have you been feeling today?" he asked. His voice changed when he asked how she felt. His voice deepened and became more pronounced. She could feel him shifting into doctor mode, and it made her want Jamie back.

"The itching is gone. I felt a little sick right after I ate, but besides that good."

The doors to the elevator opened, and he led her down the hall. It felt good to stretch her legs. The pads of her feet beat against the floor and she felt human again, even if she didn't have shoes.

"Here we are." Dr. Ash turned down a small hallway and cracked open a door. As soon as he did, Sam could feel the air get humid. Scents far beyond what she could describe filled in around her. She stepped through the room, still in socks and hospital gown, but if she closed her eyes she could swear she was outside.

"Our small greenhouse," Dr. Ash said. "We have volunteers that come in to take care of it and make sure everything is watered and maintained.

All the plants were potted, so nothing was too large. A few plants here and there, herbs, tiny bushes that were only in their infancy.

"Everything starts off in here, and when it grows too big,

216

the landscape team moves it outside."

Sam stepped toward a potted plant with deep green leaves. She ran her fingers over the leaf and down the stem until she could hear a small trickle of water off to her left. When she turned there was a small little water fountain running. She stepped forward until she was close enough that she could sit on a rock and dip her hand into the water.

Dr. Ash stayed close to the entrance. The moment she was having in the greenhouse felt like a private one. Her eyes lit up when her hand touched the water, experiencing the world for the first time. Dr. Ash thought about how a group of volunteers asked to bring butterflies into the garden, but the idea had been shot down by executives before it could go any farther. He could image it now, how the butterflies would have completed the garden. How one would have landed on Sam's knee and her face would have lit up ten-fold of what it had when she touched the water.

Dr. Ash was watching Sam when he heard her cough. It started off as a small cough to clear her throat, but after a moment of short silence, she coughed again. This time, it was louder and where the first cough had left Sam still smiling, the second cough was enough to bring the edges of her lips down.

"Sam?" Dr. Ash said. She looked over to him and her eyes were watering. She coughed again and she took her fingers from the edge of the water and brought them to her chest.

Dr. Ash didn't think, he acted. It was the only thing he knew to do. Part of him wanted to scoop her up and bring her into the emergency room to another doctor, someone else who knew what to do, but when she kept coughing, she leaned forward and soon enough the coughing turned to vomiting.

He touched her back, trying to steady her until her coughing slowed. The vomit at her feet was clear, totally devoid of any color or texture. She stopped vomiting, but her body was still shuttering and Dr. Ash realized it was because Sam was crying as she took gasping breaths. He knelt beside her as she covered her face with her hands.

"Do you still feel nauseous?" he asked.

She looked up, the white of her eyes a bright red. Tears were still streaming in ripples, but what shocked him most when he looked at her was the bright terror he saw there.

"I always feel sick," she said, and she buried her face again.

"Can you stand?" He stood up, trying to pull her up beside him. Her body was heavy, but he was able to guide her out of the greenhouse. Once he opened the door to enter the hospital, a chill of air greeted them.

"I need a wheelchair," he said, keeping Sam close beside him. He shouted the words to no one in particular, but soon enough a team of passersby came to attention.

"Here you go, Dr. Ash." A nurse came from a little way down the hall with the wheelchair in hand. She helped lower Sam into the chair. Her eyes were wide and when the nurse was about ready to wheel her away, she turned around back towards the greenhouse door.

"I don't want to leave," she said. "Dr. Ash, please let me stay in the greenhouse."

"You're sick," he said. Sam knew his words were true, but they were a crushing blow as she sunk into the wheelchair. That spark that had been there when she touched the water was gone, only to be replaced by a sense of dread. She was trapped in her own body.

"Page Jamie. She vomited in the greenhouse," Dr. Ash said. The nurse nodded her head and turned toward the greenhouse. She disappeared into the room to clean up the mess.

Sam was silent as she was rolled back to her room. She hadn't felt sick in the moments before vomiting. It felt good to finally touch water again. When she had closed her eyes she had imagined she was outside. The beeping of the machines, the constant hum of voices, it was finally gone and replaced with the sound of trickling water. And then it was gone again.

Sam's body was betraying her. No matter how hard she tried to fight it, she kept becoming sick. She imagined her body covered in small scars from being poked and prodded.

"Does she need to be stabilized?" It was Jaime's voice. She rushed over to Sam and took the wheelchair from Dr. Ash's hands. He didn't protest and walked beside her as they ran down the hall. Sam looked through each hospital room as they went by. Some people were sleeping, others watching TV, some beds were empty. It had been so long since her bed had been empty, but it was about to be filled again.

"Sam?" It was Dr. Ash talking this time. He was walking beside her, crouched down to meet her eyes. Sam looked at him and blinked too many times. She couldn't get herself to focus. His mouth kept moving, she knew he was talking, but she couldn't hear them.

Her head began to fall forward. She wasn't aware of her own motion until Dr. Ash fell from her vision and soon enough she was looking at her lap. She coughed and vomit came again.

She remembered being sick when she was little. Whenever she had the stomach bug she always felt worse and worse until she threw up. Once it was out of her system, she felt better. This wasn't the same. Sam felt fine, always felt fine, up until the moment the vomit came. Then she felt worse. That's why was she was looking at her own vomit as it sat in her lap.

The moments that proceeded were a blur. She was floating from her wheelchair and in the next moment her skin was cold and exposed. Her naked body was on display and hands were touching her arms, softly guiding her. She didn't feel scared as warm water poured over she skin.

"We're going to get you cleaned up," a voice said.

Sam felt coarse cotton against her skin. The fabric fell just above her knees and over the tops of her arms. She still felt exposed until she felt her backside come into contact with a bed — her bed. Blankets were rolled over her body until she was the only one left in the room again. The machine by her bedside beeped to remind her she was alive.

# Chapter 33

Willow was taking the blood pressure of a patient when she felt her balance tip. The patient, a middle-aged man, was lying in bed with an IV in his hand and blood pressure cuff around his arm. She was watching the computer screen reading off his blood pressure when she put her hand out to catch herself. Willow was leaning against the wall at the head of his hand, thankful the TV in the room was enough to distract him.

"Everything looks good," she said. She took a deep breath as she tried to push herself up to stand. The pit of her stomach felt like it had dropped to the floor. She was nauseous, like at any moment she might fall to the floor.

Willow's legs were shaking as she found her balance enough to lean forward and take the blood pressure cuff off the man's arm. He grunted as she lifted his arm, but even though she could feel herself swaying as she walked out of the room, she knew he wouldn't have noticed.

"Willow, did you want to order lunch?" Terry, one of the nurses on call, was the first person to walk towards Willow once she left the patient's room. Terry had a takeout menu in her hand from the Chinese restaurant.

"No, I'm all set," Willow said. She meant for her voice to be calm, but it came out as one large breath. She was walking too fast, but her eyes were on the bathroom down the hall. She just needed to sit, take a breath and she would be all right. Willow didn't want to stop walking for fear that she may tumble in front of everyone.

"Willow?" Terry said. She was behind her now and Willow knew without looking that Terry was following.

Willow's stomach bunched into a twist, and she practically ran to the bathroom, darting for the door.

"Are you okay?"

She could hear Terry behind her, just barely, but the sound of her own breathing was a loud pulsing in her ears. She got to the bathroom, tugged on the door, and it was locked.

"Damn it," Willow said in the breath. She began coughing once her body paused and she cursed at the single-stalled bathroom. Terry was close behind, shouting, but Willow couldn't hear over the buzzing noise in her ear.

She fell to the floor when her hand slipped from the door. She supposed her body made a thud as it hit the ground, but she wasn't sure. Her vision went blank, so she closed her eyes as she lay on the floor. The only thing she was sure of was the prickle of tears that were streaming down her face. She wanted to get up, to move, but she was trapped inside her own body, betrayed.

— — — — —

Dr. Ash was pacing in his office long after Sam had fallen asleep in her room. The last he had seen of her, she was flushed a healthy shade a pink and her vitals were perfect. The only giveaway that she had been sick was that her hair that was still wet from the bath the nurses had given her to clean up the vomit.

In one way, he was amazed. Her mind was healing. She

could retain thoughts, recall long-lost memories and recognize people from her past. It was as if the dementia that had been infecting her brain had never been there.

But then there were the rashes, the vomiting, the constant reactions her body made in protest to the vaccine. He hoped her body would adjust over time and that she wouldn't need any further injections of the vaccine, but if the dementia came back and she started reverting to her old ways, he would have no choice but to administer again. She was a person conscious of her own existence, but now she was aware as she suffered through it.

Dr. Ash was clenching and unclenching his fists, pacing his office that he practically lived in. There seemed to be more nights, long nights of confusion. His hand brushed against the papers laying across the desk and he wanted to throw it all away. His fingers found one paper, a sticky-note laying on the keyboard of his computer. It was Willow's soft script: I'm sorry.

The words were written small, like a whisper, but he could still hear the sound of her voice loud and clear in his mind.

He crumpled the note.

"Dr. Ash?" The was a quite knock at the door and he hid the note in his pocket.

"Come in," he said. He stood behind his desk, trying to wipe his face of the emotions and lack of sleep that he was sure was etched there across his skin.

"I'm sorry to disrupt you, but I think Willow needs you." It was Terry, a nurse that usually had the same shifts as Willow. She was an older woman, someone who took on the world with no nonsense. He'd seen her on the floor and how she took on any patient without even the slightest look of doubt on her face, but now she seemed unsure.

"Where is she?" he asked. The sticky note was still

crumpled in his pocket, but he began to unfurl it again.

"We found her unconscious on the bathroom floor."

— — — — —

If he was honest with himself, he had wanted to rip the sticky note in half or burn it or do anything but what he was doing right now. Willow had gotten them into this mess; she had let her own feelings compromise another patient and now he had to cover it up. He wanted to yell and scream, to make her find sense. Yet there he was, at the side of her hospital bed, holding her small, tender hand. Sometimes when he held her hand he could feel her spirit lifting him up, but now he could only feel her dragging him down.

Her eyes never fluttered. She was a pale pink on the hospital bed, alive and so lost. He wanted to be angry with her, he could still feel it rumbling inside him, but he could only hold her hand and hope she opened her eyes.

"Her vitals all seem okay. What blood tests do you want me to run?"

He still had his eyes on her when Terry was talking to him. For a moment, seeing her face so at peace, so still, he could imagine it was just the two of them and they were home after a long night. They were both still in their scrubs, too tired to get changed and too tired to let go of the other person's hand.

"I'll handle it, Terry," he said, taking his eyes off his wife. "Thank you." Terry smiled and rolled a cart forward, the syringe and tubes laid across it.

"Are you sure?" she asked.

"I'm sure," Dr. ash said, taking the cart and rolling it closer to his side.

"Page me if you need anything," she said as she left the room.

He worked quick to prep her arm and take her blood. She opened her eyes when he wrapped the rubber band around her arm.

"What are you doing?" she said. Her eyes were wide, more frightened than he had seen them in a long time.

"I'm just taking a sample so we can make sure you're okay." He put his hand over hers to try to calm her down but she pulled away.

"No, please, Randy, I'm fine." Willow untied the rubber band from the top of her arm and tossed it to the side.

"Willow," Randy said. He gripped her wrist. "Do you even know what happened?"

She kept trying to pull away, but Randy's grip only grew tighter. He wasn't hurting her, and that frustrated her even more. She wanted to be angry with him, but he only gave her reasons to calm down.

"I'm fine," she said. She pushed him away and pushed herself off the bed.

"No, you're not." Randy stepped in front of her and wrapped his arms around her waist, pulling her so her back was to his chest. She could imagine the two of them at home, making dinner, just another day, but his grip was too tight to be a normal embrace. "Willow, Terry found you passed out on the floor."

She was glad that her back was to him when he spoke to hide the surprise that coated her face. She shook it away quickly.

"I'm fine. Terry was just being dramatic."

She wanted to wriggle free, but Randy pulled her farther away from the door and closer to the bed until he had her seated.

"Stop it," he said.

"Randy, I'm fine!" But he wouldn't let her get up. He didn't say anything to her. He just stood while he held her onto the bed, waiting for her arms to relax and when he felt her release the tension in her arms, he leaned away.

"Dr. Ash?" Terry poked her head into the room. Her face was still as she took in Willow sitting on the edge of the bed like she was ready to jump up.

Randy sighed and looked at Willow. His eyes were a mix of anger and sorrow. He was begging her to sit.

"Terry, can you get a blood sample from Willow and send it off to the lab?" His eyes never left Willow's face. She could feel herself sinking with submission. "Willow, I'll be back soon to take you home. You need to rest."

He walked out of the room and a panic set fire to her bones. Terry stepped through the door and grasped her hand.

"I'll be quick," she said. Terry worked fast to sanitize the area, wrap the band and plunge the needle. Willow couldn't ignore the urge to pull away, to hide what was hidden in her blood. She watched the syringe as it filled with the bright red liquid.

"All set," Terry said. She covered the pin-prick in the crook of Willow's elbow with a small bandage. If the area hurt, she couldn't tell. Her body was on fire all over, begging her to run.

# Chapter 34

S am was shaking. She was burrowed under the cotton blankets of the hospital bed, but it felt like sandpaper against her skin. Her skin had droplets of sweat which only seemed to catch the cold air more.

"One of the nurses said we could use this blanket," Shelly said. She walked into the room with a fleece blanket with pink hearts. Paul took it from her and began to wrap it around Sam's body. "Feeling any better?" Shelly said as she came by her bedside.

"Fine," she said. She was trying to hide the shaking from her grandparents. The rash on her arm had finally healed, but with it left all heat in her body.

"She has a fever," Paul said. His voice was firm, aggressive. "No one in this damn hospital is treating her. She'll die because of them!"

"Paul," Shelly said.

Sam sunk deeper into the mattress. She wanted to think that her grandfather was being over dramatic, but the longer she stayed at the hospital, the surer she was that she might not ever leave.

Paul looked from Shelly to Sam, his hand in a tight fist.

There was a knock at the door and Dr. Ash entered. His body was slumping in on itself as he walked. There were things about him that seemed off, and for a moment Sam wondered if he was as delicate as she was.

"How have you been feeling, Sam?" he asked. He didn't look at Sam as he walked across the room. Instead, he walked straight towards the machine that read off her vitals. His lip slipped into a frown for just a moment before he caught himself. "I just want to take your temperature."

Dr. Ash slipped a thermometer under her tongue and the room waited in silence. His kept his eyes on the handheld device that was reading off her temperature. She wanted him to look at her. She wanted him to see what she was too afraid to say, that something was wrong. She held herself together as best she could, but the shivers wanted to be released. Her skin wanted to sweat, her body wanted to give up. But she dragged herself along, waiting for the moment her grandparents left and she could finally let the masks down. She was too terrified to let them see how much her body was betraying her.

"Nothing has improved, so I'm going to have one of the nurses bring another round of medicine," Dr. Ash said.

Paul crossed his arms and took a step closer to Dr. Ash. "And how many years of schooling did you need to be able to tell me that? I could have told you that. Look at her!" He pointed to Sam and she closed her eyes in a grimace. It felt like her grandfather had sent an electric shock through her body.

There was another knock at the door, and Sam opened her eyes to see Avery standing at the doorway, her school backpack still on her shoulder.

"I'm sorry," she said. "I can come back." As soon as she

saw Sam and her grandparents, she questioned why she had come back. Each time she looked at Sam, she only remembered the fire. Each time she looked at Sam she questioned why Sam was the one who was okay. Avery wondered why she was okay. Why was it their parents were dead but not her? Or not Sam?

"No, sweetie, it's all right. The doctor is just finishing up. Sam is going to get more medicine." Shelly stepped towards Avery and wrapped her arms around her back to guide her into the room. She let Avery take the seat by Sam's bedside, but both Sam and Avery shrunk away at the proximity.

"I'll let Jamie know to give Sam more medication," Dr. Ash said. His words were final as he walked out of the room. The air was still after he left.

Paul let out a deep sigh and dragged his fingers down his face. There were deep lines of worry around his eyes that hadn't been there before the fire. Avery looked at the three people in the room with her and saw how time had changed everyone so quickly. In the last month, each person looked to have aged ten years.

"I think we should go," Shelly said. "We'll let Sam and Avery have some time." Shelly gripped her husband's hand and looked at Sam who was resting her head against the pillow. Her eyes were closed, but she wasn't asleep.

Paul and Shelly left the room with a quick goodbye and frustration still wavering off Paul's skin. Once they were gone, it was like a weight had shifted, and Avery let herself slump into the chair.

There was a long stretch of silence before either of them spoke.

"I don't remember what happened," Sam said. Her voice was hoarse, like she was holding something back.

Avery turned and saw that Sam's eyes were still closed, but her cheeks were wet like she had been crying. His body was shaking in small movements under the blankets. Her face was tense like she was holding back.

"What do you mean?"

"Our parents are dead," Sam said. Her words were flat, matter-of-fact. "I know they're dead and there was a fire, but I don't remember why."

Avery wanted to scream at her. They'd had this conversation before, time and time again and it felt like nothing ever changed. She wanted to yell until Sam did remember so then she wouldn't have to speak the words herself. It didn't seem fair that each night she slept, the smell of smoke is what always woke her. It didn't seem fair that every time she saw a picture of her dad, she could only picture the last time she'd seen him — in a stretcher. It didn't seem fair that Avery would always have to relive those moments and Sam didn't.

Sam reached out for Avery's hand. Sam's hands were cold when they touched Avery. Sam's palm felt foreign to Avery. They had once been close, but now Avery could barely be in the same room as her. Her face reminded Avery of everything she lost, everything she continued to lose every day.

"There was a fire," Avery said. Her voice wavered. It felt like someone was choking her, begging her to stop speaking.

Avery turned her head to look at Sam, but her face never changed. Sam was never known for her poker face, Avery could remember that in every game they played. Sam would always give away the cards in her hands. It was an easy win every time. But Sam's face was stone.

"They were brought to the hospital," Avery said. Her voice squeaked on the last word. She didn't care what she was saying anymore. All she could do was stare at Sam and wait for a response or reaction that never came. "Mom died before the firemen arrived; Dad died at the hospital."

There were tears streaming down Avery's face. She was still holding Sam's hand, but her grip had tightened. If Sam was uncomfortable, she didn't show it.

Sam was unmoving. Her eyes stared at her fingers, wrapped tightly in Avery's. She didn't pull her palm away, though Avery thought of pulling away from the strain on her own hand. Sam was numb. Her soul rattled inside her body, but she was trapped. If it had been up to Sam, she'd be screaming, but she couldn't find her voice.

"Say something," Avery said. She tugged on Sam's hand and released her. Sam pulled her hand back into her lap and stared at her fingers. Avery stood beside her bed, her feet pouncing from side-to-side. "Tell me you miss them!"

Sam picked her head up and looked at Avery. Her hands were balled into fists and her eyes were a bright crimson that rolled with emotion. Sam watched her, this sister of hers, and closed her eyes. Tears rolled in a slow procession down her face. She couldn't stand to look at Avery. Avery couldn't stand to look at her.

Sam's eyes were closed, so she didn't see when Avery took a gasping breath and fell to her knees, leaning against the side of the bed. Avery shook as she tried to breathe through the tears.

"It's my fault," Avery said. Her words were muffled between the sheets of the mattress.

"It's not your fault," Same said. She could remember very little from that night. The smoke came in rivers in her mind. She could remember the feeling of not being able to breathe, but beyond that? She couldn't bring anything to the surface.

"Sam," Avery said. She picked up her head and looked up. Her eyes were tired, coated in their own layer of sleep. She wanted to curl up into a ball in the corner and cower away until people forgot she was there, but every time she looked at Sam, something sparked in her. A nervousness. It forced her to remember what happened. "I think it was my fault."

Avery could almost feel Eric's lips against hers. The moment had been so sweet, so private. It was just the two of them in the kitchen late that night. Sam, her parents, everyone was asleep. When she closed her eyes and kissed Eric, she could imagine there was no other world than theirs.

The thought of him made Avery dizzy. Part of her missed him, and she hated herself for it. How could she miss someone who brought on something so bad? But it wasn't him, was it? It had been her all along. That kiss on the front porch? It was the calm before the storm.

"Do you remember the date I had with Eric that night?"

Sam's eyes glazed over for a moment, but once she remembered, Avery could see it on Sam's face. Her face lit up, like something from the past had taken over her body and she was the same Sam again.

"How did it go?" Sam said. She sat up a little in bed and leaned in towards Avery. The moment was the type Avery had been expecting the morning after her date. The morning was supposed to sisters gossiping about a boy. Instead that morning had turned into a never-ending hospital trip.

Avery wanted so badly to take that moment and pretend like nothing had changed. She wanted to go into detail about everything that had happened on their date, from the moment he picked her up, to the final kiss he gave before he disappeared. But each time she thought of that kiss, all she could smell was smoke.

"Sammy," Avery said. Her voice was shrill, like it used to be when she was a kid and didn't get her way. "I think I left the oven on."

Sam's face dropped. The smile that had eluded to the person she used to be was replaced by one of a girl who was lost. Her body relaxed into the folds of the mattress.

"Sam?" Avery said. She reached out for Sam's hand. It was hot, almost uncomfortable to the touch. "I left the oven on, and I think it started the fire."

Sam's face was blank. Avery looked closer and closer at her, but no matter what, she couldn't find any emotion there. She watched the corners of Sam's eyes crease, but she couldn't find any other change in her face.

She was waiting for Sam to blame her, to yell or scream or to do something so it wasn't Avery who was doing it anymore. She wanted someone else to be angry. She was too tired to be angry anymore.

"Avery," Sam said. She face inched forward and her muscles tensed. A knot formed in her stomach—no, more than a knot. Sam rolled on her side in an attempt to make the pain ago away. Her hands were in fists as they were wrapping around her stomach. It felt like there was something sharp in her abdomen. Like a doctor was taking some sort of implement and twisting it just to what it would do. "Bucket."

Avery pulled away and stood up.

"Bucket, Avery," Sam said, her voice louder. Hair was falling into her eyes, but she couldn't bring herself to move her hands away from her stomach.

Avery looked around the room and found the trash can near the door. She pulled it over and pushed it towards Sam, but she didn't move from her position.

"Sam, I need you to take the bucket so I can go get a nurse," she said.

Sam's eyes were closed, the skin on her face tight. If Sam could hear Avery, she didn't show it.

"Help!" Avery yelled. She held the trash close to Sam's face and tried to lean her head out to the door of the room. Sam was curling in on herself, like a suction was making her body smaller and smaller.

A nurse Avery had never seen before rushed into the room and took Avery's place by the bed. Her hands were quick as she assessed Sam's vitals.

"Get Dr. Ash in here!" she yelled out to the hall. Avery wasn't sure if anyone heard the command out in the hall, but the nurse still worked.

"Ok, Sweetie, just tell me what hurts." The nurse tried to coax Sam out of her curled position. "Is it your stomach?" She brushed the hair out of Sam's face. "If you feel like you need to cough, just let it out. Don't try to hold it in. You'll feel better if you let it out."

Avery could only hear Sam moan at first, but within a few seconds she began to cough, and once she started she couldn't stop. Avery had to look away.

Another nurse came into the room and the two were talking to each other back and forth. They were moving fast about the room and Avery felt like she was floating farther and farther away until the two figures were moving in a blur around Sam.

Avery was backing up to the door when someone ran into her.

"Sorry," the voice said.

Avery turned and saw it was Sam's doctor. His hair, which was normally slicked back, was falling over his ears at the sides, like he had run his hands through his hair one too many times.

"How are her vitals?" he said. His voice was swift but his body moved slow.

She knew she should just walk away. She could feel something inside her, something in her core that was just begging to be released.

"What's wrong with her?" Avery asked. Her voice was soft at first, much too quiet to be heard in the chaos of the room. "What's wrong with her?" This time her voice was firm. The first nurse that came into the room to help looked up. Her face was composed, but there was something about her eyes that seemed off. Was it pity she felt? Pity towards Avery?

"I need someone to tell me what's wrong with Sam!" She took a step toward them and in that instant, she felt like a small child that wasn't getting her way. She realized her hand was in a fist at her side and she was one comment away from slamming her foot to the floor. "She's my sister," she finally said, gaining at least an ounce of composure.

If the doctor heard her, Avery couldn't tell. He kept his back to Avery as he worked. She stared into the room, the chaos of figures moving around, blurring her vision until she didn't know what was happening anymore.

# Chapter 35

The blood test results didn't take long to come back. It was a slow day and Terry helped speed the process along in the lab. It was always strange to handle the health of another co-worker. Willow certainly didn't appreciate being a coddled, but doctors and nurses always made the worst patients—they're always too close to the situation to access it properly.

For Willow's sake, Terry tried not to look at the test results when they came back in, but she couldn't help but see spikes in her blood content that weren't normally there. She glanced away before she caught any further information.

"Dr. Ash!" Terry said across the hall. He was walking out of a patient's room, the lines of his face more pronounced than they usually were. Terry had seen him with more energy after a twelve-hour shift, but she accounted it to the fact his wife was lying in a hospital bed.

Dr. Ash turned when he heard Terry's voice. When he saw her, he seemed both relieved and frightened at the same time.

"I have Willow's test results back," she said, closing the distance between the two of them. "Has your wife been taking any medications?"

He shook his head. "Just the normal ones that she's been taking for years."

Terry held out the paper with Willow's results printed out. "Looks like your wife has some explaining to do." She meant it as a joke, but once Dr. Ash looked at the paper his eyebrows cinched. Part of Terry grew curious and regretted not getting a closer look at the paper before she handed it over.

"What's wrong?" she asked.

He shook his head and lowered the paper.

"Nothing," he said. "I'm going to go talk to Willow, make sure she's okay."

"Anything I can do to help?"

"No, it's fine," he said, walking away, but keeping the paper pinned close to his body.

— — — — —

Randy was surprised to find Willow asleep when he stepped into her hospital room—he was surprised that she was even still in the room. Willow was sleeping with the bed still inclined, her head tilting off to the side. With her eyes closed, he could picture her the way he always pictured her. She was the beautiful, young and bright women he married. He could stand there in the doorway for hours, just memorizing her. The IV in her hand was the only reminder of what was so terribly wrong.

The paper with Willow's test results was folded in his breast pocket. He was tempted to shred it, but was afraid that if he did, he wouldn't believe what he saw. Part of him wanted to shred it to get rid of the evidence. He wondered whether Terry had seen, he supposed she had, but she didn't know what she saw exactly. He wasn't even sure what he saw when he looked at the papers. The only thing he knew for sure was that Willow's and Sam's blood contents were all too similar.

He wanted to deny the thought that kept surfacing. He wanted to ignore it and to just remember his wife for the women he knew. But he needed some way, no matter how flimsy, to put the accusing thoughts to rest.

Randy walked across the room and pulled a chair up to the side of his bed. He was amazed, because in all their years together, never once had he seen Willow in a hospital bed. How many times had he seen her standing beside a bed, but never in it?

She was too strong for that, yet there she was, the blood pulsing through her veins full of chemicals he couldn't begin to name off.

He held her hand, strikingly warm against his skin. His eyes followed her hand, trailing up her arm until he noticed the tone change. Her pink, smooth skin turned to a bright red. Bits of the skin at her elbow looked enflamed. He looked closer, using his second hand to lightly grip her forearm. He turned her arm towards the light and saw the red rash followed all the way up her arm into her arm pit. He pushed the sleeve of Willow's scrub shirt out of the way only to see that as it grew up her arm it only got redder.

He felt Willow pull her arm away from him in protest as he examined the rash. He brushed the tip of his finger across the skin and Willow pulled harder, bringing her other hand up to itch the skin.

"Stop," he said. His voice was clear. Randy wrapped his fingers around his wife's hand as she tried to itch at the reddened skin. Her eyes were still closed but her lids were fluttering awake. "Willow, look at me." He wanted the words to come out gentler than they had.

She turned in the bed and grimaced as she tried to pull her arm away. Her eyes opened as she tried to focus in on the room.

She blinked once, twice, confusion sketched across her face. She looked at her husband holding her hand and relaxed, but her eyes followed his other hand until she noticed it wrapped around the bright red rash coating her skin. For a moment, it felt as if she wasn't attached to her body anymore. She wished the chaos unfolding in front of her was not her own.

"Do you know what this rash is from?" Randy asked.

Her lip quivered when she looked back at her husband. He was holding in the anger as best he could, but she could still see it seething inside him.

"Willow, do you know what this rash is from?" he said it again, this time his voice shook.

He lightened his grip on her arm and hand, aware of how tense his body was becoming the longer it took for her to answer. Her eyes were darting from her arm back to his face.

"Willow," he said. His voice broke, and tears rumbled, wanting to cascade, but he wasn't sure if it was out of anger at Willow or sadness that he felt he had lost his wife.

"I don't know," Willow said. Her voice was soft, barely a whisper.

"You took the vaccine," he said. Randy let go of her hand and backed away. He was shaking and swayed a bit. The room was spinning but for some reason he stood steady. "You took the same vaccine as Sam."

Willow was still as she laid in her bed. She looked her husband up and down, but all she could see was his anger reverberating off his body. She wanted to disappear.

"You could die," Randy said. His voice was firm but broken. He had his hand out, but he wasn't steady enough to move forward. He longed to touch his wife, to hold her in his arms again, but there were some moments that he looked at her and saw a monster. He loved her too much, maybe so much that he never saw what she was going through. He saw her, her curly hair, her blue eyes and pink, flushed skin and yet he still saw the young women he married so many years ago.

Willow closed her eyes and let her head fall into the pillow. The rash on her arm was burning and only burned more when she touched it, but for a moment she used that pain to ground herself. She would rather be in pain than dead. She would rather be in pain than to lose herself to dementia.

"I'm already dying," she said. A tear skimmed across her cheek, her eyes never opened. Her lip gutted out with each breath she took. "I'll be just like my father."

Randy fell into the chair next to Willow's bed. He took her hand in his and ran his fingers across each of hers. He was seeing her for the first time: the dark circles around her eyes, the hair that had lost its luster, maybe even thinned, the way her hands seemed lifeless. Everything about her body seemed like it had given up. And her spirit, he knew her spirit had been damaged ever since she had lost her father, but he had no idea to what extent.

"I won't let that happen to you," he said. She opened her eyes to look at him and he leaned forward to his touch his forehead to hers. Her skin was muggy and cold. "I'll take care of you."

Her eyes were dark, the rims red. She was there, but he also knew he was already beginning to lose her. She was a stranger sitting in the hospital bed. If he wanted, he could pretend this was just one of his patients. Examine her, determine the next steps, and leave. Part of him wanted to do that and ignore that this was happening. But there was a part of him that, when he touched her hand, he felt like he was home.

"When did you take the vaccine?" he asked. He couldn't

look at her. He wanted to see Willow, to love her, but each time he saw her face, it wasn't her who was staring back anymore.

"I don't remember," she said. Her voice was fading, edging away.

"Willow, try to remember. I need to know so I can get you help."

"I don't know!" She let her voice raise, her arms raising to her head and slamming down again at her sides. She was jittery, like she needed to do something but wasn't sure what that thing was. "That's—that's why I took the vaccine, Randy, so I don't end up like my father, but it's not working!"

"It's not working because there's nothing to fix!" He stood and the motion pushed the chair farther behind him. She wouldn't listen. No matter how many times he tried to tell her she was okay, she insisted she was losing her memory. The matter made him want to walk out the door. He knew he could talk to her for hours trying to convince her why she's okay and why she didn't need the vaccine, but it would be no use. Her memory was fine, but something else was much worse.

"Then why don't I remember?" Tears were welling up in Willow's eyes. They poured down her cheeks in think streams and when she spoke, the words came out nasally. "I don't want to be like my dad."

Her words were softer this time, though they were lost in hiccups as she spoke. Her chest was heaving and soon it was all she could do but cry. She wasn't sure how long she had been crying, and after a few moments she forgot why she was crying. All she knew was that it was something she needed to do, something she couldn't stop herself from doing.

Randy sat beside her in the open space on her bed. He pulled her into his arms and the moment she touched his skin she curled into him. She continued to let the sobs take over her body. As the seconds passed, her breathing slowed and the tears stopped.

He didn't dare disrupt the silence. He let her stay in his arms and he listened to her breathing as she drifted off into sleep. He rubbed her back and closed his eyes, giving himself a moment to pretend the vaccine never existed.

# Chapter 36

"We need to get Sam out of this hospital," Avery said. Her words were rushed and she was pacing as she spoke. She was still in the hospital, too terrified to leave Sam there alone.

"What's wrong, sweetie?" Shelly said.

"I—" Avery's words got caught in her throat. "I don't know, but Sam started coughing again and shaking, and I didn't know what to do. Nurses came in and helped her, but they wouldn't tell me what was going on."

"Okay, Avery, deep breaths." Shelly spoke on the other line, but she could hear her saying something else but her voice was muffled.

"I don't think they're trying to help her. I just, when I was in there, it felt like something was off. I'm not sure what, but when I look at Sam, she's terrified, like she's trapped."

There was a pause on Shelly's end of the line before she spoke. "Paul," she heard her say. Her voice sounded farther away, like she was holding the phone away as she spoke.

"We're going to get Sam out of there. Your grandfather has been talking to a lawyer about what's been going on, and she wants us to get Sam out of here as soon as possible."

Avery was still out in the halls. People were moving in crowds around her but no one took much notice of her.

"What's going to happen?" Avery asked.

"Sam is going to be transferred to a new hospital where they can treat her better and while that's , our lawyer would like to look into Sam's health records and find out if the doctors here really did do everything in their control to help Sam."

Avery almost dropped the phone. Would a doctor do that? It had been thoughts that had been running through her head whenever she visited Sam, but she always pushed the thoughts away because it seemed possible for a doctor to do anything but good.

"Avery, where are you now?" Paul said. He must have taken the phone out of Shelly's hand.

"I'm still at the hospital," she said.

"Good, I need you to stay there. We weren't going to do this until tomorrow, but I'm going to call our lawyer and see if we can get Sam out of there today. I need you to go back up to her room and stay with her until we get there, okay?"

"Okay," she said. Her voice was hushed and she could feel her body swaying, barely able to keep up with what was going on.

"We'll see you in a little bit," he said, hanging up the phone.

Avery felt like she was in a daze when she got off the phone. She wasn't sure what her grandparents' lawyer had in mind or what they thought they might find, but she only hoped it meant that Sam would get the help she needed soon.

When Avery made her way back to Sam's room, the corners of Sam's lips creased into a smile, but the light in her eyes was faded. The longer Avery looked at Sam, the more it seemed like she was sinking it the sheets of the bed, just one whisper away from disappearing.

She didn't know what to say to her. The two girls stared at each other in silence, neither knowing what to say to the other. Did Sam know she was being transferred to a new hospital?

The time passed in slow lulls. A TV was turned on at the end of Sam's bed and they both watched a movie, but Avery couldn't stop herself from glancing at the clock every few minutes waiting to see how much time had passed.

When Shelly and Paul finally arrived, both the girls jumped awake.

"Sam," Shelly said. She walked into the room and went straight to Sam's bedside. Sam's eyes followed her as Shelly worked to check everything that Sam was hooked up to. Avery was positive that Shelly knew almost nothing about the medical devices, but it looked like she was looking them over out of habit rather than of knowledge. "How are you doing?"

"I'm fine," she said. Her voice was coated with a sandpaper texture.

"We're working to get you out of here as quick as we can. Until then, Avery is going to stay with you, okay?"

Sam nodded her head and as soon as Shelly turned away Avery should see Sam fall back into the pillows and let her body blend into the mattress.

Shelly turned to Avery. "Just call if you need anything," she said, wrapping her arms around Avery for a quick hug.

"I will," Avery said, burying her face into her grandmother's shoulder before she stepped away and left.

"I'm not going home, am I?" Sam said. She didn't look at Avery when she spoke, her eyes still fixated somewhere out the window. Avery thought she could see Sam's eyes glossing over, just one blink away from crying, but she held her face.

"No," Avery said.

"I'm going to another hospital," she said. Her voice was wavering. A tear slipped down her cheek and rippled throughout the room.

"The doctors at the other hospital will be able to help you." She tried to instill confidence in her voice, but in truth she had no idea what was going on anymore.

"Do you really think that or did Grandpa tell you that?" Sam said. She turned to look at Avery. Sam's eyes were sunken in, her face was pale. She looked like another person from the last time she had seen her. Wasn't that only a few hours ago?

"They told me," Sam said. Avery looked at her, how her body seemed to be getting smaller, her sentences getting shorter, and part of her began to forget what the old Sam was like. Sometimes there was a glimpse of the old Sam, moments where she laughed, and everything felt normal again, but in moments like this, when Sam was settled into the same hospital bed, Avery almost forgot Sam's life before the hospital. Before the fire.

"They told me I've been here a long time and that I should have been able to go home by now," Sam said. She lifted her hands to graze them over the top of her sheets. Her eyes stared out at her hands, but never focused on them. For now, it seemed her world was a blur. "I don't know how long I've been here."

"Over a month," Avery said. She watched the way Sam's hand skimmed every surface of the bed sheets. She should see the bones in each finger.

"And off to another hospital," Sam said. Her hands came to cover her face, her fingers long and slender across her cheek bones. "Do you think it will help?"

Her face was still covered by her hands when Sam spoke.

246

Avery watched she chest rise and fall, the rhythm growing faster as her heart sped and the tears flowed.

"Sam, it's okay," she said.

Avery came to the bedside and wrapped her arms around Sam's shoulders. She felt Sam's breaths come in frantic patterns, her mouth gaping open for more air.

"Breathe," Avery said. "Ready? Breathe in." She took a deep breath and waited for Sam to follow suit. "Breathe out." She released the breath of air and felt Sam follow in sync. They continued the breathing until Sam's heart slowed and her eyes ran dry.

"You didn't answer my question," Sam said after a long moment.

Avery frowned and let her head fall onto Sam's shoulder. Her skin was cold to the touch.

"I don't know," Avery said. "But I hope so."

Sam didn't say anything. Avery laid next to her in the hospital bed, listening to her breaths come and go. The room grew quiet and Avery began to count Sam's breaths, each one growing longer and slower. She counted until she knew she was asleep.

"Avery?" a whisper came into the room. Avery lifted her head off Sam's shoulder and saw Shelly standing at the doorway.

Avery stood from the bed, careful not to move Sam, and walked to the other side of the room to meet with Shelly. The bags under her eyes seemed heavier than usual, but there was a spark of hope that Avery hadn't seen in a while.

"Is everything okay?" Avery asked.

"Paul is just finishing up some paperwork, but a team will be here in a few moments to transfer Sam to the other hospital."

And that's when Sam's words kept echoing through her mind. *Do you think it will help?*

# Chapter 37

Randy left Willow in the hospital room overnight. He left having no plan of how to treat his wife or what to tell the other nurses. There was no easy explanation for the spikes in her bloodstream. His only hope was the same hope he held for Sam, that the vaccine would eventually fade from the bloodstream and the symptoms would disappear with time.

"Dr. Ash, there's a phone call for you on line two." It was Terry who found Dr. Ash as he was returning to his office. When he heard her voice, the muscles in his back tensed.

"Who is it?" He tried to calm himself, knowing that for now at least she wasn't asking how Willow was.

"Someone calling about Samantha Ellison."

He nodded his head and turned away from his office to find the nearest phone station.

"Dr. Ash?" Terry said, stopping him in his tracks. "Proceed with caution."

He had hoped she said the words jokingly, but the light tone he normally heard in her voice was gone.

Randy braced himself for the phone call as he walked to the nearest nurse's station to pick up the phone. The odds that it was anyone but Paul or Shelly on the line were slim and judging by their last encounter, he was almost certain it was Paul waiting for him on the line.

"Sophie, there's a call on line two for me?" he said as he approached the station. The young nurse behind the desk nodded her head.

"I would take this one in the back," she said. She pointed to the phone that was hanging on the wall behind her. Sophie pushed the empty desk chair that was next to her and pushed it towards the phone and into an inlet that the nurses used as a small break area.

Randy frowned and looked at the room, the door ajar slightly.

"Sophie, that won't be necessary," he said as he picked up the phone.

"It might be," she said, but giving him one final look of warning before she turned her back to him and faced the computer once again.

"This is Dr. Ash speaking," he said, picking up the phone. He stood just outside the small room, ready to slip through and close the door behind him if necessary.

"Good evening, Dr. Ash. My name is Olivia Williams. I'm the attorney of Paul Rhea. I'm sure you know Paul. He's the grandfather and guardian of your patient, Sam Ellison." The women's voice was crisp on the phone. She spoke with the sort of confidence that could crumble someone apart almost immediately. Randy looked over to Sophie who was already engrossed into her computer again. He stepped into the break room with the phone and shut the door behind him.

"Yes, Sam is one of my patients," he said.

"So, I'm sure you're aware that Sam has been one of your

patients for some time now. Would you be able to tell me how long she's been in your care?"

The women was playing with him, he could hear it in her voice. She had no reason to question him. She knew the answers to everything she was about to ask. There was no judge or jury to prosecute him. It was just the two of them on the phone.

"She's been here for over a month now, as I'm sure you're highly aware of," he said. The annoyance was slipping off his tongue. He let the aggravation manifest. It was the only thing holding back his fear.

"I'm well aware, thank you," she said, kindness and manner sugar coating the message she was eager to deliver. "It's been brought to my client's attention that Sam was brought into Dover Memorial Hospital in order to get care for injuries she sustained as a result of a fire that occurred in her home, yet the treatment she's been given doesn't have to do with injuries that result from fire. I'm sure that you would agree that unless a patient had severe burns, there should be no other reason for a patient to stay at a hospital for so long, correct?"

He held the phone to his ear and tried to release the tension in his body. He needed to stay calm.

"Correct," he said.

"According to Sam's medical records, she hasn't been treated for any injuries as a result of burns or a lack of oxygen to the lungs. Dr. Ash, can you tell me what she's been getting treatment for?"

"She's been receiving MRIs to discover the cause of her seizures and other various symptoms that she's been experiencing."

"That's not what I'm asking," Olivia said. He thought he could hear the smile in her voice over the phone. "What have you been treating Sam for?"

"That's what we've been trying to discover, Ms. Williams. Sam's case has become complex. Her symptoms are not ones associated with inhaling too much smoke during a fire. My colleagues and I think that the symptoms Sam is experiencing have to do with something that either occurred or was beginning to surface before she was brought into our care."

"Do you have any record of this?"

"No, of course not."

"Dr. Ash, my client and I are requesting to take Sam Ellison out of your care, effective immediately. She will be transferring to another hospital, and we will need her health records prepared within the next hour for her transport."

He felt as if his veins were icing over. His bloodstream tingled with panic and fear, leaving him frozen in place. Sam was a walking piece of evidence. Her body, her bloodstream, was teaming with evidence of what Willow had done—of what they both had done. One look from another doctor and all heads would turn back to him.

"I can prepare that," he said into the line. His palms were sweating, holding the phone to his face. He leaned against the wall, thinking of the chair Sophie had offered before he began the call. It was on the other side of the door now.

"Wonderful," Olivia said into the phone. He thought he could hear the ruffle of papers coming from her end of the line. "I also have to inform you that my client intends to jump at the slightest piece of evidence that malpractice has taken place."

He swallowed. "I assure you, that won't be necessary."

"Dr. Ash, I suggest you get a lawyer," Olivia said. She paused, waiting for a response, and when there was none, she hung up.

# Chapter 38

The skin around Willow's fingers were dry. There was a window beside her bed that let her look out over the parking lot, but she couldn't look at it. Her attention was continually being drawn back to her fingers. She picked at the cuticles, the fine skin around her fingers. She cursed herself every time she did it, but she couldn't stop herself.

A hand came out to over hers. She turned her head and saw Randy staring back at her. She didn't realize he stepped in the room. When she looked past him she saw the doors were closed. His jacket was draped at the edge of her bed and she saw car keys hanging out of his pocket.

"Are we going home?" she asked. She sat up in bed, letting her feet hang over the edge. Randy sat next to her, but he felt far away.

She felt better, or at least she hoped he did. Willow wasn't sure how long she had been in the hospital bed. For all she knew, she could have been there for days. Her stomach protested against her a lot, but every time the feeling passed, she always fell into a deep sleep. When her eyes finally opened again, she was never sure how much time had passed. If there was a clock in the room, she had yet to find it.

"Not yet," Randy said. His voice was quiet, but it sounded like he was holding something back. Willow wanted to look closer at him, but he kept his body angled away from her. She could always know everything Randy needed to say by looking at his eyes, but without that she could only assume what he was thinking.

"How was work?" she asked. She smiled and held his hand. She loved the feel of his palms against hers. She knew every inch of Randy's body. If her eyes were closed and someone held her hand, she would be able to tell if that hand belonged to Randy or not.

"Sam is being transferred to another hospital," he said. He was looking at her arm when she spoke. She could sense him memorizing the red skin on the inside of her arm. The skin burned, it seemed to always have a tingling sensation that came and went as it pleased, but the sensation grew only when Randy looked at it.

"When?" she said.

"Less then twenty-four hours."

He let go of her hand and without him, she grew cold. A deep panic set in her chest. Her breathing hitched and her limbs began to quiver. Could Randy see her shaking?

Sam and her, they were intertwined. If Willow couldn't observe Sam, where was she supposed to go from here? Was she supposed to blindly experiment on herself? How could she make accurate decisions and move forward?

"Sam's grandfather, Paul, got a lawyer," Randy said. Willow was trying to listen to him, but the world around was beginning to tilt on its side. She closed her eyes to find balance, but the room only proved to spin wildly.

"Where are they taking her?" she asked.

"Willow, it doesn't matter where they take her. If anyone does any tests on her, they'll see something's wrong and it won't be long until they put the pieces together and connect things back to us."

"I'm trying to find the cure," Willow said. She looked at Randy with half-seeing eyes. He was there in front of her, but it felt like if she reached out her hand, that she would never touch anything. For a moment, it was as if she was suspended in the world. And it was in this suspension that she wanted to say. Safe, far away from people who wanted to take her away from the cure.

"Willow, listen to me." Randy grasped her hands. She was sure his grip was light, but for this moment it felt like he was suffocating her. She could imagine his grip, too tight, leaving bruises along her wrist. No, he wouldn't do that. He would never touch her like that.

She blinked and his fingers were barely brushing her wrist.

"They're taking her away," she said. She kept her eyes on her wrist, the way his fingers so gracefully seemed to wrap around her. She told herself to take comfort in his touch.

"Yes, they're taking her away and they'll see what you've done." His words were firm. He was reprimanding her.

"I was trying to find a cure," she said. The words came out as a sob. Her head was spinning, her stomach protesting. She thought for a moment that she may just throw up again. The sensation neither passed or came. "They'll see that."

"Willow, they'll see that you intervened in the life of a healthy young girl. Someone who had a future and you took it away. You infected her, and we don't know if we can fix that."

"I can fix it," Willow said. He eyes held hope, but her

body held fear. Every limb was curled to attention. She was ready to run out of the room, but she was afraid she would fall. "That's what I've been trying to do this whole time."

Willow looked into her husband's eyes. She wanted him to see her, to know what she was trying to do. He looked back at her, but something was off. It was like he didn't see her for the person she was. There was a pain in his eyes. When she looked at him, a deep sorrow infected her core.

"I need you to talk to a lawyer," he said. His words were gentle and clear. He reached out for her hand. She longed for his arms to wrap around her, but his words made her want to push him away.

"No," she said, but she kept her hands in his.

"It will be okay, Willow. I'll protect you, you know that. I'll do everything I can to keep you safe." His words were pleading. He kept his grip on her hands tight, but she drew herself away.

"I'm not talking to a lawyer," she said. Her hand tensed, the muscles contracting. Randy began to massage her palm which only seemed to infuriate her more.

"There's no other way."

She pulled her hand away from his. The two were like Velcro, tight and intertwined. When she drew away, there was a rip, a protest, yet she could still be separated. Her hand was raw.

"I refuse to let anyone interfere with what we've been working for," Willow said. As she spoke, her lungs begin to burn. The burn was beginning to feel natural. She knew it was the vaccine that was making her lungs set ablaze, so she welcomed it with open arms. With the burn came the urge to cough. She let her lungs clear themselves, but once she began coughing she feared she wouldn't be able to stop. Each cough required her entire body and with each movement the burning in her lungs grew.

"Breathe," Randy said. He sat with his hand on her back. She leaned forward and leaned her elbows on her thighs for support. Her body was quivering, and she tried to control it. If she relaxed her muscles, she feared she would fall over.

Willow was aware of each inch of skin on her body. It was the only thing distracting her from the pain in her lungs and throat. Her body was alive with its own vibrations. Every touch against her skin was ten-fold. The fabric of the hospital gown was too abrasive, the mattress too soft, Randy's hand on her back too heavy. She was suffocating under the touch.

"Stop!" she screamed. The voice came out high. Her eyes were clenched shut, her fingers wrapped tight around the blanket that was covering her legs. The weight from her back lifted and her body began to shiver. She coughed again, this time the taste of iron coated her tongue.

"Shit."

She heard the words, but she wasn't sure who spoke them anymore. Her eyes were open but the only things she could focus on was her hands resting against her legs.

Something rough brushed against the corners of Willow's mouth and she pushed it away. When she coughed again, whatever it was came back to cover her mouth. She thought she saw something red. It was blood, she was sure of it.

She coughed again and brought her fingers to the edge of her lip. When she pulled her hand away the tips of her fingers were a bright crimson.

"Willow, hold this," the voice said. Whoever it was put something in her hand. It was some sort of fabric, rough to the touch. The person guided the fabric in her hand to her mouth. "Hold it there." The person pulled their hand away, leaving a trail of numbness against the back of Willow's palm. She coughed. She wasn't sure if she would be able to stop coughing. Her lungs were suffocating.

The room was spinning, and even if it hadn't, everything in her vision was a blur. She knew her hand was in front of her face, but all she could make out was the light pink scheme of her skin. A cloth was held to her mouth. It was growing heavier, her arms growing weaker. There was a bright red stain in the room.

She was alone. The voice that had been in the room with her was gone. She listened for movement in the room, but no matter how hard she tried, there was nothing but silence surrounding her. The stillness was deafening.

Her body started to go numb, beginning with her toes. Just when she thought she wouldn't be able to take the pain any longer, just when she thought she might scream out, begging for the pain to go away, something changed. At first she thought she had grown numb to the pain, but that wasn't it. From the tips of her toes, slowly going up, she was healing. The sensation inched its way up her body, but as it spread the places the pain remained grew deeper, urgent.

The healing spread to her feet, up her legs to her knees. She wasn't in control anymore. She was detached from the physical world. If she was still in the hospital, she was unsure. For now, she was floating. The lower half of her body was in cool water, the upper half was dancing in fire.

Willow let out a deep howl as the healing spread up her torso. She could feel it reaching her fingertips. She screamed until she felt like she couldn't anymore.

"Breathe, Willow!"

The voice startled her. Arms were wrapped around her. Fingers were touching her body, examining every inch. The fire was still there, but she could feel the healing retreating back down to her legs, her feet, her toes, until it was gone, replaced only by burning.

She opened her eyes to the hospital bed. People were standing around her, every inch of the room was occupied.

"Her eyes are open again," a voice said.

There were other words, mumbles as the team worked over her. Feeling was coming back to her body, and with it the burning began to ease enough to allow other senses to creep in. The taste of iron was thick in her mouth. A hand came in from her right side to wipe her face. From the left came another hand, this one placing an oxygen mask over her mouth. The air was cool, and as soon as she breathed it in, it was like her lungs were finally about to expand again.

"Her vitals are returning to normal."

Willow blinked. She recognized the voice. It was Randy. If she concentrated hard enough, she thought she could see him standing by her. She blinked again. Was it really him? She thought she saw him look up at her, but before she could be sure, the fire seeped back through her veins.

# Chapter 39

The room was blurry. Willow blinked but nothing came into focus so she counted each blink until her eyes found themselves in the room. She lost count and lost herself in a loop of numbers without realizing it.

"Eighteen, nineteen, twenty, sixteen, seventeen." She continued to whisper to herself with each flutter of the eye. Were the numbers in the correct order? She found her focus enough to see her feet at the other end of the bed. The room was dark.

Her senses were overwhelming. There was still a prickle of fire in her skin, begging to be put out. She hushed it away with her thoughts. She tried to count her blinking once again.

"Eighteen, nineteen, twenty," she said to herself. She forgot why she started counting in the first place or why she was in a hospital gown.

"How's she been doing?" It was a voice in the hall. Willow recognized the voice from somewhere, but couldn't pinpoint exactly where.

"Better I think. We still haven't figured out what happened in the first place."

It was a second voice. They were growing quieter. Were

they walking away?

Willow found her toes and curled her legs to her chest and twisted herself until her toes hung off the edge of her bed. Her movements were careful as she let her feet fall to the floor and guide her out into the hallway.

She was losing herself again. Her mind ran in a panic, trying to find reason. She tested herself, trying to dig up memories but they never came. What was her birthday? What was today's date? All these simple facts were slipping from her.

The lights were bright once she left the room and the hall was silent. She wandered, listening to the hushed breathing coming from the rooms to her left and right as she walked. There were sounds of soft snoring as she tip-toed through the hall. It wasn't until she looked down that she saw she was only wearing a thin pair of socks.

Some of the rooms she passed had beeping noises and she ignored them. She wasn't sure where she was going. She only knew she would find her way eventually.

The halls were long and winding. Willow's body knew where she was, but her mind had left her abandoned. She followed silently behind a nurse that scanned her card to go through the locked doors.

Her panic is what guided her forward. The simple things she forgot, but she knew a way to fix it. She had to try with all her might to remember where the vaccine had been stored. She didn't know exactly where she needed to go, only that she was heading in the right direction.

The insistent beeping stopped once the doors closed. The silence was mind-numbing, but a door stood out to Willow. Dr. Randy Ash. She stepped through before anyone entered the hall to see where she had gone.

The office smelled like Randy, like the cologne he put on every day. Her mind stirred the longer she was in the room. Randy's face, a silhouette in the dark, seemed to find her when she closed her eyes. And then all she could see was her father. Her father, not knowing who she was. Her father, dying out on the street. Her father, diseased with the same sickness that was claiming her as each second passed.

Willow stumbled to the floor, her body shaking. She felt like her father, the way he always curled in on himself, and now she feared her mind was being lost the same way his had so many years ago.

It was an instinct that brought Willow over to the safe. She couldn't remember what was locked behind the thick metal door, only that it was something that would help her. It was with desperate fingers that she turned the dial on the safe, always seeming to get the numbers wrong. Her mind, too frantic, couldn't focus on the task in front of her. The numbers ran through her mind, her fingers twisting the dial until she heard a click. The latch moved.

She wasn't sure what she had done, what sequence of numbers she had put in, only that the door to the safe opened, almost unprovoked.

The curled opened on its hinge, a loud screech filling the room. Willow looked behind her to the door to the office. It was closed.

The safe was filled with papers and a few beaten down notebooks. She skimmed her fingers over the papers but nothing seemed right. It wasn't until she reached into the back of the safe that she felt something. A lump. Cold glass. Relief was at her fingertips.

Willow pushed the papers aside and pulled out a glass

vile filled with a clear liquid. Thin memories of filling a syringe filled her mind, and almost immediately she stashed the liquid in her underwear, pressed up against her hip bones. Her hospital gown suddenly felt too thin.

She ran out of the room, never bothering to close the safe or the door to Randy's office. She didn't find her way back to her room easily. The vial held against her skin was cold, a constant reminder it was present. She walked slow, too fearful that it might fall and shatter, the glass sending shards across the hall.

She let her body guide her, rather than her mind. Her mind wanted sleep, but her body wanted something else, something hidden in the halls of the hospital. When she reached the nurse's cart out in the hall there was a sense of relief. Vials, just like the one Willow was hiding, laid out on the cart, but that wasn't what drew her eye. There was a syringe laid out, the needle perfectly sanitized, cap still on.

It was second nature when Willow reached her hand out and took the syringe in her grasp. There was a breeze at Willow's back as she reached under the hospital gown to grasp the vial she had hidden. She bit the cap off the top of the syringe and stuck it into the rubber cap of the vial, watching as the syringe filled with the liquid.

She should have sanitized the portion of her arm that she was about to stick, but there were a lot of things she should have been doing.

The pain from the needle was sharper than she remembered, or maybe it was Willow's subconscious trying to tell her to stop. Either way, it was with a steady hand that Willow administered the last of the remaining liquid from the vial. When it was finally emptied, she pulled the needle away from her arm and dropped it on the nurse's cart. The needle glistened back at her, mocking.

She watched the vial glint in the light. Her head spun, the needle feeling all too familiar in her arm. That's when she had the vague sense that she'd been here before. She had forgotten she had already administered the vaccine once, but by the time the realization occurred to her, the liquid was already working its way through her body.

Her arm was pulsing. The room around her began to spin and shift until she couldn't feel her feet on the ground anymore. Each limb in her body was turning to liquid. Thoughts ran through her head. Had she done this to herself? Was it the medication or her panic? She began wheezing and it wasn't until then that she realized she couldn't breathe.

She put her hand out for support and that's when she realized she was already on the ground. The tile felt cool against her skin, and suddenly that's all she could think about. As the fire ignited in her core and a black screen seemed to descend over her eyes, she felt the tile. Cool, inviting. Home.

# Chapter 40

They didn't let Randy finish seeing his last patient of the day.

"Dr. Ash, there's a phone call for you. I've forwarded it to your office." It was Sophie who stopped him in the hall. The corners of her mouth were pulled down. Sympathy was in her eyes that hadn't been there the last time she spoke to him.

"Thank you," he said quickly as he made his way down the hall to his office. His mind went to Willow, but if something had been wrong with Willow, wouldn't she have just said something?

Millions of thoughts ran through his head as he reached his office, none of them had a good outcome. He shut the door behind him, knowing that if the call wasn't important, Sophie would have had him take it in the break room like she did last time. He took a deep breath before he picked up the phone.

"Dr. Ash speaking," he said as he stood in front of his desk.

"Good evening, Dr. Ash." The voice was John Roux, the president of the hospital. There was new wave of panic as he waited for John to say something more. Part of himself was relieved that whatever the phone call was about, it had nothing to do with Willow, but the other part sunk into a sense of dread knowing full well that if John wanted to speak with him, it wouldn't be anything good.

"How are you doing, Dr. Ash?" John's tone was casual and Randy tried to match it, though sweat started to pool and drip down his back.

"Busy as usual."

"Do you happen to know why I'm calling?"

Randy took the cord of the old phone and guided it as he walked around his desk and sat in his chair. "I'm not one hundred percent sure," he said. His voice softened towards the end and dripped into a whisper.

"We're requesting that you go on leave until further notice," John said, his voice final.

Randy was sitting at his desk, papers astray and his world falling apart. He stared at the letters and numbers jumbled in front of him and wondered if he'd ever be able to make sense of it again.

"I'm not sure I understand," he said. He tried to keep his voice even, but it wavered and dipped. He began to sink.

"In light of the recent events with Samantha Ellison, we request that you go on leave." It was a rare day he spoke one-on-one with the president. He had hoped the next time he spoke with John it was going to be some congratulations for a discovery he had made to aid in finding the cure to Alzheimer's. The phone call was ironic in its cruelty.

"And if I don't?" The words came out like a whimper. He wasn't threatening to stay. No, he was judging just how much trouble was in his future.

"Then you risk termination," John spoke without hesitation, and it was the first time Randy could hear the doubt in his voice and hesitation towards making such a sudden move against Randy.

The phone line was silent and it was all Randy could do to stop himself from hanging up the phone.

"I want you to understand, Dr. Ash, that this does not mean we believe Mr. Rhea's accusations. However, we have reporters coming to us, asking about you, what we think you've done, and how we're dealing with the situation. An investigation is already underway in hopes that we don't find anything against you, but either way, we cannot have you working here until you've been deemed innocent."

"I understand." Randy's body revolted against him as nausea rolled up his stomach and into his throat. He feared anything the investigation might reveal. Would the serum Willow produced end up in the findings? He was almost sure it would, unless Willow found some way to tamper with it.

How had his wife done this?

"Once the findings come back, and it's revealed that what happened with Samantha had nothing to do with your care, then we invite you back into this hospital with open arms."

A knock sounded at the door and before Randy had the chance to respond, the door opened and Jenna let herself in. He was guarded when she first made her way through, afraid what his face might reveal of the conversation he was having with John, but one look at Jenna and suddenly talking to the president didn't matter. Her eyes were wide with panic.

"Dr. Ash, I'm so sorry to disrupt, but Willow was found on the ground. She wasn't breathing, and we have a team currently working to resuscitate her."

"Where is she?"

"In ER bay two."

In that moment, John possibility firing him, taking his

license to care for patients forever, all these possibilities seemed so small compared to Willow being taken from his world. His mouth hung open, not in the type of way when one looks dumbfounded, but in the way that Randy was fighting to breathe but no air could come.

The moments that followed were done without thinking. Randy blinked and suddenly he was running down the halls toward the ER bays. He vaguely remembered hanging the phone up on John, pushing Jenna out of the doorway, and running past familiar sets of eyes following him with curiosity. His feet couldn't carry him fast enough as his chest thudded against him, begging for him to slow down.

He thought he heard someone calling his name as he ran, but his body urged him forward without a moment to stop. By the time Randy pushed through the doors of the trauma bay, a crowd had formed around bay two. As people saw him coming, they moved out of the way.

"Randy, we found Willow." The man was going to say more, but Randy pushed past him and into the room.

He saw Willow behind a blur of faces. They were walking around her as she was spread across the bed, her shirt hanging open electrodes strapped to her chest.

"She was found on the floor outside her room," someone said.

Randy didn't look up to see who it was. He bit his tongue, so eager to yell at these people who took their eyes off Willow when there was something wrong with her—he screamed at himself for doing the same. He reached out for her hand and when he was finally able to wrap his fingers around hers, he was overwhelmed by how hot her skin was.

A woman was doing chest compressions on Willow,

putting all her weight into getting her heart back into rhythm, and that's when Randy heard the unsteady beat on the heart monitor. It echoed in the room full of people and soon enough it was the only sound he could hear. When Randy looked around the room he could see people's lips moving, but their voices went unheard. The only sound in the room was the irregular beeping of Willow's heart.

Randy's eyes wandered to Willow's. Her face was sunken, her skin too pale and body too lifeless. With each chest compression, her entire body moved. Her eyes were closed but her mouth hung open.

"Clear!" a voice shouted.

Someone took Randy by the arm and pulled him away. The room stopped as each person stepped away from Willow and a bolt of electivity ran through her chest and her body jumped. Once she stilled, the room was set in motion again, and everyone found their place back into rhythm. Randy watched the heart monitor, waiting for the beats to settle into a rhythm, but nothing changed.

Her heartbeat was fading, and he wasn't sure if it was his mind playing tricks on him or Willow slipping away.

"Damn it," a voice whispered behind him.

Randy reached out for Willow's hand again and put his other out to brush hair way from her face. He waited for her to open her eyes, ruffle her nose, anything but hold so still.

"Clear!" a voice yelled out again.

Someone pulled Randy away again and when his hand dropped away from Willow's, the room felt colder.

When the second jolt of electivity went through Willow's body, it wasn't the beeping of the heart monitor that Randy heard; it was the soft thud of her heart, as if he was leaning his ear against her chest. The sound was fading and when the room gathered around Willow again, Randy reached out to touch her hand but she was gone.

He didn't hear the beeping of the heart monitor shift into a long held alarm. He didn't hear the voices of the nurses and doctors as their panic shifted into something less hopeful. But most of all, her didn't hear Willow's heartbeat again.

He froze by the side of her bed. He held her hand, but he was afraid he would disturb her peace. Alive or not, she felt more delicate than ever.

Around him, bodies began to back away. He thought he felt one or two reach out and touch him on the shoulder, but he couldn't pull himself away from Willow.

He inched closer towards her, feeling his airways closing and his breathing grow uneven.

He could see her and touch her, but he knew she was no longer there. Before these last few months, Randy never cried. Until he learned what Willow had done, he reserved his tears for her. It was when he was standing at the altar and Willow was making her slow progression down the aisle. She was glowing that day and something about the moment made him cry. The tears were of happiness, but the tears that stained his cheeks now were a whole other monster.

The tears came fast and sharp, and he surrendered into them. If there were still doctors or nurses in the room, he didn't care. He scooped Willow into his arms, breathing in the scent of her hair, suddenly afraid he was going to forget what she smelled like.

He did not sob. His sorrow was silent, and it was vibrant.

Her death was a mystery, and part of him wanted it to remain that way. He could imagine her plunging a syringe full of the untested antivenom into her veins, letting panic guide her. The thought of poison in her body, poison that she willingly injected, made him want to vomit. Had it been her own doing, or was it some freak accident? He had hoped for the later.

"Dr. Ash?" A voice said behind him. His face was still hanging over Willow body, her thin frame wrapped in his arms. When he looked at her, her face didn't look the same; it was missing that piece of light in her that made her glow. "Randy?" the voice was softer this time.

Randy turned, but didn't loosen his grip on Willow. She was lighter somehow, as if the universe wanted to take her body along with her soul. He was terrified to let go.

Jenna was standing at the door. There were faces behind her out in the hall, but she was the only one brave enough to step through the door. Her face was turned down, but she gazed past Randy to Willow who was still in his arms. His grip on her loosened as the reality of the world around him began to come crushing down. Jenna took a few steps forward and stopped. She whispered something Randy couldn't hear as her eyes blinked and tears streamed over.

"Oh my god," she whispered. Jenna was more than a co-worker to Willow — she had been a friend, coffee date she could rely on every Monday morning. He forgot about that. He cursed himself for not remembering something so simple.

Jenna stood in the middle of the room, frozen, her face coated with a mix of horror and sorrow. Randy kissed Willow's forehead, a small tear dripping onto her skin. He laid Willow's body down on the hospital bed, lifting her hand one last time. His eye caught on the wedding ring on her left hand. The band was silver, the engagement ring a bright diamond against her soft skin. He ran his thumb over the ring, feeling it loosen and shift under his touch. Should he take it off?

He slid the ring away, leaving her finger exposed. He hadn't touched her ring since he had said his vows to her eight years ago.

Randy stepped away and turned around to Jenna. Her arms were wrapped around her stomach, and she was leaning forward like she might fall at any moment. Randy reached toward her, and she fell into his arms. Holding Jenna felt different, wrong. Her body was too small, her hair the wrong scent. Was this what it would be like for now on, whenever he held someone? Would he only remember how much that person wasn't like Willow?

The room shifted and soon all he could see was Willow. He memorized her face, the stillness of it. He watched her, waiting for the corners of her lips to twitch upwards like they would when she took naps. He waited for her to turn over in her sleep and curl into a ball. He waited, begging for her to wake up.

# Chapter 41

By the time Randy came back to his office, it had been searched. Papers had always littered his desk, but now every file seemed to have been touched and rearranged. To anyone else, the office looked normal, but to Randy, his secrets were exposed.

He sank into his chair, utterly hopeless in what to do. The door to the safe by his desk was open, all the contents had been removed. All the notes Willow had taken on Sam, all the chicken-scratch from when she was trying to perfect the serum was gone. All of it had been in the safe, the secrets hidden not so thoughtfully.

"Dr. Ash." When Randy lifted his head, John Roux stood at the door, two security guards behind him. His eyebrows were furrowed in, but his eyes were pleading, like he couldn't believe the investigators had found something against him. John was holding papers in his hands, and one glimpse was all it took for Randy to recognize the files he held.

Randy stood from his desk. How long had he been gone? Two hours, maybe three? Long enough for the investigators to come into his office, find what they need and get John's attention enough to cause him to see Randy face to face.

"You know why we're here." It wasn't a question, but it was John's eyes that begged for answers.

The two security guards stepped forward as John spoke.

"Files were found in your safe that documented some sort of experiment on Samantha Ellison. The notes recalled some sort of serum that was injected into her system which, at this point, leaves me to believe that this is what caused Samantha's decline."

Randy's gaze never wavered away from John's. A hint of disgust and disbelief painted his face. Was Randy supposed to say something? Pretend that the words written on those papers weren't what they seemed?

A paper was poking out from John's grip, and he could see Willow's handwriting decorating the edges. He felt he could be ripped in two. He was torn between telling John what Willow had done or defending her, even in her grave.

John was still speaking, telling Randy he was no longer allowed near the hospital and that his license to practice medicine would be revoked, all pending a court hearing. The words started to blur together, but one single light of hope kept him standing. Perhaps, through all of this, Willow would be able to remain innocent.

"I recommend you get a lawyer," John said.

The security guards walked towards Randy until there was one on each side. They gripped the tops of his arms and showed him down the hall where three police officers greeted him. Paul was standing with one of the officers, along with another man in a suit who Randy assumed was Paul's lawyer. When Randy approached, Paul looked up and scowled. He was a good grandfather, Randy had to credit him that.

One of the officers came to Randy's side and gripped him,

rougher than the security guards had, and pushed him until his hands were behind his back and his front was against the wall. Out of the corners of Randy's eyes, he saw some of his colleagues he had been working with for years. Each one of them looked at him wide-eyed, but as soon as he caught their gaze they looked away.

Handcuffs were strapped onto Randy's wrists. Out of everything that was going on around Randy, the only hint of surprise that hit him was the wonder at how heavy the handcuffs were.

"Rot in hell," Paul said. A wave of defeat coated Randy's skin, mixing with sweat and tears.

He was guided down the hall some, pulled into an elevator, and suddenly the hospital he had worked in for so long felt unfamiliar. The elevator doors opened, and the officers kept Randy in front of him as they walked.

"Come on," the officer said, pushing Randy forward.

They went through the double doors of the hospital, and a police car was waiting for him, the door back door already open. The officer kept one hand on Randy's cuffs while he used the other to push his head down and into the car.

No one spoke as they drove off. The muffle of reporters filling the streets as they filed out of the lobby and into the fresh air was the only thing Randy could hear over the hum of the car's engine.

— — — — —

The prison uniform reminded him of scrubs from the hospital. All one color, baggy, and rough like it might have been ironed too much. If anything, it made it feel like home.

"Can you explain to me your side of the story?"

Randy wasn't in his cell. He was in a meeting room with

concrete walls and a mirror that was really just a double-sided window. A small camera was pointing down in the corner of the room. The man that sat across from him was David Patrini, the attorney that had been provided to him upon arrival at his jail cell.

"What did they do with Willow?"

"In the city morgue," David said. The words were clipped and final. He brushed the words away while Randy hung onto them. Randy wasn't sure what he expected to have come of his late wife in his absence, but he had hoped she was placed somewhere peaceful. The morgue seemed too gruesome.

"Would you like to explain or would you like to rot in jail for the rest of your life?"

David was sitting back in the chair across from him, completely at ease. He looked at Randy with keen eyes like he was searching for something. He held a pencil in his hands, tapping it against the metal table in front of him even though he had no paper to write things down.

Randy watched the pencil tap. His eyes glazed over. He didn't have any options left. He had lost everything, most of all he had lost Willow. He had no chance to grieve her death. Her name would be ruined. All her life, she had been an amazing nurse that cared about her patients, but it was one fatal mistake that people would always remember her for. He wasn't sure if she did have Alzheimer's, but what was clear is that somewhere along the line, she believed she did, and to her that was all that mattered.

"Dr. Ash, would you like to explain?" David said again, this time his voice harder.

He began to speak before he thought through his actions. "I wanted to find the cure to Alzheimer's," Randy said, meeting David's gaze. His lawyer was supposed to be on his side, but it felt like he was far from it. "My wife, Willow, her father had died due to complications from Alzheimer's. Her biggest fear was always that she would meet the same fate as her father, and I wanted to take that fear away from her."

The more he spoke, the more he could believe his own lie. It's what he should have done. Willow should have never been left to face the disease on her own, yet somehow she had been left abandoned and there was nothing he could do to take that back. But even his lies made him realize Willow had suffered from exactly what she had been running from, except this time she had done it to herself.

"So you began conducting experiments on Samantha Ellison?" David looked at Randy with curiosity. He spun the pencil around between his fingers.

"There was a serum that had been produced by a team in New Zealand that mimicked the effects of Alzheimer's. They needed to first create the venom before they could create the antivenom. They did it first on animals, but they haven't gotten far enough in the clinical trials to test it on humans."

"So that's what you did," David said. "Why?"

Randy remembered the long nights of researching, finding article after article of lost hopes and failed experiments when it came to finding a cure to Alzheimer's. Randy read the New Zealand article when Dr. Gadel referenced it during Tom's treatment. He hadn't made a note of it the same way Willow had. To Willow, that experiment was her lifeline, and maybe it could have been if she hadn't let her desperation grow in the way.

"I needed to save my wife," Randy said, his voice sandpaper against his throat.

"Then why Sam? Why push things so far, that you needed to experiment on a human without her consent?"

"I didn't know what else to do." As he spoke the words,

he felt like he finally understood his wife. She was trapped, and the only way out was to trap someone with her.

"Was your wife involved?"

Randy's head shot up, and he looked at David. His eyes had softened the more Randy spoke, but he still looked at Randy with questions wavering.

"No."

The pencil David had been twirling between stopped, and he dropped it the table. His eyes bore into Randy's. His head cocked to the side, so much so that Randy thought he might have imagined it.

"So, you'll be pleading guilty?" He crossed his arms in front of him.

"Yes."

# Chapter 42

The court hearing came months later. It was long enough for the serum to work its way through Sam's bloodstream and fade away. The effects of the venom and anti-venom were just about gone. Sam found herself, re-learned life, and attempted to forget the death of her mother and father, but the length of time would never be long enough. There were still moments, blinks of moments that surrounded Sam with darkness, and she feared that there were memories gone and out of her reach forever.

Sam sat in the court room, her blonde hair braided and tucked away from her face; Avery sat close by. Most days, Sam was okay. Her short-term memory was getting better, and bits and pieces of what had happened before her accident were coming together. She couldn't remember that fire, but for that she was thankful.

"How are you feeling?" Avery said. She had a folder in her hands. It was a copy of all the documents that had Sam's name written all over them. The documents that went into detail about what had been injected into her system. Avery had read the copies just as many times as their lawyer had.

"Fine. Ready to move forward," Sam said, wrapping her

arms around her stomach.

"He's pleading guilty, you know."

She wasn't afraid to see Dr. Ash again. There was nothing about him that scared her; it was learning what he had done to her that terrified her. So much of those weeks spent in the hospital were a blur. She hadn't read the files like Avery had. If it were up to her, she would live her life, never knowing what had been done to her, but she was required to be at the trial where they would go into every detail of what had been done to her. They called her a witness, but in reality she was just the victim.

The case took hours to dissect as each attorney took turns at the stand. The serum, how it was created, how and when it had been injected. The prosecution stood up, placing his hands behind his back before he stood.

"Samantha Ellison," he said.

Randy sat in the defendant's chair. His body was hunched forward, his once groomed and sleek hair now frayed at the edges, waiting to be tamed. Any sense of the man he used to be was gone the day Willow died.

He turned as Sam stood and made her way to the front. She was a different person from when he last saw her. She cowered as she walked, but her eyes had the light that had been missing for so long. Her skin was healed and possessed the healthy glow that hadn't been there since the fire. When Sam looked around the room, she found Dr. Ash and they both looked away.

She swore her oaths and sat in front of the court room.

"Samantha, we've all heard what's happened to you, and I can only assume the thoughts running through your mind, but can you all let us know how you're doing? How long has it been since you were last injected with the serum?"

She looked to the side where the judge sat. He smiled and urged her to speak.

"Over 5 months ago."

"And how was your memory recovered after the injections stopped?"

"It was slow at first," she said. "To come back, I mean. I couldn't remember a lot, but I think the effects of it are fading. All my new memories are fine, but anything that happened before or during the injections is still a little hazy."

"Do you remember getting any of these injections?"

Sam's arms curled in and her fingers traced the blue vein in the crook of her elbow. The stinging was still there.

"Some," she said.

The prosecution stepped back and paced the front of the room. "And do you remember who it was that administered the injections?"

Sam stared wide-eyed at her lawyer, and he stepped closer. "Was it Dr. Ash?" He pointed to where Randy was sitting. Randy kept his gaze down, only looking up the moment Sam caught his eye. The two froze, their eyes locked. Sam bit her bottom lip and stared back at Randy. Moments in the hospital flashed in front of her. None of them involved Dr. Ash.

"No," she whispered so quietly the microphone in front of her almost didn't pick it up.

Behind him, Randy could feel people shifting in the room. His heart rate spiked, and camera flashes went off. The courtroom had a silent buzz of excitement.

"Do you know who it was?" the prosecution asked.

Sam shifted in her seat, placing her hands on her lap. The room was silent as everyone held their breath for an answer. "It was a woman," she said. Sam looked up and at the crowd. Avery stared back at her. Sam hadn't told anyone. She barely knew the truth herself. "It was a nurse. The same nurse that took care of me when I was brought to the hospital after the fire."

As she spoke, Avery wavered in her seat. She lost Sam's gaze and searched the room, hoping the nurse was somewhere in the courtroom.

The prosecution paused for a moment. His brows furrowed until something clicked. He lifted his head, and the corner of his lip went up into a narrow smile. "Thank you," he said and ushered her to sit.

The whispering that was already filling the courtroom grew louder as Sam left the stand and went back to her seat.

"As you can see, while Dr. Ash was in fact Samantha's doctor, he wasn't the one to administer the injections. Her nurse was Willow Ash, Dr. Ash's wife. She was the nurse that was assigned to her case when she came into the ER. While she was not Samantha's neurology nurse when she was under Dr. Ash's care, all of the medical notes pertaining to the serum are written in Willow's handwriting."

Air left the courtroom. Surprise and maybe some confusion filled the room. More whispers, but not a word came from Randy. He shouldn't have been shocked, really. Everything was in her hand. She had documented everything so clearly, for the sake of the cure.

The prosecution stepped towards his table and gripped a folder, taking it to the judge who flipped through the pages.

"What are you suggesting?" the judge asked, still looking through the pages.

"I think Randy Ash was not alone, that his wife was also a part of the experiments. All the notes are in her handwriting. Dr. Ash was just there to help cover everything up."

"You're aware Mrs. Ash is dead?" the judge said, his eyes wary.

"Yes, sir, but my client prefers to have to truth exposed, whether or not punishment can be served."

Defending his wife was the only thing he had left and even now he couldn't do that. All her career of saving lives, pouring herself into every patient she treated, all thrown aside and forgotten. She had poisoned a girl and that's all she would be remembered for now.

Randy turned to the table next to him. Paul, Shelly, Avery and Sam were all sitting together. Sam was looking down at her hands, similar to the way she had when she was infected with the serum. The only difference now was when she looked at her hands, her eyes weren't vacant. They were occupied with tears she couldn't seem to hold back.

"Randy Ash to the stand," the prosecution said.

Randy stood, and it was then he realized how shaken he was. There was nothing he could do. He could place the blame on himself all he could, but there was no denying Willow's involvement. The judge didn't give Randy a chance to breathe once he sat.

"Is this your handwriting?"

A bailiff passed the papers to Randy. He glanced it over like he had so many times before, but now it was different. It had been months since he had seen a picture of Willow or even her hand writing. Seeing the soft curves of script, the way she so meticulously recorded made his heart speed up, like he was on a runaway train and needed to jump off. Her face came to mind. Her tanned skin, clear, full of life, happiness, and ultimately desperation. He couldn't stop seeing her cold, lifeless face when she was in the hospital bed, already gone.

"Dr. Ash?" the judge repeated himself.

He thought about lying and saying the writing was his, but he knew that somewhere in the crowd there was someone ready to analyze his handwriting.

"No, it's not."

"Are you familiar with the handwriting?" the prosecution asked.

Randy looked at the man, a stranger really, who was standing in front of him, ready to expose a secret he had fought so hard to keep secret.

Randy only looked back down at the papers.

"Whose is it?" the prosecution asked.

The charts Willow drew in the notes were perfect. Each diagram was in place, not one number was missing or out of place. He never got to attend her funeral.

"My wife's," he said. His voice softened. He didn't want to do this to her.

"So, your wife had a part in Sam's care?"

Randy looked down at his hands. His wedding band on his left hand was loose on his finger. It occurred to him he was a widow. His wife was dead, but if he took his wedding band off, it felt too final.

"Yes," he said. His voice was strained, and he begged the questions to stop or to move away from Willow.

"Was she the one that administered the shots?"

Randy could hear his heartbeat from behind his ear. It pulsed until his vision blurred. He looked around the room, but couldn't make up any of the faces. He adjusted his wedding band before spoke.

"Yes," he whispered.

The courtroom stirred. There was a flash of a camera, but

Randy refused to look up. Every eye in the room was on him.

"Dr. Ash," the prosecution said. The way the man spoke was final. He was toying with Randy; he knew what Randy would say before he could speak. "Whose idea was it to inject the serum into Samantha Ellison's body?"

He took a deep breath, his heartbeat wavered. "Willow's," he said. He wanted to scream, to tell everyone that his wife wasn't there. He wasn't sure when, but he had lost her. The women he loved, that wasn't the women that injected Sam with the serum, but none of that matter. It didn't matter that she was once a good person or that she had tried too hard to save others from a fate her father had endured. All that mattered was the one mistake. The one vial of serum she had injected into Sam. But it was too late. His words had been said.

The world moved in a blur. Words bounced around the room, none of which registered in his mind. At some point, he was released from the stand and the trial continued without him.

Each attorney, the prosecutors and his own, had a chance with their closing statements, but he never heard their words.

As both lawyers spoke, he heard Willow's name being said over and over. Each time it was like a blade being dragged across his skin. He blocked out the words, but her name struck him like a dagger.

The judge sat stone-faced at the front of the room, and when everyone was done speaking, he left. Only a few minutes passed before he came back into the room.

"Under the law of our federal government and the state of Massachusetts, Dr. Randy Ash has been found guilty of charges of medical malpractice and reckless conduct. As a result, he will be serving a state prison sentence, minimum of 10 years."

Murmurs filled the room and cameras flashed around

him. The photos were all for him. He was their star. Tomorrow morning, newspapers would have his face plastered across the front, *Doctor found guilty of child experiment.*

For all that, he didn't care. He didn't care if his name was whispered across the papers. He didn't care that his license to practice was gone forever, or that he had no idea how he would support himself after he served his time in jail. He only cared about Willow, and while she was gone, her secret was not. Her name would be littered in those papers as well. He had wanted her secret to die with her, but now it would take a life of its own.

He couldn't save her. Not from herself and not from what she had done.

# Acknowledgments

I thought by the third book, this whole writing thing would get easier. Turns out I was wrong.

First and foremost, I have to thank my amazing boyfriend, Phill. I'm not a pleasant person to be around when I'm stressed, so thank you for finding enough patience to put up with me on a daily basis, especially when deadlines for this book were coming up. Thank you for being a thesaurus, a place to bounce ideas, and someone who supports me through all my crazy dreams and ideas. I love you!!!

My parents, who I also put through the ringer, but less these days because I've moved out. Do you miss me yet? Thank you both for supporting me every step of this journey.

Elizabeth Bidinger, my creative writing professor, who read one of the original drafts of this book when Dr. Ash was the evil one. Thank you for always offering feedback.

Kim Chance, my editor and amazing person in general. I can't thank you enough for the phone calls, text messages and genuine support.

All the authors and writers I've meet this year through the AuthorTube Retreat and Wander Writer's Retreat. There are moments in your career that you think about giving up. Spending the weekend with these girls reminded me that wasn't an option. I'm so glad to have met you all in person and I can't wait to see each of you again!

My beta readers, Pam Deveny, Debora Spano

and Mae LaBelle. Thank you so much for meeting my crazy deadlines!

My street team, who were my first handful of readers and helped me get this book out into the world.

Alaina Waagner, my marketing expert who taught me more things about keywords and ads than I thought my brain could handle.

Alisha from Damonza, who made my book come to life with this gorgeous cover. I still can't stop staring at it!

And most importantly, all my followers and readers, especially those who have been around since Essence came out in 2013, thank you for believing in me.

# Support the Author

If you've enjoyed this book, be sure to head over to Amazon and Goodreads and write a review!

# About the Author

Mandi Lynn published her first novel when she was seventeen. The author of Essence, I am Mercy and She's Not Here, Mandi spends her days continuing to write and creating YouTube videos to help other writers achieve their dream of seeing their book published. Mandi is the creator of AuthorTube Academy, a course that teaches authors how to grow their presence on YouTube. When she's not creating, you can find Mandi exploring her backyard or getting lost in the woods.

Newsletter: http://bit.ly/MandisNews

www.mandilynn.com

www.youtube.com/mandilynnVLOGS

Instagram, Twtitter, Facebook, Pinterest:
@mandilynnwrites